CAROLA STORMS THE CHALET SCHOOL

CAROLA STORMS
THE CHALET SCHOOL

BY

ELINOR M. BRENT-DYER

W. & R. CHAMBERS, LTD.
LONDON AND EDINBURGH

First printed, 1951

Printed in Great Britain
by T. and A. CONSTABLE LTD., Hopetoun Street,
Printers to the University of Edinburgh

Dedicated to

SYDNEY

With many thanks for a Title

CONTENTS

Chapter I

CAROLA PLEADS IN VAIN

'CERTAINLY *not*! You ought to be ashamed of yourself for behaving like this! Now let me hear no more about it, please, Carola. You will come with me to Jamaica as I have settled. I have engaged a very good governess for you—one who is comparatively young, so that she will also be a companion for you. The berths are booked, and all arrangements made, so that's the end of it, I hope.'

'But, Cousin Maud——'

'Did you hear what I said? I want to hear no more talk about the affair. You are a very lucky girl to have such chances as you have. I wonder how many other girls of your age have seen as much of the world as you?'

'And I'm *sick* of it!' Carola flared out. 'I'm sick—*sick*—*sick* of perpetually travelling about! I want to go to school like other girls, and have the fun of games with them, and proper lessons—not footy little lectures from a governess—and everything! I want to go to the *Chalet* School——'

'I thought I said I wished to hear no more about that?'

'I can't help what you said—you're *always* saying! I tell you I won't go! You'll have to carry me aboard the beastly liner, if you get me that far! I won't stir a step by myself! I—oh, I hate you!'

Realising that tears were very near, Carola suddenly

9

stopped her wild diatribe and made for the door. She rushed out of the room and upstairs to her own bedroom, regardless of her cousin's stern: 'Carola! Come back at once and shut the door after you!', slammed and locked the bedroom door after her, and then casting herself full-length on the bed, howled like a small child.

Cousin Maud got up and shut the sitting-room door herself before she went to sit down and try to recover the self-possession Carola's outburst had so rudely—in more senses than one—disturbed. Really, the child was abominably impertinent, not to speak of being utterly ungrateful. She didn't deserve the treat of a trip to Jamaica. But she, Maud Curry, knew her duty too well to be turned from her purpose by a naughty, ungrateful child of fourteen. She had promised her cousin Andrew and his wife, before they left for him to take up his post in West Equatorial Africa, that she would look after Carola; and no amount of tantrums and temper on that young lady's part should make her break her word. It was a pity that the girl had taken this extraordinary wish for school, but that could not be helped. Once they were well away from England, she would settle down with the nice governess who was young enough to be a friend for her, but old enough not to be silly. In the meantime, she was to be ignored until she chose to apologise for her rudeness. Probably that would be the end of all this foolish fuss. Miss Curry decided all this complacently, and when she saw the new vicar's wife coming up the path she hurried to the door to welcome her, and put the young recalcitrant who was sobbing her heart out upstairs right out of her mind.

Meantime, Carola cried till she could cry no more. For a long time after the tears were dried, she lay, still shaking and gulping, for the storm had been a violent one. Her face felt stiff with tears and her head was aching. She lay still, and presently, worn out with the force of her emotions, she fell asleep.

When she woke up, it was to find that night had come and the room was in darkness, the only light being from the street-lamp at the gate. Her head was better, but her eyes were sore and she was stiff and chilly, since to lie and sleep outside your bed on New Year's Day is hardly a warming process. She got up, switched on her light, and pulled the curtains over the windows. Then she went to the toilet-basin and turned on the taps and bathed her face till it felt more comfortable. That done, she looked at the clock on the mantelpiece. Seven o'clock! She must have been asleep for hours. She might as well undress and go straight to bed. Carola had no wish to go downstairs to meet a righteously indignant Cousin Maud over the supper table. She was still much too upset to feel hungry, and if she woke up during the night she could always slip down to the kitchen and get some bread-and-butter and milk.

To think was to do where she was concerned, and ten minutes later she was curled up in bed, her hot-water bottle filled at the hot-water tap and hugged close to her, and she was gradually losing the shivery feeling with which she had awakened. She had switched off the light again and opened the curtains so that the lamplight could shine into her room, and she lay watching it, thinking of her one deep desire, to go to school, and especially to that school of schools—anyhow, that was how Miss O'Ryan had described it—the Chalet School.

Cousin Maud kept on her pretty house in a small seaside town on the south coast as a *pied-à-terre*, to which she

returned at intervals varying from two to six months. She
herself had a passion for travelling, and during the past year
she had taken Carola to Dublin, Edinburgh, Switzerland,
and the Gower coast in South Wales, with only the shortest
possible intervals between each visit. Having promised
her cousin to be responsible for his girl, she insisted on
keeping that girl under her own eye, travelling a governess
who could also be useful to herself. Christmas had been
spent at a delightful guest-house in Cornwall, where Carola
had struck up a great friendship with a Miss O'Ryan,
rather to Miss Curry's relief, since Miss O'Ryan had been
quite willing to have Carola with her, and it had freed the
elder lady so that she could indulge in her twin passions,
bridge and gossip.

Miss Curry had made a few inquiries, and found that
the Irish girl was a graduate of Oxford who was returning
to her own old school as history mistress when the Easter
term began, having hitherto been in Australia. Evidently
she had told Carola the most enticing tales about the school,
for ever since they had come home that young person had
worried and teased to be allowed to go to this school instead
of accompanying her father's cousin on the trip to Jamaica
which had been arranged for some months. Miss Curry
had treated the idea as a passing whim at first. Then as
the girl became more and more urgent, she had grown
annoyed and wished that she had never permitted the
friendship. It had ended in today's outburst, when it must
be admitted that Carola had behaved about as badly as
possible before she had fled to the refuge of her own room
to cry so heart-brokenly.

Lying in the lamplight, Carola had to own to herself that
if Cousin Maud were angry, she had every reason for it.

'All the same,' she thought sullenly, 'she might listen to me. Who wants to be for ever on the go? It's all very well for her, but I'm sick and tired of it. I'm getting all behind in lessons, too. I'm sure Dad and Mother wouldn't want that to happen. But how can you do lessons decently when you never have the same person to teach you for longer than six months and you're always moving about, anyhow? I ought to be at school like other girls. I've never played hockey nor cricket and I've no friends of my own age—not a single one! I just haven't had a chance to make friends.' Her eyes brimmed over again with tears of self-pity as she thought this, and she gulped for a moment. Then she drove them back, for she had no time for crying now. She had resolved firmly that she was going to do something about school since Cousin Maud either could not or would not see sense. Go to Jamaica she would not! She couldn't quite see how she was going to avoid it, and she had only fourteen days in which to lay her plans, so she mustn't waste a moment.

At this point she fell asleep again, and when she woke up the street-lamp was out, and a waning Christmas moon was sailing serenely across the deep blue of the skies. Carola felt hungry by this time. Once she was properly awake, she got up, huddled on her dressing-gown and bedroom slippers, padded quietly across the floor, switching on the light on her way, and unlocked and opened the door softly. It was as well that she paused to look up and down the passage in case anyone else should be stirring. If she had not, she must have walked right on top of a tray left at the door. With an exclamation she stooped and picked it up. When she had set it on the bed, she went back to fasten the door again. Then she returned to the bed and, feeling rather guilty, lifted the napkin laid over it. There was a well-filled plate of bread-and-butter and another holding a banana and an apple. A glass of milk and a slice of currant loaf completed it. Under the glass was a note. Carola decided to eat her supper and then read the note.

'It's Cousin Maud and she's sure to say something beastly,' she thought as she bit into her first slice.

The plates and glass were all empty in less than ten minutes. Carola carried the tray over to the little table in one of the windows and dumped it down. Then she refilled her bottle at the hot tap as it was little more than lukewarm by this time. She straightened the bed and beat up the pillows. Finally, when she could find no further excuse for delaying any longer, she climbed back into bed, having switched off the centre light, and switched on her bedside lamp and opened the note—very reluctantly, it must be confessed.

'Dear Carola,' she read, 'I hope that by the morning you will have come to your senses again and be ready to apologise to me for your most uncalled-for rudeness of this afternoon. A girl of your age ought to be ashamed to speak so improperly to an older person—especially one who is your guardian and in the place of your parents. Unless you reform very soon, I am afraid your father and mother will be deeply disappointed in you when they return to England. I will say nothing about my own feelings, though I think you should know that I am very deeply hurt by your ingratitude for all I am doing for you.

'However, if you are prepared to beg my pardon when we meet at breakfast, we will say no more, and I will forgive you. But I must impress on you that I will listen to no more talk of school—of *any* school. I cannot be expected to rearrange my whole programme just to suit you, and as I have promised to look after you I must take you with me. Please believe that, as you are behaving at present, this is no pleasure to me, but rather an unpleasant duty. If, however, you make up your mind to accept what must be, and to try to be pleasant and accommodating, that should end. Your parents are returning home next year and they can then decide whether or not to give in to you and let you go to school—personally, I can see no need for it. You have had good governesses, and the lady I have engaged for this trip is better than any you have had before. I considered you when I fixed on a person much nearer your own age than usual; and I expect you to consider me and try to make yourself rather more agreeable in future than you have been lately.

'Now this is the last time I intend to discuss the matter with you. We go to Southampton today fortnight and sail for Jamaica on the Wednesday. I will listen to no arguments on the subject, so please make up your mind to that and do not attempt to produce any.

'If you show yourself properly penitent tomorrow, I will, as I said, let the matter drop, so long as you behave properly to me and let me see no more such outrageous exhibitions of childish rage as you gave me this afternoon. I was shocked to think that you could act like that!

'I shall be taking you to London to buy some clothes tomorrow, so come down prepared to set off as soon as possible after breakfast.

'I have no more to say, so I will close. I am putting this on the supper-tray I shall leave at your door; and *remember* that in the morning I shall hope to see you a very different girl from the one who left me in such a fit of temper a few hours ago.

'Your affectionate cousin,

MAUD CURRY.'

Carola read the last word. Then she sat up in bed, and tore the paper across and across.

'"Affectionate cousin" indeed!' she cried. 'There's not much affection in *that*, anyhow! I've a good mind not to go down at all.'

She threw the pieces on to the floor, turned off the lamp, and lay down, seething with anger. However, she was really too tired for that to last long, apart from which, she was an honest girl, and she had to admit to herself that Cousin Maud had some excuse for being indignant. All the same, her purpose of not going to Jamaica was strengthened. She felt that she must apologise for her rudeness, now that her first fury of disappointment was over; but she could do that with a clear conscience. Only, if Cousin Maud really thought she would give in as easily as all that, she had another think coming to her!

Having settled all this in her mind, Carola rolled over for the last time, curled round comfortably, and fell asleep once more. She woke at seven, and when she had switched on the light again she saw the scraps of the note where she had tossed them and remembered that she had to dress for a trip to London. With a groan, she tumbled out of bed and made for the bathroom where she speedily attended to washing. That over, she raced back to her bedroom, not anxious to meet her cousin before she must. She dressed quickly, stripped her bed, and then, with a slight reddening,

She had been wondering how on earth she was to slip away from her new governess. If there was only Cousin Maud to consider, she might be able to manage it. She applied herself to her bacon and Cousin Maud drank her coffee in a frowning silence which lasted until her young cousin, having finished her breakfast, asked to be excused to go and make her bed.

'Yes—run along,' the lady said absently. 'Be as quick as you can. We are going by the nine-fifteen train and it's twenty-past eight already, so there is no time for delay.' She scrambled the letter which had so disturbed her back into its envelope and stood up. 'Never mind about the table. Mrs Pascoe is coming in later and she will see to it. Go and make your bed, and be down here by ten to nine at latest.'

Carola departed, thankful to have got out of the trouble so easily, and when Cousin Maud, still frowning, came bundling down the stairs, she found the girl waiting for her, looking the picture of a neat, trim schoolgirl. They left the house, and when they were walking briskly to the station Miss Curry informed her young cousin that, among other things, she was to have a new suitcase.

'Oh, may I have an expanding one, please?' Carola begged.

'That is what I intend to buy for you,' Cousin Maud told her. 'They are much the best for long voyages, as they hold so much. You will do your own packing, of course. With this happening, I shall be far too busy to do more than give you occasional oversight. When you begin to pack, please put everything you are likely to need during the voyage in this new case and the bigger one of your other two. Then your trunk can go to the hold and picked up the paper and put it in the waste-paper baske Somehow, she was not anxious for Cousin Maud to see ho she had treated the letter.

The gong sounded as she did this, so she opened th windows widely to air the room, picked up her handke chief and went downstairs, prepared to eat humble-pi with what grace she might.

Much to her surprise, Cousin Maud seemed scarcely t listen to her very halting apology.

'I'm sorry I was so rude to you yesterday, Cousi Maud.'

Miss Curry hardly glanced up from the letter she wa holding to say, 'Then that finishes it. Sit down, Carola and begin on your porridge. We haven't any too much time.' Then she returned to the letter, while Carola, who had been ready for a long lecture on ingratitude and impertinence, slid into her seat, and began to empty her porridge-plate in silent wonder as to what could have happened.

Presently, Cousin Maud put the letter aside and started on her own breakfast. She looked thoroughly vexed and worried, and Carola, having emptied her plate, and received a helping of bacon and sausage, ventured to ask what was wrong.

'I am very much annoyed,' Cousin Maud said, pouring out her coffee. 'Miss Bacon, whom I had engaged for your governess, now writes to say that she has had a cycling accident and broken her leg, so will be unable to accompany us. At this late date I do not see how I am to find you another governess before we sail, so we must just go without. It really is most annoying!'

Carola said nothing, though inwardly she was chuckling.

we need have no further trouble with it till we reach Kingstown.'

'Yes,' Carola said meekly.

Cousin Maud went on talking, but, sad to say, Carola heard not one word of her discourse. She was far too much occupied in rejoicing over the extending suitcase to think of anything else. Really, it did seem as if the luck were coming her way for the moment.

Thanks to Miss Bacon's falling out, Cousin Maud had far too much to think about to worry further over Carola, and that young lady contrived to possess herself of a brown coat and beret and a brown velveteen frock without any comments from her guardian. Brown, it should be noted, was one of the Chalet School colours, according to Miss O'Ryan. She also turned down her cousin's suggestion of a green raincoat in favour of a brown one; and though she could hardly ask for a brown tunic, she felt when they returned home that, on the whole, she would not show up too badly so far as school colours were concerned. Carola went to bed that night thoroughly satisfied with herself and the world.

Chapter II

ENTER BIDDY!

JO MAYNARD sat by the drawing-room fire darning stockings. It was a job she loathed with her whole soul; but when you have a long family of youngsters, never to speak of husband who could only be described as 'hard on his socks,' you have to see to it sometimes. Jo was expecting a visitor—a visitor whom she had not seen for the last four years—and was wildly excited over it inside, so she had determined that darning was the most subduing occupation she could find and, anyhow, it had to be done!

Tall and slim was Jo, with black eyes that could dance with mischief or soften to pools of darkness in a pale, delicately-featured face under a broad fringe of black hair, with earphones of the same at either side. Despite her long family and many responsibilities, she looked amazingly girlish, and everyone who knew her could have told you that there were times when she seemed very little removed from the most beloved Head Girl the Chalet School had ever known.

She was alone for once save for Rosa in the kitchen. The entire family had spent Christmas at the Quadrant, the queer old house where her brother Dick Bettany lived with *his* long family, and Jo had been persuaded to leave the children in her sister-in-law's charge when she came home to look after her husband. Today he was away at the big Sanatorium up in the Welsh mountains, where he

held an important post. Her adopted sister, Robin
Humphries, had left the week before to go to Switzerland
for winter sports with one Zephyr Burthill, a friend of hers;
and the other two members of the family, Daisy and
Primula Venables, who were 'nieces-by-marriage' to quote
Jo, were staying with friends outside Armiford near their
old home. Anna, her faithful maid, had gone to Plas
Gwyn, which was undergoing severely necessary repairs,
in order to see to several odd jobs there, so the only other
member of the family was Rufus, Jo's big St Bernard, who
never left her for long these days, for he was a very old
dog, nearly eighteen now. He was lying on the rug at her
feet, every now and then thumping the floor with his tail
when she spoke to him.

'You know, Rufus,' she said gravely as she poked her
needle in and out of the meshes she had woven over a
huge hole in the heel of one of her husband's socks, 'I am
so wondering if Biddy has changed much. And do you
think she'll see any change in me? Four years is a long
time.'

Rufus banged the floor with his tail and then got up
stiffly. He had heard the creak of the gate. So had Jo,
and the sock went in one direction, her darning-wool in
another, while her thimble flew off her finger and rolled
away by itself into a corner of the room, giving Jo a good
deal of trouble when she came to look for it. Jo herself
made a wild leap for the door and wrenched it open to run
to the front door, Rufus at her side, his tail going like a
flail. The front door was yanked open before the newcomer
had fairly reached it, and the light from the hall-lamp lit
up Jo standing with arms wide open, exclaiming with joy
in every note of her voice: 'Biddy!'

'Joey! 'Tis yourself, acushla!' came the equally joyful reply in the soft tones of southern Ireland as the visitor tossed her case down and hurled herself on her hostess, hugging her ecstatically.

Rufus forgot his years and his rheumatism and bounced round the pair woofing excitedly as if he were a good ten years younger; and when Biddy O'Ryan had recovered her senses a little, she dropped on her knees beside him and submitted to having her face thoroughly swiped with his tongue as she flung her arms round his neck, calling him love-names in creamiest Kerry brogue.

'Where's your luggage?' Jo demanded, interrupting this touching meeting and looking round severely.

Biddy looked up at her and laughed. 'At the station. Sure, there wasn't a taxi to be had for love or money, so I just grabbed me case and left me cabin trunk to be called for tomorrow. The rest's gone straight to the School. I've all I need here, really. 'Tisn't as if I was staying for a real visit.'

'Well, when you and Rufus have quite finished making amorous idiots of yourselves, I think we'll bring the case in and shut the door, or the neighbours will be thinking I've taken on a tame lunatic in addition to everything else,' Jo told her with mock severity.

Biddy laughed again. 'Ye couldn't expect anything else after all this time. Sure, I've often wondered if I'd ever be seeing dear old Rufus again.' She went out and picked up the case, came in, and Jo closed the door. She led the way into the drawing-room, and Biddy, having dumped her case down in the hall and dropped her cap and coat on top, followed her.

'Joey, how do you do it? Rufus is *old* and yet he looks

almost in his prime.' She turned to him again, to lay her hand on the great head nuzzling joyfully against her. 'Ah, acushla, machree! So you haven't forgotten Biddy, even after all this time?'

Jo laughed back at her. 'Is it likely? Rufus, bless him, is as loyal as they come. Oh, we take the very greatest care of him, and except for rheumatism, he's amazingly well. I'm so very glad. I wanted the children to grow up with him as far as possible and even Michael will have some faint recollection of him. The vet says he ought to be good for two or three years yet.'

She pulled Biddy over to a chair, and then sat down herself. 'Let me look at you, Bridget Honora O'Ryan. Have you altered at all?'

'Older, maybe,' Biddy retorted.

Jo chuckled. 'Not even that.' Her black eyes dwelt thoughtfully on the pretty face with its gloriously blue eyes under their long lashes—real Irish eyes, 'put in with a smutty finger'—and the mass of waving black hair which was drawn back from a centre-parting into a big 'bun' on the back of her neck. Biddy had the Irish oval face and softly pink and white colouring. Her mouth was generous, and when she smiled she showed a row of white teeth that would have gained her a fortune as a toothpaste advertisement.

'Well?' Biddy demanded, flushing under the steady gaze.

'Not changed a scrap. Biddy, it's fine having you here. I only wish it could have been for Christmas, but we'd fixed up to go to the Quadrant—that's Dick's place— weeks before I had your letter. I'd have taken you with us, but you couldn't have got another creature in with a shoehorn. Six Bettany kids, five of my own, Robin, Daisy and Primula, and four grown-ups, never to mention my own Anna, and Mollie's nurse and Nurse's two nieces! You add that up, my lamb, and see for yourself!'

'Five of your own?' Biddy gasped. 'Where's the sixth, then? You've *six* of your own, Jo Maynard!'

'Six it is; but Margot is with Madge and Jem in Canada. I'll tell you about that in a minute. I've heaps of news for you.'

'And the first you can tell me is why you are here at all, at all. What's happened to Plas Gwyn?'

'Oh, my dear! It very nearly wasn't! Half the foundations were going and it was only a miracle that it hadn't collapsed on our heads. Jack had us all out in short order, and luckily this house belongs to a friend of his who has let it to us for as long as we want it. They've had to renew a good half of the foundations, so we're doing some work that needed doing, now half the place is in pieces, and we're likely to be here some time. You'd hear that the School had to move because of the drains? They're at St Briavel's —that's an island just across the road from Carnbach, so to speak. It's really quite convenient, for I *didn't* want to part with the girls full term just yet. They aren't much more than babies, after all. As it is, I can see them quite often and they come home for two or three week-ends in the term.'

Biddy had sat up alertly. 'But this *is* all news to me! Why wasn't I told of it before?' she demanded. '*When* did all this happen?'

'But you *were*—told, I mean. It happened last Easter, and Daisy wrote you sheets and sheets about it. Do you mean to say you've never had it?'

'I have *not*! Ye could have knocked me down with a

feather when I got your letter saying you were here. I couldn't think what had happened.'

'Well, all I know is that Daisy spent the whole of one Sunday with my typewriter, giving you the gen. She produced about fifteen sheets of my thin typing paper, with the whole story. You'll have to thrash it out with her when she comes home again—there's the gong! Supper's ready. Come along; or do you want to wash first?'

'I'll wash. Where's the bathroom?'

'That can wait. We've a box of a place at the end of the hall that is dignified by the title of "cloakroom." Come along and I'll show you.'

Jo led the way, nodding at a door opposite the drawing-room as she went. 'There's the dining-room. And here's the cloakroom. Towels—soap—nail-brush—you have everything. You wash and brush-up and then come along. I'll go and begin on the serving.'

Biddy was in the dining-room within five minutes, and sitting down to a smoking plateful of goulash which she ate hungrily. 'Oh, but it's nice to be eating the good old Austrian dishes again!' she said as she passed her plate for a second helping.

'You won't get too many of them, I'm afraid,' Jo told her. 'We can't get the stuff to make them, though Anna does her best. She's made apfeltorte specially for you, so leave a *little* room!'

'The nice creature she is! But I'm hungry, I can tell ye!' Biddy fell to in a way that proved the truth of her remarks, and found plenty of room for a lavish helping of Anna's apfeltorte after.

'We'll take our coffee into the drawing-room,' Jo decided when she had finished. 'Then I want all *your* news. I've talked myself nearly hoarse and I should think you were fairly well up-to-date by this.'

Biddy laughed and picked up the coffee-tray to carry it into the drawing-room. They settled themselves by the fire, Jo poured out and then looked expectantly at the guest over the rim of her cup.

'I'm disappointed about one thing,' Biddy announced as she sat back in her chair. 'I wanted to see your family. Where are they?'

'You'll see them soon enough,' Jo told her cheerfully. 'They're at the Quadrant until school begins. Peggy will bring the girls with her own crowd and I'm going off for a few days to retrieve the boys. You'll see them all soon enough. You'll be coming over when you can, won't you?'

'Oh, I know; but I wanted to see them *now*!' Biddy lamented. 'D'you happen to remember that Charles was just a baby that no one thought would live when I went to Australia? And I've never seen Michael *at all*. How old are they all now?'

'The girls were nine last November, and Stephen will be six next month. Charles is five in June, and Michael two in July. Anyhow, you're all wrong about Charles,' she added. '*I* was never really afraid for him. Oh, I know there was a great fuss made when he arrived so suddenly and was such a miserable specimen; but I *knew* he'd make a go of it all right, misery or not. Can't tell you why, but I knew all right.'

'No one would have thought so from the way ye carried on about him.'

Jo laughed. 'He was so tiny and looked so frail that I felt I had to give him the greatest care; but underneath it all I knew we should pull him through, and we have! Actually, we've had nothing like the worry over him that we've had with Margot. However, we're hoping that that is over, too. See here, Biddy!' She made a long arm, and pulled open a bureau drawer from which she took a sheaf of photographs. 'These were part of my Christmas present from Canada.' She handed them over.

Biddy looked at them—beautifully tinted photographs, one each of a little girl, and one of the three together. 'Well, no mistake who this is,' she said. 'That's Margot with the wicked twinkle in her eye. Yes, Joey; you're right. There oughtn't to be any need to worry over *that* any more. Now—Jo Maynard! Ye're niver telling me this is Josette!'

In her excitement she became richly Irish, and Jo laughed. 'A bit of a change, isn't it? Yes; that's Josette. And that one Ailie, the youngest of Madge's girls. She's not nearly so pretty as the other two but she has a dear little face of her own, don't you think? Now,' she drew a fifth photo from its envelope with a flourish, 'here's the pick of the bunch. What do you think of *that*?'

Biddy gaped at the portrait of a graceful dark-eyed woman sitting in a big chair with a tiny baby on each arm. 'Jo! That's Madame! But—are ye telling me those are *hers*?'

'I am indeed—twin sons, so David has brothers at long last. The only snag,' Jo went on ruefully, 'is that he's nearly old enough to be their father—sixteen in May!—so they won't be much of pals for him. Still, he's very thrilled about them. The girls, of course, nearly went crackers when we told them. One's Kevin and the other's Kester—the old English form of Christopher.' She stopped to laugh. 'Madge is so bucked with herself for having caught up with Mollie and me! I say it's her own fault for having such enormous intervals between babies. *We* were much more reasonable.'

'Yours aren't so close as all that,' Biddy argued. 'You went and had triplets as a beginning; but there's three years between them and Stephen, and isn't Michael three years younger than Charles?'

'That's a lot closer than Madge's crowd, anyway. Fifteen and a half years between David and this pair, and only three girls between. I admit there's not quite two years between David and Sybil, but she was four and a half when Josette arrived, and Josette was nearly five when Ailie came along. There's a book of snaps as well, but you can see that later. I want to hear *your* news now I've told you our biggest piece. First of all, what about Australia? How did you like it?'

'Quite good in spots. I'd never want to live there—it wouldn't suit me as a home at all, at all. Still, I've enjoyed me four years.'

'I've never said anything about it to you before, Biddy,' Jo said gravely as she refilled Biddy's cup, 'but we all thought you played up splendidly when you offered to go back with that poor child and see her safely home. Only —why on earth did you stay so long?'

Biddy looked thoughtful. 'Sure, I couldn't do anything else. She—well, she sort of clung to me. She'd loved Oxford so, and I was the only bit of it left to her. We all knew it couldn't be for long—she was too ill for that, though she did revive for a while once we got her home and she lived for fifteen months, which was more than Dr Jem gave her when he saw us off on the boat. Her folk begged me to stay with her till the end and I'll never be sorry I did. Then there were three quite little ones and their place was right up in the bush, so school was a difficulty. I helped out by teaching them, and when Mavis died, Mrs Grant asked me to stay on until Lydia—that's the baby—was old enough to go away to school with the others. So I stayed. That's all.'

'I see. Then Lydia is old enough for boarding school now?'

'Ten last August. She went with the others when they went back. So then I wrote to Miss Annersley and asked her could she find me a job back home, and she wrote and said Mary Burnett was leaving to be married and they would need a history mistress and would I like to come? There was only the one answer to that as ye know yourself. I couldn't leave Burra-Burra until the girls went, and Mrs Grant wanted me to stay on with her even then; but I couldn't do it. There wasn't any real place for me there and, anyhow, I've always wanted to teach. But I've a standing invitation to go back whenever I like. Maybe I will one day.'

Jo chuckled. 'I'm glad you turned it down. I filled in last term, but I can't go on, of course. I've got my own job here, with all my family. It wasn't awfully convenient, either, for there were days when I couldn't cross to St Briavel's—or else I was there and couldn't get back. Besides that, Madge and Jem want us to go out to Canada at Easter with all the kids and stay until they come home —June, some time, they think—and I'd love to go. I've always wanted to see Canada and I'm dying for Margot again, not to speak of Madge and Jem and the rest. I couldn't go if the School had to depend on me for history, so you see it all fits in beautifully. Now, tell me how you liked Penny Rest.'

'Och, Joey, 'tis a real home from home it is. I'd a good time there, I can tell you. I made a new friend there,' she added with a gurgle.

Jo gave her a quick look, but Biddy's face was transparently innocent. 'Who was it?' she demanded.

'A girl of fourteen—rather a jolly kid. Not pretty in the least, but such a vivid little face, and full of bright ideas. She has the queer mix-up in her life—shall I take the tray out to Anna, seeing neither of us wants more coffee? I'll go on when I come back. Shan't be a minute.' Biddy picked up the tray and vanished with it, to return ten minutes later and find Jo placidly going on with her darning.

'I like your "minute"!' she said. 'Come along, now, and tell me about this girl.'

'So I will—but I can darn, too.' Biddy produced a pocket hussif from which she took her thimble and a darning-needle; picked up a stocking from the heap in the basket, and set to work while she talked.

'How did you mean about a queer mix-up?' Jo asked.

'Well, her parents are on the West coast of Africa, so they can't have her with them, and she's in charge of a cousin who likes to globe-trot. Carola told me it was fun at first, but she hates it now, never having a home, or going to school like other girls. Sure, she nearly had the face off me for stories about our School.' Again came that low chuckle as Biddy added sweetly, 'I told her all about *you*!'

'Didn't tell her any of your own evil doings, I suppose?' Jo snapped.

'I did so! But sure, Joey, there's never a one of us has had so many queer adventures as you have. 'Tis a fly-paper for adventures you are!'

Jo chuckled in her turn as she remembered some of her weirder exploits. 'They do happen to me,' she admitted. 'What about this kid?'

'She told me she was going to beg and beg her cousin to let her come to the School.' Biddy rested a prettily-cleft chin on her hand and stared into the dancing flames of the wood-fire for a moment. 'I only hope Miss Curry— that's the name she has on her—will see reason, for that child needs school more than most in my opinion. What's more, she *wants* it more than most. Sure, 'tis the main idea the creature has in her head just now. Of course, after all I told her about the Chalet School, nothing would serve her but that she must go there. Dear knows what will happen!'

'Let's hope this cousin of hers sees sense. It's absurd for a girl of that age being dragged round the world from pillar to post! We had one specimen of that kind of thing in young Lavender, poor kid!'

'Yes; but Lavender liked it. She'd never known any-thing else—or not to count, anyhow—and she hated school at first. Carola *wants* school, I tell ye. Miss Curry means well enough I dare say,' Biddy continued honestly, 'but she's not unselfish enough to give up her own fun, so poor Carola has to be a kind of wandering Jew. There's one pair of stockings done for you, anyway,' she concluded with a yawn.

Jo got to her feet. 'Time you were in bed when you gape like that. You'll swallow the whole room, me included, if you go on like that. Come on, Biddy; bed!

I've put you into Robin's room as she won't be home for a while yet, and school begins in two days' time for you.'

'I'm longing to see her again—Daisy, too. What's Rob doing now, by the way? I know Daisy's heart and soul in her doctoring.'

'Oh, my dear! Of all things she insisted on taking up social service! We let her try, but she isn't strong enough, and she caught a cold which she couldn't shake off. That's one reason why she's in Switzerland. You know what sort of a heritage she has from her mother, and how anxious we all used to be about her years ago. She's far, far stronger now than anyone ever hoped; but she can't do strenuous things like social service. What she'll do when she comes back—which won't be until that cold is cleared up for keeps—I couldn't tell you. Rob's a darling and the light of my eyes—one of them, anyhow—but she knows her own mind, I can tell you. Mercifully, she's generally open to reason. There's a lot to be said for bringing up children to be obedient, Biddy.'

'I agree with you. Mavis was an example of what happens when ye do *not*! If she'd done as she was told and rested and kept out of draughts and damp, she might be alive this moment, poor little soul!'

Biddy looked very serious as she followed Jo upstairs to the pretty bedroom at the top of the house. Biddy had picked up her case as they passed through the hall, and when they had reached their goal she dropped it with a sigh of relief. 'This looks good! You're right, Joey: I'm very tired. I'll sleep well in that bed.'

'I should hope so! You get undressed and into it and I'll bring you a glass of hot milk presently to make sure of it. We can go on with our gossip in the morning. "Tomorrow is also a day,"' Jo quoted the old Spanish proverb as she left the room, and Biddy wearily turned to open her case and take out what she needed for the night.

She was in bed when Jo came up twenty minutes later with the promised hot milk. She found her guest half-asleep, though she roused up enough to sip the milk and say good-night before she sank back on her pillow, and was literally drowned in sleep before her hostess had closed the door behind her after tucking her in with a kiss and switching off the light.

Chapter III

ESCAPE!

CAROLA glanced round with a hunted air. Cousin
Maud was busy chatting with some old acquaintances
she had just met who, so they had informed her, were
taking the same cruise as herself. She was still indignant
about Miss Bacon. She had made a few inquiries but had
been able to find no one to play governess to Carola and
helper in general to herself. This meant that not only
must she see to everything for herself, but also she must
look after Carola on the voyage, whatever she might be
able to do when they had reached Kingstown. She
almost regretted her decision to keep the girl with her.
If Carola had been packed off to school, life would have
been that much easier. Then she reminded herself that
she had promised Andrew and his wife to look after their
girl, and unless she had given up the trip altogether she
had no choice but to put up with this inconvenience. Part
of her wrath had descended on the head of Carola, who
had never found her so fussy and trying before. Needless
to state, it required only this to confirm that young person
in her decision not to sail. After the first she had wavered
a little; now she was determined. Go to Jamaica she
would *not*!

During the sixteen days which had elapsed since New
Year's Day, Carola had laid her plans carefully. She had
some money—four or five pounds—for her father had sent

her a cheque to buy her own Christmas present, and Cousin Maud had cashed it for her while they were at Penny Rest. Carola had not spent a penny of it, having no need and not seeing anything she particularly wanted. In addition, she had saved her pocket money for some weeks. Money was the thing that least worried her, therefore.

Clothes might have been a difficulty, but Cousin Maud had left her to do all her own packing and the young monkey had made full use of her new expanding suitcase, cramming it with everything she was likely to find useful at school. She had rejected her own old ones, routing out one of her cousin's which was twice as large, and the trunk which had gone to the hold marked 'Not wanted on the voyage' contained little but summer clothes. Everything else was in the cases. She had taken the precaution of fastening straps round them, for really they were so crammed she was afraid they might burst if she trusted to locks only.

'I wonder,' the naughty girl muttered to herself as she stood to one side, watching her cousin talking animatedly to her friends, 'if it would be safe for me to get off now? She's awfully keen on these people, and I don't believe she'd notice if I did slip away.'

She eyed her cases doubtfully. They were very heavy, and she simply must have them with her. Carola felt sure that she would need everything in them at school. She fully intended writing to her parents once she was settled there, and getting their permission to stay on; but it would be some weeks before she could hear. Of her cousin's feelings when she discovered that her charge had vanished, Carola never troubled. It is doubtful if she even thought of that side of it.

At that moment Cousin Maud turned for a minute from her friends and came to the girl. 'It's time we were going on board, Carola. Pick up your cases, child. You know our cabin, so take them there and begin unpacking until I come to you. I won't be long and we may be separated in the crowd—why, Mrs Barnett, are *you* coming, too? Quite a gathering of the clans, isn't it?' She beamed at a tall, pretty woman who had just come up.

Mrs Barnett gave an exclamation. 'Miss Curry! Well, isn't the world small? Are you coming to Jamaica? What fun! I've just been seeing my young monkey off to her school; and I suppose you've been doing the same by your small cousin? Oh, there goes the bugle. We'd better make a move, I expect.'

Carola picked up her cases and moved forward—exactly six steps. Then a sudden rush of the crowd separated her from Cousin Maud and she slid back to the outskirts of the throng, while Miss Curry moved forward, gaily chatting with her friends and quite satisfied that Carola would go straight to their cabin and she would find her there presently. Carola, however, was now behind a pile of cases, watching what was going on with interested eyes and clinging to her cases like grim death. A man came up to ask her if he could carry them aboard for her, but she coolly informed him that she was seeing her cousin off before going on to her school, so he advised her to move back out of the way, and left her.

Presently, the bugle rang out again. Gangways were cleared; hawsers were cast off; gaily-coloured streamers were flung from those on deck to those on the wharf; and with great hooting, the liner swung slowly and majestically round, headed by her guardian tugs, and set her course for the open sea. The crowds struck up 'Auld Lang Syne,' and the great vessel moved forward to the sound of a great wave of melody. Carola watched her, wondering secretly if she would manage to get safely through the dock gates. She saw a little party of a woman and two girls standing waving violently. Tears poured down the face of the middle-aged woman, and the two girls kept mopping their eyes. She slipped forward, and when, the liner now well away, they turned to leave, she tagged on behind them. The dock officials seeing her there, made no demur, and she passed through and out on to the road with triumph in her heart. She had accomplished the first part of her plan in safety.

From the tales she had coaxed out of Miss O'Ryan at Penny Rest, Carola had learned that the Chalet School was on St Briavel's, a tiny island off the coast of South Wales. It was reached from Carnbach, a small port, and she had heard that the girls went to Swansea by train and were met there by motor coaches which took the shortest way through the mountains, thus saving them the tedious journey in a stopping train along the coast. Her plan was to find her way to the shopping centre of South-ampton, get lunch somewhere, and then make for the station, buying food for the journey on the way. She and Cousin Maud had reached the city the day before, and while that lady had taken an hour's rest on her bed at their hotel in the afternoon, Carola had slipped out and made inquiries about trains, so that she knew what she must do. Once she had reached the School, she reckoned that they must keep her, at any rate until someone in authority had been contacted, for the house at Boncombe was closed, and she had no relations in England.

The first part of her plan was easily carried out, for a bus arrived just then, and took her and her cases to the shopping centre, where she found a café and made a meal of welsh rarebit, cake, and coffee—all she could have just then, as the liner had sailed at nine forty-five. That finished, she found a taxi and drove to the station, where she was just in time to catch a train for Cardiff where she had been told she must change. She had bought jam puffs and sandwiches in the café and even found time to rush into a bookshop and invest in a book.

At the station a kindly porter, seeing the schoolgirl in difficulties with her cases, book, handbag, and parcels, came to help her. He found her a corner-seat, swung up the cases on the rack, and left her extremely pleased with herself. She took a packet of chocolate out of her handbag and settled down to enjoy it and *Because of Vivien*.

So far, so good; but at Cardiff she had the first of her real difficulties. She had never been in the big station and she lost her way and nearly lost her train into the bargain. However, she caught it by the skin of her teeth and then found that she had somehow lost the remainder of her food. She faced a long journey with nothing more substantial than what was left of her chocolate and a bag of boiled sweets.

Well, it couldn't be helped now. The best she could hope for was that she could buy something from a platform trolley at some station on the way, and that, she guessed, was a somewhat faint hope. Anyhow, she had caught the train and that was something. Miss O'Ryan had told her that the last coaches for Carnbach left Swansea after this train arrived there, and if she had lost it, she would have been stranded overnight.

She was tired of reading by this time, so she sat staring out of the window as the train ran through Welsh valleys disfigured by ugly mining villages. When darkness fell, she returned to her book and contrived to keep herself from thinking too longingly of those jam puffs and sandwiches. There were no Chalet School girls in her carriage, for they travelled in specially labelled compartments, and in the circumstances Carola had decided it would be better to keep clear of them until she was as near the School as possible. She had put on her brown coat and beret and hoped that in the darkness and on the motor coaches she would pass muster as a new girl.

At long last they arrived at Swansea, and she tumbled out. A kindly fellow-passenger lifted down her cases for her and she thanked him as prettily as she could, picked them up, and staggered off with them to the exit, hoping no one would say much to her yet.

Outside the station three big coaches were drawn up, and already the girls were climbing in. She noticed that they added their cases to a pile at one side, so she did the same, and then advanced rather timidly towards the second bus where girls were filing in under the eyes of two mistresses. A third one was already in the first bus, settling various people in their seats. Not very sure what to do, Carola went up to the two ladies still outside.

'Please,' she said in a tired voice, 'I'm Carola Johnstone. I couldn't get into the proper carriage because I nearly missed the train.'

The elder of the two ladies promptly pulled out a list and scanned it, much to Carola's horror. It had never dawned on her that mistresses on escort duty would be armed with a list of the pupils they had to meet. The younger lady smiled at her sympathetically.

'New, and very tired, aren't you?' she said. 'What a horrid situation for you!' She turned to her companion. 'Found her, Miss Slater?'

Tired as she now was, Carola noticed that she had a charming voice, fresh and sweet, and even under the somewhat dim lights, it was plain that she was very pretty.

Miss Slater, busy with her list, shook her head. 'Not a Carola in the list—unless this queer scrawl at the bottom is it. It might be anything! Rosalie must have been in a mighty hurry at the end and just scribbled it in anyhow. You *are* for the Chalet School, aren't you?' she added doubtfully to Carola. 'What's happened to your beret badge?'

'I—I didn't get one,' Carola stammered, blushing violently.

'Didn't? Oh, those posts!' She groaned loudly. 'Well, it must be all right, and we can see you get your badges at school tomorrow. Now, let me see. Annis Lovel! Come here, dear.'

Annis Lovel, a sturdy, dark-eyed girl with a short mop of thick black curls, detached herself from the group of girls with whom she had been chattering excitedly and came up, saying, 'Yes, Miss Slater?'

'This is Carola Johnstone—isn't that what you said?— a new girl. Take charge of her, will you? And you people stop gossiping and get into your coach or we'll be here all night.'

'Yes, Miss Slater.' Annis turned to Carola. 'Come along, and I'll show you what to do. How old are you?'

'Fourteen,' Carola said, staring. She had never expected to be asked her age so soon.

'Good enough. Here you are—Clem Barrass!' She caught a red-haired girl of about Carola's own age, who was chattering eagerly with two or three others. 'Clem, I want you to look after Carola Johnstone. This is her. Take her along with your crowd, will you?'

'O.K.,' Clem nodded. 'Come on, Carola.'

Carola went, and Clem, with an arm through hers, took her back to the group, and introduced them. 'Here's a new girl, you folk—Carola Johnstone. This is Jean Ackroyd, Carola, and Anne Whitney and Gillian Moggeridge. We're all in the same form.'

The others said, 'Hello!' and then Jean added in a rather different tone, 'There's Miss Burn signalling to us to get a move on. Come on! We're to go in her coach.'

They moved over to the last of the coaches where the pretty young mistress was standing, and clambered in, Clem taking care to see that Carola sat beside her. Other girls followed them, and when the coach was full Miss Burn climbed in and settled down at the back, and they rolled away.

They were soon out of the town and running through the valleys where here and there they saw lights from farmhouses and cottages far up the hillside. Sometimes they swept through villages; once or twice it was a small town; but for the most part they went in darkness. The girls chattered eagerly among themselves and Carola sat silently listening to them and trying to suppress yawns. She was very tired, not only with the journey, but also with the mixture of emotions she had felt through the day, and she was beginning to feel terribly hungry. Presently

Clem, who seemed to live somewhere in the Hebrides and have artist parents, turned to her politely.

'This your first time at school, Carola?'

'No; not quite,' Carola replied. 'I went to a Kinder when I was little. Then Dad got a job in Equatorial Africa and I couldn't go with them, of course——'

'Why ever not?' demanded someone sitting in front who had turned round to listen when the new girl began to speak.

'Because it isn't the right sort of climate for English children—too hot,' Carola informed her.

'Oh, I see. Why didn't you go to school in England, though?'

'Well, you see, I've been living with Dad's cousin and she liked travelling about and took me with her. Now she's gone to Jamaica, so I'm coming to school, as I didn't want to go.'

'Oh, I see. Won't you be rather bored after going about like that, though?'

Carola shook her head decidedly. 'Not me! I'm sick of it!'

She was interrupted by a screech from the girl in front. 'I say, you people, I've just thought of it! She's exactly like Lavender Leigh!'

Carola stared. 'Lavender Leigh?'

'Don't you know the "Lavender Laughs" series? Well, Lavender Leigh who was at school till the end of last summer term was "Lavender." Oh, you ought to read them. They're *wizard*!'

Carola shook her head. 'I've never read them. I think I've seen them in the shop windows, though. Was she really at the Chalet School?'

'Rather!' Half a dozen voices chimed in on this.

'Well, I wonder why——' she suddenly stopped.

'Yes?' Clem prompted her. 'You wonder why—what?'

'Oh, nothing. Tell me about Lavender. What a jolly name!'

Clem shot her a quick glance and then decided to change the subject. 'Oh, Lavender just hated school at first. She'd travelled just about everywhere since she was a tiny kid, and she didn't like school in the least.'

'Well, that's not me,' Carola said with decision. 'I'm only longing for it. I'm sick of trains and planes and boats. It'll be a rest to settle down somewhere for a few months and not be for ever on the move.'

'Oh, I see,' said Clem, clearly not seeing at all. She added politely, 'I hope you aren't too awfully tired with today's journey?'

'It'll soon be over now, though, won't it? I'm awfully sleepy, but I think I can keep awake a while longer. Have we very far to go?'

'Oh, not so terribly far,' Clem told her. 'Look here, if you're sleepy, change places with me and tuck your mack under your head. I'll wake you when we get near Carnbach—if I know it in time,' she added with a giggle.

'Why won't you know it?' Carola asked when the change had been made and she was sitting next the window, while Clem expertly rolled up her raincoat and tucked it between her head and the side of the coach.

'Well, you see, this is only the third term we've been at St Briavel's, and before, it's always been daylight when we arrived; but now it's dark and I may not recognise my landmarks,' Clem explained. 'Are you all O.K.? Then you tuck down and have a nap. We'll probably see the lights, anyhow.'

Carola was thankful to do as she was told. She did not exactly sleep, for she was conscious of a murmuring all the time; but she certainly dozed, and when Clem woke her fully with a gentle shake and the news that they were running along the coast-road, she sat up, yawning widely.

'Feel better?' Clem asked. 'Have you been travelling far today?'

'It feels like hundreds of miles. We set off at half-past eight this morning and I seem to have been going ever since—especially since I left Southampton after seeing the liner off.'

'And it's a good bit after six now! Oh, poor you!' the girl in front sympathised with her. 'Well, it's early bed for everyone tonight. Keep going for a while longer and then you can do all the sleeping you want till seven to-morrow morning.'

Somehow or other, Carola contrived to keep awake now, and when they finally reached the ferry-landing at Carn-bach and tumbled out of the buses, the fresh breeze from the sea swept the sleepiness from her eyes for the time being. She stared round at all she could see under the light from the arc-lamp. The black water rippling against the land-ing, reflected back the rays, and tied up to the posts were two broad-beamed ferryboats, clearly waiting for them. They were lined up in pairs and each girl took charge of her own case as her name was called when it came from the boot. Suddenly, Miss Slater paused in her calling.

'Carola Johnstone!' she read. 'How is this, Carola? I thought I had called your name already?'

'I have two cases, Miss Slater,' Carola said, going red under the startled eyes of the girls about her.

'But the instructions distinctly say that each girl must

bring only a night-case with her—no more. Everything else should have been put into your trunk.'

'I—I haven't brought a trunk,' Carola faltered. 'It's all in the cases.'

Miss Slater raised her eyebrows; but Miss Burn interfered. 'Oh, well, Carola can explain when we get to the Big House. Take the thing, Carola, and let's get on. We shall be here all night at this rate! Here you are!'

Carola took the case; no more was said; and presently the last girl was on board, the gangplanks were wound up, and the ferries swung clear of the landing-stage and set their course for the island. From the chatter of the girls, Carola discovered that this was the first time most of them had been on the water after dark. She joined the excited crowd thronging round the sides to watch the reflections from their own lights as the lumbering ferry steadily ploughed her way through the tranquil water. She sniffed the salt air with appreciation and felt quite wide awake.

'Ooh! Doesn't it look *wizard*!' said a small, clear voice close to her.

Carola looked round. The speaker was a sturdy twelve-year-old, with two fair pigtails bobbing about her shoulders. She looked up at the new girl with dancing blue eyes, and grinned companionably. 'Hope you'll like us,' she remarked. 'We're a pretty good school, if I do say it. What's your name? Clem did say it, but I wasn't really listening, so I didn't catch it.'

'Mary-Lou, you hush up!' retorted Clem herself who was close at hand. 'I never knew a kid with as much cheek. You've enough for fifty your size.'

Mary-Lou remained unperturbed. 'I was only being

polite. I'll tell her my name first, if you like. I'm Mary-Lou Trelawney,' she turned to the new girl. 'You know that this ginger creature is Clem Barrass, and this,' drawing forward a slight, dainty girl of her own age, 'is my other great pal, Verity-Anne Carey. Now tell us your name.'

'I'm Carola Johnstone,' Carola replied rather dazedly. She knew so little of other girls that Mary-Lou's unruffled calm rather stumped her.

'Really? Then you're jolly lucky!' Mary-Lou informed her.

'Lucky?' Carola stared at her. 'Why? How do you mean, lucky?'

'Having a name like that, of course. There's not another Carola in the place, though we've dozens of Annes and Pamelas and Elizabeths and things like that. How d'you spell it, by the way?'

'C-a-r-o-l-a,' Carola spelt for her, and Mary-Lou considered it.

'But isn't that "Carōla"?' she asked at last.

'Rather not! It's Carola, without any accent anywhere,' the owner of the name told her.

'Well, I'm glad to know. If you hadn't told me I'd have thought it was spelt like the Christmas wait carollers,' Mary-Lou explained. She gave a sudden deep chuckle. 'I say, Auntie Jo will be all over it! She's always on the look-out for new names for her books. She's a writer, you know. Her name's Josephine M. Bettany—at least her writing name is. Of course, really, she's Mrs Maynard now. Have you read any of hers—*Tessa in Tyrol*, or *The Rose Patrol in the Alps*, or any of those?'

By this time, Carola knew where she was. Biddy O'Ryan had told her all about Jo Maynard, and she was a Josephine

Bettany fan and owned most of the books. 'Of course I've read them. Is she really your aunt? You lucky soul!'

'Well, actually she isn't,' Mary-Lou replied honestly, if reluctantly. 'Only, she and Mother are pals, so she said I was to call her Auntie. Two of her triplets are at school, you know——'

'You're talking too much,' Clem interrupted. 'I always did say your tongue was hung in the middle and waggled at both ends. Anyhow, we're nearly there, so you'd better put a lid on it, Mary-Lou, and go to your own form. See you later.' She gave Mary-Lou a shove and that young chatterbox departed after making a weird and wonderful grimace at her.

'Mary-Lou's quite a good kid,' Clem airily informed the new girl as the ferry drew in, 'but she talks till she nearly has you *deaved*!'

'Till *what*?' Carola demanded with interest.

'Deaved,' Clem repeated. 'It's Scots for—well—dazed.'

Carola began to laugh. That was exactly what she had felt. There was no time for more, for the ferry had reached port and already the mistresses were calling the girls into line. The gangplanks rattled down with a great clanking of chains and such part of the School as was on board marched off and through the little turnstile on to the high-road which, as Clem informed the new girl, wound right across the island. The young mistress had wrenched the larger of Carola's cases from her as she passed, remarking, 'You can't possibly walk the whole way to school loaded down like that! It's a pity your people didn't abide by the rules, but it's too late to worry about that now.'

She gave the girl an infectious grin and Carola murmured

'Thank you,' and walked on with Clem Barrass who had paired off with her.

It was not really a long walk—about a mile—and the girls were glad of the chance to stretch their legs which were cramped after the long journey in the motor coaches. They chattered gaily among themselves as they wound up the road which ran between high hedges. Before long they were turning in at big gates and going up a drive walled on either side by a high holly hedge. A dark mass loomed up at the farther end and then a sudden stream of light poured down the drive as someone opened the front door.

'Welcome back, girls!' said a deep, very musical voice; and as the girls replied, Carola realised that here was one of the Heads.

They marched in, depositing their cases in a deep pile in a corner of the wide hall and then were sent to the cloakrooms to hang up berets and coats and change their walking-shoes for house slippers.

'I expect you'll be in our Splashery,' Clem told Carola. 'Come away and we'll find your peg and locker. Oh, you'd better take your slippers out of your case first. All of us who were here last term left ours in our lockers, so we haven't to bother.'

Carola stared at the two cases. 'They're at the bottom of one of them, but I can't remember which,' she said helplessly.

Clem began a whistle, but broke off short with a guilty look. 'Help! What a position! In that case, I should say you'd better leave it alone for the moment until you can unpack,' she said. 'After all, you're new. No one is likely to say much to you, if anything.'

It seemed the only thing to do. Carola meekly followed

her new friend into the long, narrow room with pegs round the walls, and peg-stands set down the middle, and Clem began a hasty search for her name—something that naughty Carola knew would be quite unavailing, but she didn't see what she could do about it at present. Presently Clem turned to the new girl looking blank.

'Someone's slipped up. Your name's not here,' she announced. She scanned the pegs again. 'It's most unlikely you'd be in a junior Splash, and this is the only one there was any room in. Let's see. Oh, *luck*! Here's one vacant! You snaffle it and we can see Miss Dene about a label for you later. Hang up your coat and cap and wait till I come. I'm at the other side.' She hurried off to her own peg, leaving Carola to do as she was told, but was quickly back.

'Now then, it's just on supper-time and I'm ravenous, and I guess you are even more so. There's the gong! Come on!'

She took Carola's arm and pulled her out into the corridor where they joined a long stream of girls of all sorts and sizes on the way to the big dining-room where Clem seated her beside herself, and after Grace, jumped up and went to the buttery hatch to come back with two plates of cottage pie, steaming and savoury and very welcome to Carola, who suddenly felt famished.

'Wire in!' Clem commanded as she set the noble plateful before the new girl. 'You look starved!'

'Oh, I *am*!' Carola said fervently. 'Thanks fearfully much, Clem.'

Clem sat down with a grin, and proceeded to tackle her own while carrying on half a dozen conversations with as many people, who all seemed to want to know what she had done during the holidays. The silent Carola, steadily eating her way through her share, noted that everyone seemed to like Clem, who kept a watchful eye on her and saw to it that she had all she needed, but was too busy to say much to her. The girl on her other side, who had been saluted as 'Lalla,' made a few friendly remarks; but on the whole Carola felt herself very much one alone. She was the only new girl at this table and, from what she heard, she gathered that there would be only a few of them this term. However, all things considered, she got through supper very well. The brisk walk through the fresh January air had roused her thoroughly, and she felt decidedly better when she had finished her meal, which was topped off with a plateful of junket and bottled plums. But after supper came Prayers; and after that, dismissal to the dormitories; and now her troubles began in real earnest.

'Are you Protestant or Catholic?' Clem demanded as, supper over, they marched along to the school hall.

Carola stared at her. 'I'm Church of England,' she said. 'Why?'

'Oh, well, that's O.K. then. If you were Catholic you'd have to go with the Catholics for Prayers, you see,' Clem explained. 'In here!'

She gave Carola a friendly little shove, and the new girl found herself in her first school hall. She looked round eagerly as soon as Clem had steered her to her place. It had originally been a big double drawing-room, but was now cleared, and the walls had been colour-washed a sunshiny yellow with dark green woodwork. Prints of famous pictures hung at intervals round the walls, interspersed with boards of golden oak, bearing names and

dates in gilt. Carola knew that these must be Honours
Boards, and she simply longed for a chance to go round
and read what they said. There was no hope at the
moment, for a bell rang and the quiet buzz of chatter that
had filled the Hall hushed at once. A minute later the
mistresses came through a door at the far end of the room,
with Miss Annersley last, and formed into a semi-circle
behind the tall reading-desk where the Head took up her
stand. A slender, very fair girl rose from her seat at the
end of one of the seats, which stood to one side of the daïs,
and gave out the number of the hymn. Clem had seen
that Carola was supplied with a copy of the School's own
hymnbook, so that young lady was able to join with the
others in singing 'Lord, behold us with Thy blessing.'
As her voice rose, sweet and clear, and amazingly powerful
for a girl of fourteen, two or three people in front turned
to stare, and the mistress at the piano also turned her head
with startled look to gaze at the ranks of singing girls.

The parable of the talents came next; and then they
knelt while Miss Annersley read the collect for the day
and the 'Lighten our darkness' before they all joined in
in repeating 'Our Father,' and—for the little ones—'Gentle
Jesus.' The blessing followed and then they all stood up.

'Sit down, girls,' Miss Annersley commanded; and they
sat down on the long forms and waited for a moment or
two until the door at the top of the room opened again,
this time to admit a stream of girls who went quietly to
take their places beside the others on the forms. Two or
three mistresses joined those on the daïs, and a tall, white-
haired lady with an amazingly young face went to the
reading-desk. Carola knew this must be the other Head
and looked at her with interest.

When everyone was in her place, Miss Annersley spoke again, welcoming all back to the School for the new term and hoping that the new girls would be happy with them.

'Now it is getting late,' she finished, 'so I shall say no more tonight. Miss Wilson will call the roll and then you must all go to bed. Tomorrow, those of you who have not yet unpacked will be excused from lessons while Matron wants you. All new girls who have not done our entrance test must go to the prefects' room after Prayers—someone will show you where to go—and a mistress will see to you. Just one piece of news for you. I know that most of you have heard of Biddy O'Ryan and many of the Seniors will remember her from their own Junior days. Miss O'Ryan has come to take the place of Miss Burnett, another old girl, and I am sure you will all want to give her a hearty welcome.'

Led by the Head Girl, the School welcomed Miss O'Ryan with a quick outburst of hand-clapping, and Carola, who had already discovered her sitting among the Staff, noted that the charming Irish face went crimson for a moment before the young mistress rose to acknowledge the clapping. Then the girls quieted down as Miss Annersley held up her hand, and Miss Wilson, producing a long roll, began to read the names rapidly, every girl answering 'Adsum' as her name came.

On and on she went and naturally no Carola Johnstone was among them. When she closed the roll, saying, 'That is all, girls,' Clem turned to her new acquaintance, open-mouthed with surprise. Miss Slater, however, had already risen and crossed the daïs and was saying something, and before Clem could do more than gasp, 'What on earth ——?' the Head had turned to the girls once more.

'Is Carola Johnstone here?' she inquired.

Carola was dumb with shock. In all her planning, she had never bothered to think what must happen once she was safely at school. She remained glued to her seat and never stirred until the watchful Clem poked her.

'Go on, you mutt! Stand up and say it's you!' she muttered.

Thus urged, Carola slowly rose to her feet and faced the gaze of not only the two Heads, but the wildly startled look of Miss O'Ryan.

Miss Annersley had been Head for too long to show much sign of the amazement that was inwardly consuming her. All she said was, 'Ah! I see. When you leave the room, will you come to the study, my dear? Ask someone to bring you, please. I want to see you.'

Carola pulled herself together. 'Y-yes, Miss Annersley,' she said faintly. Just at the moment she felt as if the world were composed of *eyes*—eyes that were all fixed on herself.

Perhaps the Head guessed that. She gave the command to stand, and the School rose to its feet while the mistress at the piano turned round and struck a chord. Like one girl, the ranks turned and then, to the tune of a bright quickstep, they filed from the room. Clem had caught Carola's arm and made her stand back so that the rest passed them. When the room was empty, even the mistresses departed, she led her off, down one corridor and along another, where they came to a door before which she paused and tapped. Miss Annersley's voice bade them enter, and the helpful Clem opened the door and shoved Carola through, hissing as she did so, 'Go on in, and don't forget to curtsy!'

Chapter IV

CAROLA HAS TO EXPLAIN

CLEM'S last injunction completed Carola's state of confusion, and it was a very discomforted young person who advanced into the room after closing the door behind her and executing a jerky bob of her knees which was intended to be a curtsy. Miss Annersley was alone, seated by the fire in a tall arm-chair, gazing into the heart of the flames. As Carola came towards her, she lifted her head and looked gravely at the girl.

'You are Carola Johnstone?' she said quietly. 'Come to the fire and sit down. I want to hear what all this means. Take that pouffe, child. Not too near the fire, are you? Good! Now begin and tell me what all this is about.'

Carola sat down and looked dumbly at the lady. When she had planned this interview in her own mind, it had taken place in a very official study, with herself standing very properly at attention before a severe-looking desk and a stern Head, draped in her gown, with perhaps a mortar-board lying beside her and looking portentously at her through black-rimmed glasses. She had never expected to be called on to explain herself sitting informally in a pretty room with the Head leaning back in her big William and Mary chair, looking like anyone else in her soft green dress.

'She doesn't even wear glasses,' was her rather muddled thought. 'I thought all Heads wore them.'

Miss Annersley had not taught for twenty-seven years for nothing. She knew girls, and she could make a very good guess at what Carola was feeling.

'You know you aren't entered for this school, don't you?' she asked.

'Yes,' Carola replied.

'What school *were* you entered for, then?'

'None at all. Cousin Maud wanted to take me to Jamaica with a governess, and I'm so tired of travelling about and never having anywhere for a real home—not even staying anywhere for long. I wanted school, but she said she'd promised Mother and Dad she would look after me while they were away, and she couldn't do it properly unless I was with her, and she wasn't going to alter the whole plan of her life just for me, and I ought to be grateful to her for seeing so much of the world. I'm not! I hate the whole thing; and so—I ran away.'

Miss Annersley looked a trifle startled. 'Do you mean that—my dear child, where *is* this cousin of yours? She must be told at once where you are. She must be frantic with worry about you!'

'She sailed for Jamaica this morning,' Carola said, looking startled in her turn.

This was a jolt for the Head. She had fancied that the girl had slipped off from home or wherever she had been staying with this Cousin Maud, and it would be merely a case of ringing up somewhere—the police, if necessary—to tell the lady where her young cousin was, and returning the child to her in the morning. This news complicated matters horribly. Leaning over, she touched a bell, and there was silence until a tap at the door heralded the entrance of a slight, fair woman in the early thirties, who came quietly in and stood waiting.

'Oh, Miss Dene,' the Head said pleasantly, 'I want you to send a radiogram for me as soon as possible.'

'Certainly, Miss Annersley.' Miss Dene went over to a small secretaire in the window, and picked up a pad lying there. 'To whom do I address it?'

Miss Annersley looked at Carola. 'What is your cousin's full name and the name of the ship in which she has sailed?' she asked.

'Maud Curry—Miss—and the ship is the S.S. *Pantyne*,' Carola replied mechanically.

'Thank you. Very well then, Miss Dene. "To Miss Maud Curry. S.S. *Pantyne*. Carola safe at Chalet School, St Briavel's Island, South Wales. Please cable instructions." You had better sign my name and add "Principal" after it.' She paused and looked at Carola. 'One moment, Miss Dene. Carola, have you any friends or relations in England to whom you can go?'

Carola shook her head. 'No, Miss Annersley. Mother and Dad are in Equatorial Africa, west coast. That's why they couldn't have me with them. I've no uncles or aunts except Uncle Jim in Canada.'

'I see. Then please add, "Can keep if necessary," Miss Dene. Thank you.'

Miss Dene, with a bewildered look at Carola, withdrew, and Miss Annersley turned to the culprit. 'And now, child, I think you must tell me the whole story. Of course we must keep you for the night, at any rate. Presently you will go up with Matron, who is putting you into a vacant cubicle in Clem Barrass's dormitory; but I must get this straightened out as far as possible first. I won't keep you long, though. You are too tired for any discussion. Now begin and tell me all about it. You say you hate travelling? Tell me why.'

Thus urged, Carola contrived to tell the bare outline of her story, aided here and there by questions from the Head. It took some time, but at last Miss Annersley had a very fair idea of the whole thing. She sat back in her chair as Carola concluded with a final statement of her hatred of travel, and a passionate plea for school, and there was silence in the room for a minute or two, save for the gentle hissing of the flames.

Carola felt better now that she had relieved her mind. She was quite satisfied to sit there, watching the dancing firelight. There was an atmosphere of peace in this room that soothed and calmed her fretted nerves. Presently, however, the Head turned to her.

'Now, Carola, it is much too late for me to talk to you properly. I will see you tomorrow and then we will go into the whole matter thoroughly. In the meantime, please give me your father's full name and address. I must send him a cable at once. Did you ever think that one of the first things your cousin would do when she found you were missing would be to let them know at once? We must relieve their anxiety as soon as we can. I expect your mother is frantic about it.'

Carola jumped up with a cry. '*Oh!* I never thought of that! Oh, Miss Annersley, Mother will be nearly crackers! Oh, what *shall* I do?'

She was so nearly on the verge of wild tears that Miss Annersley sprang up, too, and put an arm round her. 'Steady, Carola! If I cable at once, I expect it will be all right. Probably the cables will arrive together—or very nearly so.' She touched the bell once more. 'What is your father's full name and address?'

'Dr Andrew Johnstone, Calabar,' Carola replied, fighting back her tears with an effort. 'It's in Nigeria.'

'Thank you, my dear. Oh, Miss Dene, I want you to send another cable—Nigeria, this time.' She dictated a reassuring message to Nigeria, and then, as Miss Dene was leaving the room, she added, 'When you have sent that off, would you mind asking Matron to come for Carola? It is growing late and I think she had better go to bed at once. We can discuss the whole position to-morrow.'

Miss Dene went off, and the Head turned to the pupil who had so calmly foisted herself on to them. 'Now, my dear, Matron will come and take you to bed. Tomorrow you will go into School with the rest of the girls, and you must remain here until I can get into proper touch with your people. In the meantime, I am going to ask you to say nothing at all about this very foolish escapade of yours. If, by any chance, your parents should decide to leave you with us, it would do you no good for the girls to know what you have done. All the best of our girls would think you very childish and absurd to have done such a thing, and the sillier ones need no encouragement from such an example as you have set. Promise me, please.'

Very red, Carola gave the required promise. It had never dawned on her that there might have to be all sorts of explanations to the School at large; nor that, as Miss Annersley said, the more sensible of the girls would look down on her for carrying out such a wild plan. She knew from her reading that a bad start in school might hang about her for the rest of her school-life, and she realised dimly that the Head was being very generous in trying to prevent that for her.

A knock at the door sounded, and when Matron appeared, very trim and crisp in her uniform, with spotless apron and angel's wing cap, the only thing Carola wanted to do was to go to bed and to sleep and forget for the next few hours all about her mad action.

'This is Carola Johnstone, Matron,' Miss Annersley said. 'She is very tired and should go to bed now. Will you take her up to her dormitory and see to her? We must leave all questions until the morning, I think. I want her to go to sleep as soon as possible.'

Matron nodded. 'I quite agree. Come along, Carola. It's more than time you were in bed, especially after your journey. Be quick, child!'

Carola turned to say good-night to Miss Annersley. 'I'm sorry if—if I'm being an awful nuisance,' she said shyly, 'and thanks most frightfully for being so kind to me.'

Miss Annersley smiled at her for the first time during that interview. 'I'm glad to hear you say that. Now good-night, and go to sleep as fast as you can. Remember,' she added warningly, 'we have a good deal to do tomorrow and you must be fresh and rested.'

'Come along,' Matron said, touching the girl on the shoulder. 'I haven't any too much time to spare.'

Carola followed her from the room, and once they were gone, Miss Annersley departed for the secretary's office where she found her closeted with Biddy O'Ryan, Miss Burn, and Miss Wilson, all three sitting round the table having coffee.

'Come on, Hilda!' the latter exclaimed. 'We've been talking over the School's latest adventure. Did you know that it's all Biddy's fault? I *thought* we should have considered a dozen times before we decided to readmit her to our peaceful fold! Come and tell her what you think of her.'

'Sure, how was I to know the little ass would think of such a thing?' protested Biddy O'Ryan indignantly. 'I only told her a few stories about Tirol. *I* wasn't to know she'd go off at half-cock like this. Not that I altogether blame her, mind you,' she added. 'Trailing about from one place to another is no life for a kid of fourteen at all, at all.'

'One moment!' Miss Annersley checked the riot. 'Rosalie, did you get those two cables off safely?'

'I sent them all right. The post office didn't seem to have much idea when they'd reach their addressees,' Miss Dene said doubtfully. Then she added eagerly, 'Did you get the whole yarn from her? What had she to say for herself? What on earth is it all about?'

'An overdoing of travel plus a very natural desire to be with girls of her own age,' Miss Annersley said as she sat down. 'Coffee, Hilary? Oh, thank you. I can do with a cup of coffee, for my head's reeling. That wretched girl had actually disappeared from the *boat* and left her unfortunate cousin to imagine all sorts of ghastly happenings! I only hope my radiogram reaches her quickly before she manages to cable the child's parents. I also think she might have kept a closer watch on the young monkey. She seems to have left her to go by herself to the cabin without bothering to see that she got there. When I taxed Miss Carola with unkindness, she simply said, " I never thought of *that*!" I do wish girls would learn to *think* before they start out to do mad things!'

'I seem to have heard you say that in the dim and distant past,' Miss Wilson murmured.

'I seem to have had occasion for saying it most of the time I've been connected with this school,' her friend said ruefully. 'I said it *about* Joey and *to* her on more than one occasion, and I've gone on saying it about sundry pupils ever since. But I must say we've never been in quite such an awkward position before. Carola wouldn't think of that, however.'

'At her age? Is it likely?' Miss Wilson demanded.

'The story—the story!' Hilary Burn clamoured. 'You keep your diatribes for young Carola and tell us the yarn.'

'Very well; here you are.' And while she sipped her coffee, the Head repeated the tale she had heard from Carola.

'What do we do next?' Miss Wilson asked when it was ended and they had all said what they thought about it.

'I don't see what we can do but wait until we hear from this cousin and the child's parents. If they agree, the best thing will be for her to remain here. Mercifully we have a vacancy. If we hadn't——'

'If we hadn't you'd have made one—I know you!' Hilary Burn gave the Head an affectionate look. 'You may pretend to be very angry——'

'It isn't pretence, I assure you—or not altogether. I really feel very much annoyed when I think of our own situation. At the same time, I do sympathise with the girl. She has been very silly, but she had *some* excuse. If this cousin wasn't prepared to stay at home to look after her, she should have let her have her way and go to school. Wrong-headed as Carola has been, I do feel that she is not entirely to blame.'

'Oh, so do I! Well, Rosalie says you cabled that we could keep her here if necessary.'

'In the circumstances I don't see what else we could do. And now,' she went on, looking round them all, 'I want you people and Miss Slater—I must see her before we go to bed, by the way—to promise to say nothing about the thing to anyone else until I give you leave. If Carola stays with us the best thing will be to suppress the definitely irregular way in which she has come to us. If not, then I suppose we must give it out that her people have had to change their plans and she is not coming after all. That will depend, I suppose, on what Dr Johnstone has to say about it.'

'They mightn't want to pay our fees,' Rosalie Dene murmured.

'Oh, I don't think there will be much difficulty on that point,' Miss Annersley said briskly. 'Obviously they are well-to-do people. What I *am* afraid of is that he may think she ought not to be indulged in her wish after the way she has tried to attain it—yes, Nell? What is it?' She looked at Miss Wilson.

'I only want to say that if she is the child of Dr Andrew Johnstone of Calabar, he isn't very likely to think that way. I know some people who are friends of his and they say he's a bit of a psychiatrist. In that case he'll understand the child, I expect. Well, as you say, we can only wait and see.'

'I suppose Jo doesn't count?' Hilary asked in a detached manner.

'What *do* you mean?' Miss Annersley demanded, looking at her with the liveliest curiosity. '"Jo doesn't count"? In what way may I ask?'

'Not telling anyone. Jo isn't any one, is she?'

Miss Annersley looked her up and down and then burst into peals of laughter. 'I wish she could hear you! Oh, tell Jo by all means, if you like. Most likely we shall call her into consultation, Madge not being available.'

'Excellent!' Hilary jumped up. 'Bags me to tell Joey first that we have one more pupil than we expected this term, and just *how* we've got her!'

'You've missed the bus,' Biddy O'Ryan informed her calmly. 'Wasn't I on to her over the 'phone with the whole tale, so far as I knew it, an hour ago? Jo's coming over tomorrow to join in the fun, let me tell you.'

'Oh, bother you! I was just yearning to hear what she had to say on the subject.'

'Sure, I can tell you that. She said, "Well, I'll be jiggered!"'

Hilary considered this. 'Very poor for Jo! With her vocabulary I'd expect something much more thrilling. I say,' Hilary looked round them all, 'has it dawned on you folk that we've got to do a certain amount of rearranging with this unexpected new kid?'

'I thought of it at once,' Miss Annersley said, rising. 'Therefore, it means early rising tomorrow, so I'm going to bed now. Good-night everyone. Don't be late, please. Nell, are you coming?'

'Yes; we'll leave the youngsters to clear up,' Miss Wilson replied, laughing. She suddenly swung round on Hilary, as Miss Annersley left the room. 'I wonder, Hilary, has it dawned on *you* that now Biddy has joined our ranks you are no longer Staff baby? You'll have to grow up at last, my child!' With which she fled, laughing as she went.

Chapter V

THE FIRST TASTE OF SCHOOL

BY the time Carola reached her cubicle, she was too tired to take in much of its details, even if Matron had given her any time to do so. Just outside the door that lady stopped and warned her to be very quiet, as all the rest would be asleep now, or ought to be. Then she opened the door, switching on the little hand-lamp she carried, and lighted Carola down the narrow aisle between cretonne curtains that fluttered in the breeze from the open windows. She stopped before one cubicle where the curtains had not been drawn, a fact she swiftly remedied after she had waved Carola inside. Then she set her lamp down on the bureau.

'Undress as quickly as you can,' she said in low tones. 'I'll be back in ten minutes to take you to the bathroom.'

Carola undressed quickly, being almost morbidly careful about hanging her clothes over the backs of the two chairs to air and setting her shoes side by side in a corner. She untwisted her long pigtail and brushed it out, and then Matron arrived, picked up her lamp, and escorted the girl to a bathroom where she bade her wash and be quick about it.

Carola obeyed meekly; but she found time to wonder who had unpacked her cases for her, for she had found everything she needed, even the towels she had taken the precaution of bringing from Cousin Maud's. When she

64

was ready, Matron took her back again to the dormitory, set the lamp down again, told her to say her prayers, and departed once more.

Carola was so nearly asleep that it is to be feared that her prayers were mainly lip-service. She tumbled into bed, where Matron found her when she came back, almost asleep, but wide awake enough to say, 'Thank you, Matron. Good-night.'

'Good-night,' Matron responded after she had tucked the bed-clothes firmly in, and seen that all was as it should be. She picked up her lamp once more and left the cubicle. Before she had reached the dormitory door, Carola was sound asleep.

She was awakened next morning by the switching on of the lights and the sound of a big bell solemnly pealing for the beginning of the day. Still drowsy, she nevertheless threw back the clothes and jumped out of bed. Then she looked round, and triumph swelled her heart, driving away the last remnants of sleepiness. She was at school! Whatever happened now, at least she had had one night of it, and most likely one day to come, too. She hardly thought that Cousin Maud would break her journey to come back for her now. Most likely she would be told to stay where she was at the present. Then voices rose round her and put an end to her thoughts, and she listened eagerly.

'Oh dear! It simply *can't* be time to get up yet!' came from the cubicle on her right hand.

'Don't you believe it, young Polly!' was the reply from over the way. 'It's seven o'clock, so out you get!'

'Oh, how I loathe early rising!' Polly groaned; but a thud told that she was out of bed, and sundry scrabblings probably meant that she was hunting for her slippers. 'I say,' she went on, 'anyone know what's happened to that new girl—the one the Abbess yanked after her Prayers last night, I mean? Clem, weren't you sheep-dogging her? What became of her?'

'Not knowing, can't say,' came in Clem's voice.

'I wonder why the Abbess wanted to see her?' This was someone else.

At this point, Carola decided that she had better let them know she was there, so she said with some diffidence, 'I say, I'm here, you know.'

'*What?*' There was a rush of feet, and then Clem, her red-brown mop tossing wildly about her, pulled the curtains aside. 'When did you come up? What was all the fuss in aid of?'

Carola was in a quandary. She had promised to say nothing, and she was not very sure how to parry these questions. Luckily for her, the door at the end of the room opened, and someone came in.

'Clem Barrass!' said a stern voice. 'What are you doing there? Why aren't you getting dressed?'

Clem went pink. 'Please, Peggy, I was just talking to Carola Johnstone, the new girl,' she said.

'Well, be quick, and tell her about the bathroom and so on, and then go and dress at once or you'll be late as usual,' Peggy responded briskly.

'Yes, Peggy,' Clem said meekly.

'Anyone still in bed?' Peggy demanded.

'I'll just see.' Clem whirled round, but Peggy was before her.

'Out, everyone!' she called sharply.

There was an instant rustle, and every girl suddenly

appeared round her curtains in various stages of undress. Clem pulled Carola forward and that young lady realised that the fair, very pretty girl standing at the door was the same as the one who had given out the hymn at Prayers, and must be the Head Girl.

'All right,' Peggy said briefly. 'Be quick and dress, all of you. Carry on, Clem.'

She turned and left the room; everyone returned to her cubicle, and Clem, with a hasty 'I'll just find out which your bather is,' ran off down the dormitory to return with the information that the new girl came after her in bath-room 10. 'So you'd best come along with me now,' she concluded. 'Strip your bed—I'll help you—and then grab your towels and sponge-bag, and come on.'

She plunged at the bed, and in two minutes the sheets and blankets were hanging over the chairs; the pillow over the footrail; the mattress had been turned and humped up in the middle.

'Come on, now,' the competent Clem ordered, 'we'll have to scram, or it'll be a cat's lick and a promise for us!'

She hurried Carola out of the dormitory and down the corridor into a short passage whence came sounds of splashing. Before one door she paused.

'Here we are. I take my bath cold, but you *can* have it lukewarm if you like. Shan't be a sec and don't you be, either,' she added from the other side of the door to the accompaniment of the sound of running water. 'There are two more folk to come after you.'

Judging by the sounds, she was in the bath by this time, and three minutes later she was out, still drying her face, and remarking in muffled tones through her towel, 'In you go! I've set the tap running, and come straight back to the dormy when you're done.'

She raced off, and Carola entered the somewhat messy bathroom and plunged into the cold water once she had tossed off her clothes. She sluiced down as quickly as she could, but with all her haste she could not hope to rival Clem who seemed to have the makings of a quick-change artist about her, and the next girl was thumping impatiently on the door before she had finished her teeth.

'Sorry if I've kept you waiting,' she said, recognising Jean.

Jean gave her a nod as she shot in and slammed the door behind her. 'O.K., but you can't waste a minute at this time of day. You get back and dress,' she called; and Carola scuttled back to her dormitory, aware that she was only half-dried, but glowing from the sting of the cold water. She finished drying, and then hurried into her clothes.

'Tunic, etc., mind,' Clem called, still 'doing sheep-dog,' as the School called it, with all her might. 'Don't forget your blazer, and leave your cubey tidy or Matey will have something to say.'

Having neither tunic nor blazer, Carola was unable to obey her Mentor, but she put on her brown skirt and cream blouse, and knotted the flame-coloured tie she had coaxed Cousin Maud to buy for her before she pulled on a brown cardigan—the best she could do. Then she hurried to hang up her dressing-gown, place her bedroom slippers neatly together under the bed, and set her brush and comb straight on the little bureau top. Clem arrived before she had done, and demanded her brush and comb bag. Slippers, too, it seemed, were to be put on the shelf underneath the bureau. You were not allowed to leave anything about. This done, Clem turned to her charge, and gasped when she saw her attire.

'Where on earth is your tunic? Only people above Middle Fifth are allowed to wear blouses and skirts for lessons.'

'Cousin Maud didn't get me one,' Carola told her truthfully.

'Oh!' Clem seemed rather floored by this. Then she noticed the new girl's woolly cardigan and demanded, 'Didn't she get you a blazer either? No? Oh, well, I suppose they'll see about it here. Pity she was in such a rush to pop off to Jamaica she couldn't take time to see you were properly fitted out, though. It's such a nuisance to have to get things like that after you come to school. Well, come on now. It's high time we were down.'

They left the dormitory, Clem pausing at each cubicle to call the owner's name and make sure that the last girl had gone down before she left the dormitory herself.

'I'm dormy prefect here,' she explained, as finally they shut the door behind them. 'It's my job to see that the place is clear before I leave. Luckily, most folk are quite good about it, and everyone always is on first mornings. Hi! Not that way!' as Carola began to make for the main staircase up which Matron had brought her last night. 'Only prefects and Special Sixth and Staff use the front stairs. *We* go down here.' She dived down a narrow flight of stairs, Carola following, and presently the new girl found herself being piloted into a large, pleasant room where little groups of girls of their own age were standing about, laughing and chattering together.

Clem was hailed by half a dozen people as they entered,

and Carola guessed that she was a favourite. She was really kind, too, for though she was speedily in one of the groups, she kept the new girl with her, and introduced her all round. Carola was to learn that at the Chalet School it was the tradition to see that new people were made to feel welcome until they had found their feet a little. After that they were expected to fend for themselves. Any girl given charge of a new girl was expected to look after her and tell her anything she ought to know. Everyone did it, but it was a recognised fact that Clem Barrass was one of the best. Not only was she a friendly creature in her own brusque way; she possessed a conscience, and was reliable. Carola had fallen into good hands, and by the time the gong sounded for breakfast she felt that she was fast settling down.

Breakfast, she found, meant porridge, a portion of scrambled eggs on toast—Vanna Ozanne, who sat next her, explained that they were 'only dried stuff, of course'— toast and marmalade, and as much milky coffee as she liked. The girls talked quietly among themselves, the prefect at the head of each table being responsible for seeing that no one became rowdy. The Heads were seated at a long table running across the head of the room, with the rest of the Staff sitting with them.

'And that's one thing that's so nice here,' Clem said as she pressed the marmalade on her 'lamb.' 'In crowds of other schools mistresses take the tables, and then you have to be careful what you say. Well, I don't mean the prees don't jump on you if you use certain slang words or make a nuisance of yourself; and on French and German days they jolly well see to it that you talk which ever language it is—or sit silent until you can. They help you out, though, if they see you're trying. Can you, by the way?'

'Can I what?' Carola asked, startled.

'Talk French and German, of course.'

'French a bit; German not at all,' Carola told her promptly.

'Oh, well, you'll soon pick it up. We all do. I couldn't talk myself when I first came. Sure you won't have any more?'

'Quite sure, thanks. I've had heaps.'

'Well, that's just as well, perhaps, 'cos there's the Abbess getting up to say Grace. Up you get! Push your chair right in.'

Carola stood up with the rest, and went behind her chair and pushed it close to the table. She noticed that every girl moved to the right to do this, except one small girl at another table, who caused a little confusion by bumping into her next-door neighbour.

'Con! Wake up! Do think what you're doing!' exclaimed the prefect in charge. 'You know quite well which side to move!'

'I'm sorry, Dickie,' Con replied gravely.

Then there was silence, and Miss Annersley said Grace. The Heads left the room at once, and so did a slightly-built, pretty woman in the early thirties, whose brown hair crisped and curled over a beautifully-shaped head. Carola wondered who she was but she had no time for wondering. To her amazement, every girl was piling up her own crockery and cutlery and, beginning with the bottom table, marching to the buttery hatch and handing them through to the maids waiting to take them. Then they marched back, picked up their table napkins, and pro-

ceeded with them to a big press, while the prefect folded
the cloth after having swept it, and followed to put it in
the same drawer. Carola noticed that each of the six
tables had its own drawer, and Clem, seeing her surprise,
kindly explained it to her.

'Help is short, of course, so we always clear the tables.
We each have a drawer, so that if one table has a spill it's
got to keep its own messy cloth until they're changed, and
not to go bagging another table's clean one. It's a good
scheme, because if a girl is careless, her own table see to
it that she doesn't go on. No one wants to sit down to a
messy cloth. Now we go upstairs and make our beds and
dust. I'll show you your dusters.'

She not only did that, but also showed Carola the one
and only way Matron passed for bed-making. When that
was done, the cubicle spick and span with everything un-
necessary out of sight, the cubicle curtains were flung up
over their rods to allow the fresh air from the open windows
have free passage through the rooms, and the girls streamed
off to the Splasheries to get ready for the morning walk.
This lasted half an hour, and when they came in, Carola
learned that they would have Prayers, and then lessons.

'D'you know which form you're likely to be in?' Clem
asked as she strode along beside the new girl.

'No; I didn't do an entrance test,' Carola explained,
turning very pink as she spoke. She was keeping strictly
to the truth, but she felt that she was not being absolutely
honest about things, and she hated it. Clem was so
straight herself.

Clem gave her a shrewd look. 'I rather think you'll be
in our form. They don't like infant marvels of learning *or*
duds in this place; though I must say the duds are given

a real chance. When they can, they put folk of the same age together. You aren't a marvel of learning by any chance, are you?' she added.

'Not very likely! But,' Carola said with some bitterness, 'it wouldn't surprise me if I didn't turn out a good deal of a dud. You can't work decently when you're for ever on the move and always changing governesses. It just isn't possible.'

Clem gave her a grin. 'I don't believe *you* are a dud. You don't look it, and you certainly don't talk like it, either. And as for moving about,' she added, 'I *should* know all about that. My Dad's an artist, and we've always stayed in a place just so long as he could find places to paint. When he'd finished everything he liked, we upped stakes and trekked for somewhere else. This is my——' she stopped short to count on her fingers. 'Yes; my seventh school. Thank heaven it's to be the last—unless, of course, they get so fed up with me that they turf me out.' Again she gave that infectious grin which Carola found herself returning.

'How did you manage when you came here first?'

'All right so long as the lessons were in English; but my French was feeble, and my German not there at all. Don't worry, Carola. I expect you'll do all right. Folk are quite patient with you and help you out at first, so long as they see you're trying. If you don't—well, you've had it. That's all.'

Carola remembered something. 'Who was the mistress who went out after the Heads? She played for Prayers last night.'

'That's Miss Cochrane, one of the first of the Chalet School girls. She teaches music. They say she's awfully good, but she's got a tongue that nearly takes the skin off you. Thank goodness no one's ever even suggested I should learn music! There'd be battle, murder, and sudden death if I did.'

At this point they were halted and turned, and began to walk back again. While this was happening, Carola remembered something else she wanted to ask.

'Who was that jolly kid that went the wrong way round at breakfast? She's awfully pretty, and I liked the look of her.'

'That,' said Clem, 'is one of Mrs Maynard's triplets. She's always in a dream, and Len wasn't sitting by her for once. She generally sees to it that Con wakes up in time. The third one is Margot, but she's in Canada with Madame —Lady Russell to whom the School really belongs. Mrs Maynard, by the way, is Josephine M. Bettany, the authoress.' She eyed Carola to see how she reacted to this.

'I knew that,' Carola replied. 'Miss O'Ryan told me all about her when we were at Penny Rest for Christmas. She said that she lives in that place across the water— Carnbach, isn't it? Does she often come to the School? I'm dying to see her.'

'Oh, she'll probably be over some time next week,' Clem returned. 'She never can keep away from the School for long. You'll like her—she's a real sport.'

Carola said no more. She knew there was a good chance that she would *not* see Mrs Maynard after all and, secretly, she was bitterly disappointed. However, Clem was off on another tack now.

'You'll be doing tests after Prayers, I expect, and then we'll know which form you really are in, so you won't have long to wait.'

Carola said no more. She thought to herself that if her parents or Cousin Maud should say she must leave this marvellous place she should want to die. She wondered if she would ever be asked to take those tests. However, when they reached the School again and had changed, she was told to go with the others, and after Prayers she was sent to the long, narrow room, usually dedicated to the use of the prefects, and set to working test papers which she did with fair success on the whole. The mathematics, apart from arithmetic, floored her badly, for she had done so little. The English and history, however, just suited her, and she was able to manage most of the French. When the mistress sitting with the girls gave her the German paper, she shook her head.

'It's no use, Miss Bell. I've never done any German at all.'

Miss Bell picked up the paper without comment. 'What about Latin?' she asked, offering her another.

'Yes; I've done some Latin. May I try it?'

'Please do.' Miss Bell gave her an amused look. 'Here you are. See what you can do with it.'

Carola settled down to the Latin paper, and soon found that though she could manage most of the grammar questions she was all at sea when it came to construing, for she had never gone further than the second book of 'Ora Maritima.' She picked out what sentences she could do, but that part of her paper had a markedly blank look when she had finished with it.

Break came next, with milk or cocoa and biscuits. Half-way through, a message came that Miss Annersley would like to see Carola Johnstone when it was over.

'Good! That's to talk over your papers and tell where

you're going,' Clem remarked. 'They never keep you hanging on for very long here.'

Carola was still none too sure. It might mean that she was to leave this gorgeous place almost at once. Having tasted its delights, she felt that she just couldn't bear it if it was that and she was sent away, and it was with considerable trepidation that she went to the study for that interview.

Chapter VI

CAROLA GOES ON TASTING

CAROLA tapped at the study door, and Miss Annersley's voice called, 'Come in!' She entered, feeling decidedly quaky about the knees. The room seemed to be full of people at first. Then she saw that apart from the two Heads there really was only one lady, a very dark, tall person, who gave her a smile and a quizzical look as she shut the door behind her and stood waiting.

'That's righ , Carola,' Miss Annersley said briskly. 'Come along in, child, and don't stand there by the door. Sit down on that chair. Now,' she continued when Carola had seated herself, 'we have heard from your cousin, Miss Curry. The boat had to wait a couple of hours at Queenstown, so she was able to make a telephone connection and I have had a long conversation with her.' She paused to give full weight to her words, and Carola squirmed uneasily inside her. What had Cousin Maud said?

She was to know almost at once. Miss Annersley decided that her victim had taken the point, and continued. 'You have given her a great deal of anxiety, for of course she had no idea what had become of you when she first discovered that you were nowhere on the liner; and that wasn't until everyone had been searching for you. You seem to have made a complete nuisance of yourself all round.'

It was impossible by this time for Carola to go any

redder, but she hung her head and regarded the toes of her slippers fixedly and wished that she was anywhere else than here. Miss Annersley's very cool judicial manner made her feel that she had made a complete idiot of herself. Miss Annersley, of course, was quite aware of this, and was satisfied at the impression she was making. The last thing anyone wanted was for Carola to imagine she had done something rather clever, and the Head was well aware that there were plenty of empty-headed girls in the School who would be inclined to make a heroine of the girl who had run away to school like that, if the story ever leaked out.

Miss Annersley went on. 'Your cousin—and quite naturally, in my opinion—tells me that she wishes to have nothing more to do with you. She flatly refuses to be responsible for a girl who could treat her in such a cavalier manner.'

Not knowing what 'cavalier' meant as Miss Annersley had used it, Carola remained dumb. On the whole, she felt she would rather have endured one of Cousin Maud's tirades than this calm, reasonable way of putting her sins before her. Besides, to quote herself much later, the way the Head was eyeing her left her feeling like a down-trodden cockroach!

Miss Wilson suddenly took a hand. 'If you felt that you *must* rush off in that way, may I ask why you couldn't leave some message for your unfortunate cousin?' she asked in the blandest tones.

'I—I didn't think,' Carola mumbled.

'Then you ought to have done,' Miss Annersley told her severely. 'A girl of your age—fourteen, aren't you?—should have enough common sense to realise that she can't just disappear in that way without giving a great deal of trouble and worry to all concerned.'

Carola had nothing to say. It was by no means the first time she had been told that 'didn't think' was no sort of excuse.

'Well,' Miss Annersley continued, 'your cousin has already cabled to your father since she got my own radio, telling him that he must make other arrangements for you in future. In the meantime you are to stay here, as there seems to be nowhere else for you to go, and he will tell us what his wishes concerning you are as soon as possible, I expect.'

Carola raised her head, a flash of joy in her eyes at this information, but she encountered Miss Annersley's grimmest glare, and remembered just *why* she was to stay— always supposing the School would keep her. For the first time she began to grasp exactly what she had done, and while she felt no sort of regret for all she had given her cousin in the way of anxiety, she did begin to see that things would have been better all round if she had left some sort of message for Miss Curry. For the first time, too, she began to wonder what her father would have to say about it.

The two Heads, watching her expressive little face, knew very well what she was thinking, but they forbore to say anything. They meant to keep her, of course, unless Dr Johnstone should propose another plan; but they had talked it over and agreed that she would be none the worse for a few hours of suspense. Nothing could be heard from West Africa until next day at soonest, and Carola could very well wait to know her fate until then. So she sat there feeling rather unhappy and wondering what was going to happen to her, while the three grown-up people in the study watched her.

At length Miss Annersley took pity on her. 'I have your test papers here,' she said, picking up some sheets. 'In English subjects, arithmetic, and French, you should be able to work with Lower Fifth B. Your Latin grammar is good; but you construe badly. Still, that is largely a matter of vocabulary and practice. Have you done no algebra and geometry?'

'A little algebra, but no geometry,' Carola explained in subdued tones.

'I see. It would mean coaching in those subjects, then. What about science?'

'I did botany about a year with Miss Wilkins, but no chemistry or anything like that. My other governesses weren't interested.'

'Then if Miss Wilson thinks you could work with—which set, Miss Wilson?' She turned to that lady questioningly.

'Set VB,' Miss Wilson replied. 'They are all Fifth Form girls. If she can work with them, I expect she'll soon pick up as much chemistry as they have; but I'll test her some time before Monday and see.'

'Yes; I think that would be best. Very well, then, Carola.' The Head turned back to Carola who was listening to all this, wide-eyed. 'As you *have* had a year's botany, and seem to have done practically no maths, we had better concentrate on the botany and cut the maths out. No need for you to do both.'

'No, Miss Annersley,' Carola replied meekly.

'Well, we must see. I think we won't worry too much about coachings, though, until we hear from Dr Johnstone.'

The stranger lady evidently thought it was time she took a hand. 'Of course, Mrs Johnstone may very well decide to come back to England to make a home for Carola and send her to day school,' she suggested.

'Oh, I'm sure she won't do that!' Carola cried, forgetting that she was a very naughty girl in deep disgrace, who might be supposed to keep well in the background for the present. 'Dad is fearfully absent-minded and he'd never be able to look after himself if she wasn't there to see that he did it. She's told me so often in her letters.'

'That may be,' Miss Wilson suppressed her. 'At the same time, when it comes to choosing between a husband who is absent-minded and a daughter who doesn't take the trouble of thinking before she does mad things, she may decide that her chief duty is to her daughter before she gets herself into really serious trouble, and she must leave him to do the best he can for himself.'

Once more Carola's face burned, and she said no more. The stranger lady glanced at her with wicked dancing eyes and then remarked, 'Well, we can't say either way until we hear from them. I suppose the only thing we can do is to wait until we do. In the meantime, Carola can't afford to waste time at her age, so she'd better join Lower Fifth B—isn't the redoubtable Clem Barrass a shining light there?—and do her best to show everyone that she repents her insane behaviour up to date by working like a trooper. How about it, Carola?'

Carola looked up. 'I'll do my best,' she promised. Inwardly she was wondering who on earth the lady was.

Miss Annersley guessed, and proceeded to introduce them. 'This is Mrs Maynard, Carola, though I expect you know of her best as Josephine Bettany.'

'*Oh!*' Once more Carola forgot she was in disgrace, and her blue eyes sparkled. One more wish fulfilled!

'Then I think it's all settled.' Miss Annersley spoke crisply. 'I am not going to provide you with any uniform, Carola, until we know that it is necessary. If your parents decide to leave you here, you must have a tunic and blazer and your badges. Matron will provide you with bed-linen and towels for the present. I imagine you have brought none with you.'

'I brought three bath towels,' Carola said, suddenly flattened out again.

Mrs Maynard gave her a friendly grin. '*That* won't see you very far; and whatever your folk do they can't settle anything for at least two or three weeks. I'll lend you what you need—table-napkins, too.' She turned to the two Heads. 'I suppose Bid—Miss O'Ryan, I mean—can't run over this afternoon, can she? If she could, I'd give her what Carola needs. She can? Good! Then I'll be off now, or I'll miss the ferry.'

'One moment, please.' Miss Annersley held up her hand. 'Miss Wilson, would you mind taking Carola to Lower Fifth B? Clem Barrass is being her shepherd just now and will look after her. Carola, tell Clem from me to see that you get your stationery and text-books after Mittagessen and rest, please.'

Miss Wilson rose while Carola was saying, 'Yes, Miss Annersley.'

'Come along,' she said. 'After you've got your books this afternoon, ask someone to bring you to me in the lab, and I'll see how you shape in botany. Hurry up, or you'll miss the next lesson, and you've missed the whole of this!' as the big bell clanged out.

She led Carola off, and presently that young person found herself standing rather forlornly by the door of a pleasant classroom while Miss Wilson conferred with the little dark lady, obviously French, who was sitting at the mistress's desk. Presently the Second Head turned to the girl standing by the door and waved her forward after a stern look round at the other girls who promptly stopped staring, buried their heads in their books, and looked as studious as they could.

'This is Carola Johnstone, Mademoiselle,' Miss Wilson said. 'Carola, Mlle de Lachenais takes you for French and Latin. Please do your best for her.' Then she left the room, the girls rising until the door closed behind her.

'Welcome to Lower Fifth B, Carola,' Mademoiselle said kindly. 'You speak French, hein?'

'Only a very little,' Carola said shyly.

'Eh bien, ça s'arrangera, n'est-ce pas? Eh maintenant, assieds-toi. Ah, Clem! Qu'as-tu, ma petite?'

'There's a spare desk here, Mademoiselle,' Clem replied in French with a good British accent.

Mademoiselle waved the dazed Carola towards the seat, and that young person went and sat down thankfully. At least the twenty-two pairs of eyes could hardly fix themselves on her now!

Mademoiselle turned to the board, and soon they were hurled into a brisk oral test on the uses of pouvoir and valoir, in which Carola, who had been thoroughly well-drilled in French irregular verbs by her last governess, acquitted herself fairly well, and merited the 'Bien fait!' that Mademoiselle awarded her.

The last lesson of the morning proved to be history, much to Carola's delight, for she had a real affection for Miss

O'Ryan. That young lady proved to be an excellent teacher, and the lesson she gave was an eye-opener to the governess-taught girl who had been accustomed to preparing two or three pages from her history book for questioning. Biddy O'Ryan knew what the tradition of the Chalet School history lessons was from experience, and insisted that her pupils should take the facts and reason out the effects for themselves during her energetic lesson on the growth of trade towards the end of the Elizabethan era.

'I don't see *why* all this happened so suddenly,' Jean Ackroyd observed rather plaintively. 'Why didn't the English get round to it sooner, Miss O'Ryan? After all, America was discovered ages before Elizabeth's time. *Why* didn't they get on with it under Henry VIII or Edward VI?'

Biddy gave her a quizzical look. 'Suppose you work that out for yourselves? You can do it for homework. Take this down, girls.'

There was a rustle as everyone opened her homework notebook and waited. Carola had one, too, Clem having supplied it from her own store during French. Miss O'Ryan considered a moment. Then she went to the board and wrote quickly. The girls took it down, lazy Jean heaving a sigh as she did so.

'Find at least four reasons for the sudden expansion of trade towards the end of the sixteenth century, and prepare to discuss them in detail.'

'I loathe preparing discussions,' she grumbled when, the bell having rung for the end of morning school, they were putting away their books. 'I never can think of a thing to say in the discussions, either. It strikes me,' she added as she shoved the last book into her locker and slammed the door, 'that Miss O'Ryan is going to be a bit of a burden. Miss Bell was a lot more to my liking. Why can't she go on teaching us?'

Clem grinned. 'You mean she didn't force you to use your brains all the time. Hard lines, Jean! You'll have to begin again. Miss Burnett always gave us that sort of lesson, and it's only a term since she left. You ought soon to be in practice again. As for why Miss Bell isn't going on with us, she really came for Junior work, and only filled in for the term.'

'I like a *quiet* life,' Jean sighed. Then they left the form-room, and as school was in full swing, no talking was allowed in the corridors, so she had to relapse into silence.

After lunch—which the School, reverting to past custom with an eye to returning to Tirol at some not too distant date, now called 'Mittagessen'—they all sought deck-chairs, carried them to the common-rooms, and rested for half an hour, during which time they must be silent, though they might read if they liked. When this was over they marched to the gymnasium, which had once been part of the stables, where they spent an exhilarating forty minutes that Carola enjoyed intensely. She had never done apparatus work before, but she showed an aptitude for it that delighted Miss Burn, who was wont to groan to the rest of the Staff over the plump and lazy Gillian and one or two other young persons in Lower Fifth B who were careless and untidy in their work. Carola, lightly built and neat, soon showed that she was an asset to the form in this way at least, and Miss Burn, with Parents' Day and the gym display given then in mind, decided to keep an eye on this particular new girl.

Gym was followed by an hour's needlework which was taken by Mademoiselle's compatriot, Mlle Berné, and here, Carola was very much at a disadvantage. She disliked sewing, and did it badly. Mademoiselle had quite a good deal to say to her about her uneven 'dog's-tooth' stitches, and made her take out all she had done and begin again. Clem, who after two years at the School had managed to learn to sew really well, smiled sympathetically at her when she set to work to unpick the really appalling sewing she had just shown up.

'Rotten luck!' she remarked in an undertone, with one eye on Mademoiselle who was scolding Polly Winterton for using a number six needle and twenty-four cotton for stitching fine nainsook. 'They do it here, though. That's the worst thing I know about this place, I think. They do insist that you sew decently——'

'Clem, you are talking too much,' stated Mademoiselle over her shoulder. 'Do more work and less chattering, I beg you.'

Clem made a face at Carola and fell silent, and Carola went on picking out her stitches with a long face. She was thankful when the hour came to an end and Clem escorted her to the lab for her botany test with Miss Wilson.

She left it with the satisfaction of knowing that the Second Head, who was also science and geography mistress, thought her quite capable of working with the Fifth Form botany set, and settled down to make the most of the half-hour's 'prep' left to her.

Prep was a strenuous time as Carola found. It was strictly limited, but while it lasted the girls were expected to work really hard. Even when they were left without supervision it was the 'done' thing to concentrate on your lessons. Carola got down to her French exercise with all her might and by the time the bell rang for the end of afternoon school she had finished it.

Tea was as jolly as all other meals had been, and when it was over they all fled upstairs to change into their evening velveteens. There was very little time, for evening prep began at half-past five and went on till seven, after which they cleared up and went straight in to Abendessen, as supper was called. That over, their time was their own until Prayers at half-past eight and bed for everyone who was not a Senior. For the first time since her parents left her Carola found her entire day planned out and there was not a moment to waste over being bored. The one fly in her amber was that she kept wondering at times what her parents were going to say about her running away and what they would do with her. She had forgotten them to a certain extent and she had no idea what their reactions would be.

As they went upstairs at bedtime after saying good-night to Miss Wilson who was standing at the foot of the stairs for that purpose, she ventured to ask, 'Please, has there been any news from—from Africa yet?'

Miss Wilson shook her head. 'There hasn't been time. They would only get the cable today. I don't suppose there will be any reply before noon tomorrow at earliest.'

'I see. Thank you very much. Good-night, Miss Wilson.'

Miss Wilson's clear-cut, rather stern face softened. 'Good-night, Carola. Don't worry until you must. You go to sleep, and when morning comes remember that it will probably mean waiting only a few hours longer, and those hours will be busy ones for you.' She finished up with a smile and Carola went on, somehow cheered.

'What were you saying to Bill?' Gillian Moggeridge asked inquisitively when they were in the dormitory.

The warm colour flooded Carola's face. 'It was only about a cable from my people,' she said.

'Oh? I hope there's nothing wrong with them?' Gillian asked. She was a kind-hearted girl though she suffered from almost insatiable curiosity which had earned for herself the name of 'Elephant's Child,' generally shortened to 'Jumbo.'

'I shan't know until the cable comes,' Carola said, vanishing thankfully into her cubicle and pulling down the curtains from the rods.

Gillian gave it up and attended to her own curtains. Half an hour later they were all fast asleep and no one stirred, not even Carola, until the relentless bell called them out of bed next morning.

Chapter VII

THE CABLE ARRIVES

'PLEASE, Miss Wilson, Miss Annersley would like to speak to you.'

Miss Wilson—'Bill' to the School—turned round from the board whereon she was illustrating various proofs of the earth's curves. 'Very well, Lalla, I will come at once. Go back to your own form quickly.'

Lalla Winterton, younger sister of Polly Winterton, made the little curtsy that was considered 'good manners' in the School, and withdrew, Miss Wilson hurriedly finished her diagram and then swept the board clean.

'Repeat those from memory in your scribblers. If I have not returned by that time, you may turn to pages 122-124 in your geographies and begin preparing them for next time,' she said. 'Don't forget to use your atlases while you work. No talking, please.'

She dusted the chalk off her hands and departed. Lower Fifth B, left to itself, relaxed the absorbed attention it had been according the mistress, and a distinct groan sounded from one or two people who found the scientific side of geography distinctly hard.

Clem, prefect of the form, uttered a warning, 'Hush! Get on with the job and don't yatter!'

As the Chalet School laid great stress on girls having the decency to behave properly whether a mistress was there or not, and Clem was, in any case, a strong prefect, the

89

malcontents subsided and silence reigned as the girls did their best to remember what they had been told.

Polly Winterton was the first to give up. She regarded her page with a long sigh, then took out her geography text-book and atlas, and set to work on the preparation. Carola finished in company with one or two others, and by the time Gillian had given it up as a hopeless job, the entire form was occupied with the description of fruit-farming in Canada.

Miss Wilson returned ten minutes later. Her eyes swept round the room and singled out the new girl. 'Carola, go to the study, please,' she said. 'Now, girls, let me see what you have made of the lesson.'

Carola rose from her place beside Clem, went to the door where for once she remembered her curtsy, and fled across the stableyard to the house. The geography-room was beside the gymnasium, as well as the laboratories and the domestic science kitchen, and girls who had lessons in one place had lessons in the others on the same morning to save continual passage to and fro.

By this time, the new girl was finding her way about and needed no one to show her how to reach the study. It seemed to her as if she had spent a good part of her first days at School going there. She did not need anyone to tell her why Miss Annersley had sent for her. She was certain that at long last the cable had come from West Africa and she was to learn her fate. This thought slowed her steps once she was inside the house, and it was a very anxious young lady who tapped at the door and entered the room in answer to the Head's 'Come in!'

Miss Annersley was standing by the window, but she swung round as she heard the door close. 'There you are, Carola,' she said. 'Well, I have had a cable from your father. He is flying home at once to see about you, and expects to be here early next week. In the meantime, you are to go on here.'

Carola gulped at this unexpected news. 'He's coming home?' she faltered. Then, 'Oh, Miss Annersley, do you think he's awfully mad with me?'

Miss Annersley went to her desk and sat down. 'Come here,' she said.

Carola went. When she was standing before the desk, the Head gave her a sudden unexpected smile. 'Why, you silly child, I believe you're afraid!' she exclaimed. 'Well, I am going to ease your mind about one thing. Your parents wish you to remain with us.' Then, as Carola's whole face lightened, she laughed outright. 'That pleases you? I am glad to know it. But, Carola, I want you to remember that, though you are gaining your great wish, you hardly deserve it. You had no possible right to run away as you did. If you wanted school as much as that, your business was to write to your people, telling them so. It was very wrong of you to take the law into your own hands as you did.'

'I—I didn't think,' Carola faltered.

'That is no real excuse. If you stay here, you must learn to think. However, I am not going to say any more on the subject. Your father will tell you what his opinion of your behaviour is, I don't doubt. We'll turn to a pleasanter subject. You need your uniform. You are to go to Matron after rest this afternoon, and she will fit you out. I'm afraid it will mean missing your games but that can't be helped. Now,' she picked up her pen and a printed form, 'we have very few of your details. Sit down on that chair and help me to fill this in. What is your full name?'

'Carola Elizabeth Maud Johnstone,' the name's owner said.

'Thank you. And your birthday and the year you were born?'

Carola did some frantic arithmetic on her fingers. 'March 10th, and I was born in 1936.'

'Then you are nearly fifteen? Now, your father's name, please.'

'Andrew Charles Johnstone—that's why I'm "Carola,"' she added. 'He's a doctor. Do you want his degrees and things?'

Miss Annersley gave her a look of amusement. 'I don't think that's necessary yet. He'll give me those when he arrives. Now, you attended a Kindergarten when you were small, I think? Where was it?'

'In Edinburgh, where we used to live. It was called Monan House. They kept girls up to the age of twelve, but after that we had to leave.'

Miss Annersley, who had already had one or two pupils from Monan House and knew their ways, nodded. 'Do you remember Kathie Robertson?' she asked.

Carola nodded. 'Yes; but she left six years ago, when I was very young,' she said; and again amusement lit up the Head's eyes.

'Kathie was here until last summer,' she said. 'She has gone to Edinburgh University now. She was one of our prefects.'

Carola's eyes widened. 'Was she really? We all liked Kathie,' she added. 'She was awfully decent to us little ones.'

'I am sure she was. Kathie was a great favourite here, and we were all sorry when she left. Well, Carola, I think that is all at present. You must go back to your lessons now—ah! Too late! There goes the bell for the end of morning school. Don't forget to go to Matron at two o'clock.'

'No, Miss Annersley.' Carola went to the door, curtsied, and then hurried off to the Splashery, intent on getting there first. One day and a half of school had already taught her that if you loitered you had a struggle to wash before Mittagessen.

'Anything wrong?' Clem asked when they were seated at the table.

Carola shook her head. 'Miss Annersley sent for me to tell me to go to Matron for my uniform after rest period,' she explained.

Clem's brown eyes opened. 'Mean to say you haven't got it *yet?* Oh, well, we haven't been back two days yet, and Matey is always up to the eyes at the beginning of term. It's rotten luck, though. That means you'll have to miss hockey—or most of it. You've never played before, have you?' she added.

'No, and I'm dying to begin; but it just can't be helped today. Anyway, I haven't a stick, so it doesn't matter so much.'

Clem said nothing but she thought the more. There was some mystery about this new girl. First of all she hadn't been entered on the roll, and that was something that had never happened before so far as anyone could tell. Then she had no uniform. To crown all, it seemed that her folk had let her come without a hockey-stick— and that, to Clem's mind, was the greatest lack of all.

Carola had no idea what she was thinking. She was wondering if her father would be so angry with her that he would refuse to let her play games. She knew from her reading that games were often compulsory at school, but so far she had not heard that they were here.

'Do you know if the Head has told Miss Burn?' Clem asked at this point. 'If not, you'll have to see her and explain.'

'See who?' Carola demanded.

'Miss Burn, of course. She takes games as well as gym.'

'Are games compulsory, then?'

'Why, of course! Oh, folk who aren't frightfully strong don't play hockey or lax——'

'What's lax?' Carola interrupted her.

'Lacrosse; but you don't play that till you're sixteen. As for a stick, you can have my old one until your folk buy you one. Auntie Doris gave me a new one for Christmas because I'd got into the Second Eleven, and my old one is still here, so you can use it.'

Carola went pink at this generous offer. 'That's super of you, Clem. Thanks a million! I'll take care of it.'

'Oh, rot!' Downright Clem looked uncomfortable. 'And I say! You watch out for slang. I told you that certain words aren't allowed here, and if you use them you're fined. That reminds me; have you taken your money to Teddy—I mean Miss Edwards?'

'I don't know which she is, and I haven't taken any money to her. *Why* must we?'

'She runs the School bank.' Then, seeing the new girl's bewildered look, Clem explained. 'It's this way. We all get weekly pocket money—our crowd have two shillings.

You've got to give to the church collections from that, of course. Then you may bring money back with you, but it has to be paid into the bank, and if you want anything for a special reason, like someone's birthday, you go to Teddy on the Saturday before and ask for what you want. And while I think of it, you don't ask for too much or she wants to know why you want it exactly. At the end of term you can either draw out what you have left or else leave it for the next term. Most folk leave it at Easter and summer and draw out for Christmas,' Clem added. 'You please yourself, of course.'

Carola thought with inward dismay of the few shillings she had left. Here was another problem for her until her father came. Would he give her some money for the bank or would he think she didn't deserve any for this term?

'Why can't we just keep what we bring and use it as we like?' she queried.

Clem gave her a grin. 'Because we mightn't use it as other people would think right. There was one girl,' her grin deepened, 'who had got into a frightful row with a Head we had pro tem when Miss Annersley and Miss Wilson were both smashed up in a motor accident. Miss Bubb—that was her name—wouldn't let Gay go home to say goodbye to her brother who was off to China. No one had taken bank—Teddy was mixed up in the accident, too—so Gay had all she had brought, and she was so mad that she got out at night and just went home. She had plenty with her, you see.'

'That was ages ago,' put in Sybil Russell who was sitting opposite and overheard this. 'I remember the fuss there was. Auntie Jo was teaching at the School then and she wrote pronto to Miss Wilson who was less badly hurt than the others, and Bill came haring back to School and Miss Bubb left. You weren't here then, Clem.'

'No, but I've heard all about it,' Clem retorted. 'But you can see, Carola, just why no one wants us to have enough cash to do a mad thing like that again.'

For no reason that anyone could see, Carola went pink again. Luckily for her, Mittagessen came to an end just then, and they had to clear the table and then go to rest. After rest she had a session with Matron, who left her in no doubt as to her own tiresomeness in having to be fitted out after school had begun. It took the whole of the games period to supply her, and prep came next, so Carola was left to reflect that it was her own fault that she had been obliged to miss the first hockey practice of the term. She was beginning to realise that by taking the law into her own hands as she had done she had let herself in for all sorts of consequences. Worst of all, at present, was the doubt that filled her as to how her father would look at the whole thing, and whether he would be very angry with her. Well, that was something that could not be decided until he came, and Miss Annersley had said he would arrive early next week. She must just bear it all as patiently as she could until then. All the same, Carola felt that she was being well punished as it was, and she hoped he would not consider it necessary to administer much more.

Chapter VIII

THE DOCTOR ARRIVES

D R JOHNSTONE arrived on the Wednesday. At
the suggestion of Jo Maynard he did not go to the
School but stayed at Carnbach with her and her husband,
an old friend of his.

'You know, I can't get over Jigger Maynard being the
responsible head of a family,' he told Jo while they were
having tea.

'What's that you called him?' Jo demanded, while
Jack Maynard scowled at his friend.

'Hang it, Andy, you needn't have let that slip! Here
I've been carefully keeping it hidden from Jo and you
must needs go and spill the beans!' he protested. 'O.K.,
Jo—it's "Jigger." But let me catch you trying to use it
and heaven help you!'

'Shouldn't dream of it,' Jo retorted haughtily. 'It's a
very poor effort when I think of all the things I can call
you off my own bat.'

The two doctors chuckled, and Jo decided to change
the subject.

'What about that girl of yours, Dr Johnstone?' she
asked. 'I'm interested in her. It was a mad thing to do
all right, but a jolly plucky one. You're letting her stay
with us, aren't you?'

Dr Johnstone frowned. 'Yes; I shall let her stay. My
cousin flatly refuses to take any more responsibility for

her, and she certainly can't join us. Calabar is no place for small girls.'

Jo gave him a startled look. '*Small* girls? What *are* you talking about? Carola's quite a well-grown specimen, and she's nearly fifteen!'

It was Dr Johnstone's turn to look startled. 'Fifteen? Oh, no; she can't be nearly that age,' he protested.

'But she *is*. She told the Head that she was born in '36. That makes her fifteen this year.'

'She's right about the date, but—good heavens! My wife and I have been visualising her as not much bigger or older than she was when we went away. One forgets how time goes, and I've been so busy. I'm on to a very interesting piece of work. This'll interest you, Jigger—'

'Not before the wife!' Jack protested. 'Wait till I get you alone in the den and I'll be glad to hear all about it. Jo loathes medical shop, though, and won't have it. Besides, I know she's just aching to discuss your girl.'

Dr Johnstone turned a rueful glance at Jo. 'You know, Mrs Maynard, you've given me a bad shock,' he said. 'If Carola is nearly fifteen, then she was certainly right in saying she needed school. I wish, though, she had chosen some other method of attaining her wish. This means that so long as we are out of England she has no home, and even at fifteen we can't have her out in Calabar.'

'How much longer are you likely to stay?' Jo asked.

'Oh, another three or four years at least. I'm on an official job—don't be afraid: I'm not going to bore you with it.' He twinkled at her as he spoke and she had the grace to blush.

'I didn't mean to be rude and, anyway, it was Jack who said it. I do dislike shop, though. You wait till after dinner and then you two men can retire to the den and yatter to your hearts' content. Dr Johnstone, didn't either you or Mrs Johnstone realise that Carola was growing up very quickly? I've seen her, and she's quite a big girl. It was more than time that she was at a good school. She wants some sort of career, I suppose? Governess training can be good; but when you have it in conjunction with leading a regular nomadic existence I should say it wouldn't be much help.'

Dr Johnstone accepted another scone and bit into it before he replied. 'The fact of the matter is this chance came quite suddenly. I had to make up my mind at once—within twenty-four hours, in fact. I had to be on the way within a week. That didn't leave us much time for anything. And—well—my wife has it fixed in her head that I'm not to be trusted alone. She was sure I should get into some sort of sticky mess if she weren't with me. My cousin, who is also Carola's godmother, offered to take the child off our hands, close the house, and see to everything of that sort. I've known Maud all my life, and whatever else she may be, she's conscientious enough. We accepted her offer and let it go at that.'

'I see.' Jo nodded gently. 'There's no doubt that for the first year or two it was quite good for Carola. Now, however, she's been coming up against people of more or less her own age and I expect she felt a lack in her life. The trouble is that the early teens are quite a good age, but fussy. If the little ass had written to you and explained in full, I expect you'd have done something about it. Unfortunately, she seems to have gone off at half-cock and now the washing *is* in the mud.'

'Mixed metaphor!' Jack said severely. 'You're leaving

the kid where she is, aren't you, Andy? Our own two beauties are there, not to speak of Jo's being an Old Girl.'

'Oh, yes; Carola can stay there now she's taken things into her own hands. The trouble is I don't want anyone else to know what she's done. At that age there are prob- ably plenty of her friends to think she's been rather clever, and that's the last sort of thing we want.'

'You needn't worry about that,' Jo told him. 'The Head thought of that first go-off. Carola's been forbidden to say anything about it to anyone. I was present at that interview and I can assure you that by the time Hilda and Nell—I—I mean Miss Annersley and Miss Wilson—' she added in some confusion, 'well, by the time they'd finished with her you could have put the pieces that were left into a pint pot. She was awfully upset, too, when she was reminded of the anxiety you and her mother must be feeling.'

The doctor's eyes lightened. 'She's a good enough lassie, but she does go at things bull-headed,' he admitted.

'Takes after Pa,' Jack Maynard observed detachedly.

Dr Johnstone suddenly chuckled. 'I'll have it out with you later. In the meantime, Mrs Maynard, thank you for having our meeting here. It may make things a bit easier if I don't turn up at the School this time. When are your Head Mistress and Carola coming?'

'Tomorrow afternoon. Carola hasn't half the things she needs, so we're making that the excuse for bringing her over to Carnbach like this. I don't quite know how much shopping is likely to be done then, but I've got her some warm undies, and we hope there'll be time to see about a pair of wellingtons which she definitely needs at this time of year.'

Dr Johnstone thanked Jo gratefully, she refilled his cup, and the conversation passed into a discussion of all Carola would need.

The next afternoon brought her over to Carnbach, escorted by Miss Annersley. Jo met them at the ferry-landing and took charge of the girl while the Head went off on a shopping expedition, promising to appear at Cartref in time for tea. This would give Carola plenty of time to make her peace with her father, and also, as Jo, quoting from 'The Mikado,' observed, add a little veri-similitude to an otherwise bald and unconvincing narrative.

'I—I didn't know you knew Dad, Mrs Maynard,' Carola said as she and Jo walked briskly along the streets shining with wet, for it had rained steadily all night and most of the morning.

'Not me, my child—my husband,' Jo informed her. 'They were at the Medical together. But enough of that! I've something to say to you, Carola.'

Carola turned questioning blue eyes on her at this.

'When you see your father,' Jo said gravely, 'don't try to hide anything from him. He's had your cousin's side of the story. Now let him hear yours. You're lucky, you know. Your dad's a good chap. He's *not* pleased with what you've done—don't run away with that idea—but he can see *why* you did it. You've got your chance to thrash it all out, and if you don't take it to the absolute limit, you're a most awful flat.'

'Yes,' Carola meekly agreed. Privately, she was thinking that Mrs Maynard talked more like one of her own nieces —Sybil Russell, for example, or Bride Bettany—than any other grown-up she had ever met. All the same, Jo's remarks put heart into her, and though she felt anxious

to have the first part of her interview over, she was prepared
to accept any scolding in store for her with becoming
meekness.

As for Dr Johnstone, when Jo ushered his daughter into
the drawing-room where he was waiting, he quite literally
gasped, for despite her words of the previous evening he
was still not fully prepared for what he saw.   In his inmost
mind was still a picture of the eleven-year-old he and his
wife had left behind them, and this tall, sturdy schoolgirl,
with her wavy, light-brown hair drawn back from a centre
parting into a long thick tail, her decided chin and
firm mouth, was a very much older person than he had
expected.

'Well, my lassie!' he said, holding out his hand.

Carola gripped it as Jo left them alone, and was drawn
close to her father for a warm kiss.   Unconsciously, she
had been building up a defence against any strictures he
might make, but it all melted away at that kiss and she
clung to him as if she were the little girl he had been
expecting.

'Oh, Dad!   Oh, Dad!' was all she said.

'Now I want to hear all about it,' the doctor said
presently.

Mindful of Jo's words, Carola began and gave him a
very fair picture of her life with her cousin.   She made no
attempt to hide her discontent during the past eighteen
months or so, and by the time she had finished, he felt he
knew where he was.

'I see,' he said.   'Well, Carola, the first thing you have
to do is to apologise to Cousin Maud for all the worry and
annoyance you have caused her.'

'I've written,' Carola said humbly.   'Miss Annersley

told me to do it on Saturday during letter-writing time.'

'Good! Maud won't be unforgiving once she has got over the shock you gave her. Now listen to me. Mother and I have decided to let you stay at the school of your own choice, but you must justify this by your behaviour and your work. Don't give us any reason to regret our decision. I shall say no more about what you did: that is past and done. Only you *must* try to think before you act. You are nearly fifteen, and it's high time you had a little sense. If you go on as you're doing, you may end up by involving not only yourself but other folk in bad trouble.'

'I'll try,' Carola murmured.

'Mrs Maynard has very kindly said she will get you what you need. Is there anything else I should know?'

Carola blushed. 'There's the bank.'

'The bank? What do you mean?'

She explained it to him and he nodded approval. 'A very good way of teaching you lassies the value of money. Very well; I'll consult Mrs Maynard and leave you what she suggests. You are to have a hockey-stick, which she will buy for you. The rest, I think, I must arrange with your Head Mistress.'

Carola was almost overcome, and she vowed inwardly to do her best in every way to prove to them that she was really grateful for all they were doing. A ring at the front-door bell announced the arrival of Miss Annersley, Jo ushered her into the drawing-room, and there was no further opportunity for private talk that day. Dr John-stone explained that he must return to Calabar as soon as possible, so the Head suggested that Carola should be allowed to spend the next afternoon with him, and then said goodbye after a business talk in Jack Maynard's den.

She took Carola back to school, for that young lady must not miss any lessons; but next day, after rest period, while the others were enjoying their hockey practice, Carola was walking about Carnbach, making the most of her time, for the doctor was returning to Africa next day.

'Cousin Maud said you and Mother were coming back next year,' she said to him suddenly as they walked along the coast road in the pale January sunshine.

'Quite true. I shall have a furlough then and we are coming for three months. My work isn't finished out there, though, nor likely to be for a few years yet.'

Carola sighed. 'Well, you'll be at home then, but I wish you were here always.'

'Mrs Maynard tells me that when she returns home to her house at Howells she will have you for the holidays,' he said soothingly. 'I understand there is some talk of her going to Canada for a visit at Easter. Miss Annersley will arrange for your holidays then, but Mrs Maynard has promised to attend to the summer ones. Don't worry; you will have happy holidays, I know.'

Carola said no more about it but turned to the exciting subject of the extras she was to take. He had arranged for her to continue with music and to begin verse-speaking. She had wanted singing lessons, but the School music authorities had strongly advised against that for another two years, so she must wait.

Finally, he took her to the best café Carnbach boasted and treated her to a gorgeous tea, after which he took her to Cartref where Jo left them alone to say goodbye. She herself had arranged to return Carola to the Chalet School, for the doctor was off to Cardiff by the evening train as his plane left early next morning.

When he had gone, Jo left Carola to herself for half an hour. Then she went to the drawing-room where she found a very red-eyed girl standing staring unseeingly out of the window.

'It won't seem so long after a week or two,' she observed as she shook up cushions and straightened chairs. 'In the meantime, I vote that the first opportunity there is you should come with me to Armiford where we have an excellent photographer, and have your photo done to send out to Calabar. How's that for an idea?'

'S-super!' Carola gulped hard.

'O.K. That's a date, then. Now scram and wash. The ferry leaves in half an hour, so we'd better think about going. You know the bathroom, don't you?'

Carola nodded and departed, to return looking more like herself. Jo would have kept her for the night, but that might have aroused suspicion at School, apart from which, everyone felt she would be better among her own kind. The best thing was to keep her mind occupied, and all the way over, Jo told tales of her own wicked Middle days until she had the girl laughing despite herself. At the front door of the Big House she stooped and kissed her.

'Your dad has left Jack and me *in loco parentis* for the moment,' she said. 'If ever you get into a sticky mess, just remember that, Carola, and let me know if things get too much for you.' She paused to look steadily at her new charge's face under the porch light. 'I don't think I need tell you to stand on your own feet when you can—oh, and try not to stand on other people's! Off you go!'

Carola went off laughing at the conclusion to Mrs Maynard's speech. At the same time, Jo had awakened a deep devotion to herself in the girl. If ever Carola Johnstone could do anything for Mrs Maynard she would do it, regardless of any cost to herself.

Chapter IX

COMPLICATIONS!

'WHAT I don't understand,' said Clem, balancing on the back of the big chesterfield in the common-room, 'is why on earth your aunt—oh, well, cousin, then! —had to go haring off as she did without seeing that you had everything you needed. After all, the School *does* send out a complete inventory, and all she had to do was to take you round the shops and get all it said.'

Carola, very flushed, had nothing to say to this. It seemed horridly mean to let the girls blame Cousin Maud because she had turned up at school so poorly equipped, but as she was still forbidden to say anything about her exploit she had to put up with it. As she was not, by nature, crooked or untruthful, this part of the affair was almost the worst part of her punishment.

'You just can't account for grown-ups,' Polly Winterton put in cheerfully. 'I say, Carola, what are you going to do for Hobbies?'

'Hobbies?' Carola asked blankly.

'Didn't you know? We have Hobbies evening twice a week when we all work at our hobbies. This term we have the Sale for the San up in the hills, so we're all hard at it for that,' Clem explained. 'We had the first evening of the term last Thursday when you were over at Mrs Maynard's. Our form and Upper Fifth are making a dolls' house and furnishing it. Tom Gay has *made* the house, and the rest of us are doing the furnishings. It's a smashing affair this year——'

'Clem Barrass! What was that you said?' demanded a stern voice.

Clem, looking sheepish, slid down from her perch. 'Er—I forgot, Dickie,' she said.

'No excuse at all,' the big, fair prefect who had spoken told her austerely. 'Fine, please. And don't use that ghastly word again. Is Carola Johnstone here?'

'This is her,' Polly replied, waving her hand towards Carola.

'Oh, good! Carola, Nita Eltringham who is Hobbies prefect is in bed with a bad cold, so I'm taking it tonight and I've come to ask what you want for your hobby.'

Carola gazed at her in silence. Oddly enough, no one had said anything to her about Hobbies until tonight, and she had no idea what to say. Dickie waited a moment or two. Then her patience was exhausted and she said, 'Hurry up! What do you go in for—leather-work—basketry—painting? Come *on*! Don't be all night about it!'

'But I don't know what to choose,' Carola said at last. 'No one ever told me anything about it and I don't know what I ought to do.'

'Something for the house, I hope,' Clem put in severely.

'But what *can* I do?'

Dickie took the decision out of her hands for the moment. 'Can you sew?' she asked.

Giggles arose from those of the girls who had been privileged to hear Mademoiselle on the subject, and Carola went redder than ever. Luckily, Dickie knew the signs.

'Oh, it's like that, is it?' she said, her basic good nature rising uppermost. 'Well, if you can't sew, what *can* you do?'

'I don't know,' Carola said truthfully. 'Oh, I can knit a little. Would that do?'

'It'll do if that's all,' Dickie told her. 'You go to Mademoiselle and get wool and needles from her and begin on a scarf for the Sale. That'll keep you going for the moment. Bride, you people shouldn't be hanging about like this. See that everyone has everything she needs and all of you settle to work, please.'

She turned on her heel and left the room, and Bride Bettany and Clem Barrass, the two form prefects, set to work to get everyone busy.

'Sybil, you take Carola to Mademoiselle and ask about the wool and needles,' Bride ordered her cousin.

Sybil, a really lovely girl of nearly fourteen, turned to the new girl. 'Come on, Carola. What colour do you want?'

'I—I don't know,' Carola stammered.

'Oh, well, we'll ask Mademoiselle what she's got and then you can choose. She keeps all the wool and needles, you see, because often we can't get what we want at Carnbach,' Sybil explained as she led the way to the sewing-room, where Mlle Berne pulled open a deep drawer filled with skeins of wool in a rainbow variety of colours and told Carola to choose which she liked.

Still rather dazed, Carola pitched on the first she saw— a pretty cherry colour. Mademoiselle asked what she was going to knit, gave her what was needed and provided the needles, and then bade them hurry back or they would have no time to do anything.

'Didn't you really know about the Hobbies Club?'

Gillian asked inquisitively when finally they were all settled down and Carola was seated near her. 'Why not? It's all in the prospectus.'

'I—I don't know,' Carola stammered.

'Well,' remarked Clem from her treadle fretsaw machine, where she was carefully cutting the backs of some tiny chairs, 'all I can say is that your grown-ups must be *most* casual.'

Carola, busy casting on stitches, said nothing once more. Some of the girls gave her curious looks. The Chalet School had housed some queer characters in its time, but never anyone quite like Carola Johnstone.

Once she had begun, Carola proved herself a practised knitter. She was using a pretty basket-stitch, and before the evening ended she had done six inches of her scarf.

'Jolly pretty,' Sybil Russell said as she looked at it when they were putting their work away. 'All the same, buck up and finish it and then you can start on something for *our* stall. We're doing toys this year, and dolls' things. If you like, I'll ask Dora to let you see what we've done already. Audrey Simpson is making some super carpets to sell separately; and some of the others are doing sets of dolls' bedding and curtains and things like that.'

Carola opened wide eyes at this information. 'I say! That's a jolly decent idea! But what could I do?' she went on plaintively. 'You all know what my sewing's like, and I've never done any woodwork or things like that. You can't when you're for ever moving around.'

'I suppose not. But you do knit awfully well. Why don't you knit some sets of dolls' clothes—you know, knickers and frock and vest. P'raps you could do a suit and jumper to match. I'm sure those would sell.'

Carola looked at her scarf. 'But I wouldn't know how many stitches to cast on. How'd I manage about that?'

'Ask Mademoiselle. I expect she has patterns some-where.'

'Well, it's a wizard idea. I'll think of it.'

Sybil nodded. 'Yes, do. What do you collect, by the way?'

'Collect?' Again Carola was befogged.

'Yes; we all have some sort of collection. Mine's shells since we came to the island. Clem Barrass collects copies of famous pictures. She's got a super collection. Jean Ackroyd collects models of animals, and so do three or four others. My *real* hobby,' Sybil went on as she handed the doll's counterpane she was embroidering to Dora Robson who was responsible for the Hobbies cupboard, 'is embroidery. I just love it. When I leave school I'm going to the South Kensington School to be properly trained. They teach you all sorts of stitches, and how to make your own designs, and how to copy ancient ones, and—oh, everything of that kind. Mummy promised me the training if I'd work hard at my lessons till I was seven-teen. I'm not a brain like Peggy and Bride,' mentioning her two elder cousins, 'but I'd work like a nigger to have my training later. What are you going to do, Carola?'

'I—I don't know. I've never thought about it,' Carola confessed.

To tell the truth she was utterly taken by surprise at Sybil's words. She knew the girl to be a hard worker. Clem had told her that Sybil's mother, Lady Russell, was the owner of the Chalet School. If anyone had asked her, she would have guessed that Sybil meant to train as a teacher and come to teach at the School as quite a number of the Old Girls had done. Perhaps she meant to take over the needlework.

'Shall you teach when you've had your training?' she asked.

Sybil shook her head. 'No jolly fear! I should hate it! Besides,' she added honestly, 'I haven't enough patience. I'd be throwing things at my pupils in ten minutes. What I want to do is church embroideries, like altar frontals and stoles and copes.'

Whereat Carola was once more left gasping, but as they had left the common-room and were now in the corridor she had to be silent.

The next day a further need was shown her. Lower Fifth B had extra art the first part of the afternoon as the weather was so bad there could be no games.

'Take your paintboxes with you, girls,' Miss O'Ryan, who had come to tell them, said.

Carola had never thought of a paintbox, and she had never owned such a thing. She turned to Clem who was standing near.

'Clem, what shall I do? I haven't a paintbox.'

Clem's red-brown eyes became saucerlike at this. 'No paintbox? But it was in the inventory. Oh, my stars and garters! That cousin of yours seems to have made a nice mess of your outfit!'

Carola forgot in her sudden indignation at Clem's remark.

'Well, you can't say it was *her* fault exactly!' she retorted crisply.

'*Not* her fault? Then whose was it?' Clem demanded naturally enough. 'Don't tell me she left you to see to your own outfit!'

Carola was in a quandary. If she said Cousin Maud had done so, it certainly wouldn't be the strict truth. She couldn't say she hadn't, Cousin Maud having never seen the thing.

'Oh dear!' the distracted Carola thought. 'This is simply awful! What ever I say it can't be the truth and I mustn't explain to Clem. If this sort of thing is going on right through the term I shall go crackers!'

Before she had decided what to do, Miss O'Ryan herself unconsciously came to the rescue. 'Carola, here's your paintbox,' she said, presenting the stunned Carola with the regulation affair that most of the girls had. 'Ask Herr Laubach if you can have one of the studio painting jars and get your own from Cook some time before next lesson.'

Carola thankfully grabbed the box with a murmured, 'Thank you, Miss O'Ryan.' She had been saved this time.

In the art room, which was an old army hut attached to the stables, Herr Laubach presented them all with some leafless twigs and set them to making a brushwork study. The others were more or less accustomed to this sort of thing, but to Carola it was quite new. Hitherto, she had done geometrical designs from copies, or freehand work, all of which she had hated. This was rather fun and she settled down to do her best.

Her best was very far from satisfying the art master who was *not* a patient creature—indeed, there *was* a story current in the School that in the days when Mrs Maynard had been just Jo Bettany and a schoolgirl, he had, on one occasion, flung paper, pencil, and rubber at her head!— but Herr Laubach somehow seemed to realise that this new girl was at least trying her hardest. He sat down in her seat and pointed out that a finer brush might have produced better results and that it was not necessary to load her brush with paint. He even brushed in a twig to show her what he meant and then left her to try with another. On the whole, Carola enjoyed the lesson.

Music came next. She was to learn with Miss Cochrane, who was also an Old Girl and considered a fine teacher.

'Poor you!' was all Clem had said when she heard the news.

By the end of the lesson, Carola felt like saying, 'Poor, *poor* me!' If Herr Laubach had very little patience, Miss Cochrane had none at all, and she did have a tongue that could nearly take the skin off you. Carola could play well for her age, Cousin Maud having always insisted on her doing two hours' practice every day unless it were utterly impossible. Her scales passed muster, being smooth, swift, and fluent. But when it came to pieces it was a very different thing.

'You've learnt all these?' Miss Cochrane asked, quickly running through the sheaf of music Carola had remembered to pack in her case. 'Let me hear this Mozart, then.'

Carola began to play the air at the beginning of the variations sonata, but had not finished the first six bars before she was pulled up and told to make it sing more.

Carola began again, and contrived to get through the air without further trouble, but when she began on the first variation she was once more pulled up and bidden to make the air ring out. She went on, honestly doing her best, but it was very difficult, and by the time the lesson came to an end she was almost ready to write to her father by the next mail, begging to be allowed to drop the piano.

Finally, she left the music room, running into Sybil Russell who came next, and who was looking apprehensive.

Sybil raised her eyebrows in a mute question and Carola grimaced eloquently. The younger girl's face fell and she went into the room looking very gloomy. Carola went to put away her music and then ran off to make the most of what was left of prep before tea.

'Was it *very* ghastly?' Clem asked pityingly as they sat munching bread-and-butter with lavish libations of plum jam.

'Simply *awful*!' Carola told her feelingly. She glanced across the table at Sybil who was looking flushed. 'Was she as bad to you, Sybil?'

'Hair-raising!' Sybil said simply. 'I do wish I could learn with good old Sally-go-round-the-moon! *She* never loses her temper, but Cockey seems to keep hers on edge all the time.'

'Who on earth is Sally-go-round-the-moon?' Carola demanded.

'Don't you know *that* yet?' Jean queried as she helped herself to a bun. 'She's Plato's sister—he takes singing— and she sort of helps out with most things like music and German, and teaches Italian if anyone wants to learn it. About ten people do,' she added.

Carola gasped. 'We learn French and German and Latin, anyway. Now you say we can do Italian, too, if we like. How many more languages do they teach here?' she asked.

'Only Greek that I've ever heard of,' Jean replied. 'But it says all about it in the prospectus. We specialise on languages. Didn't your people show you the pros?' she added.

'I've never seen it,' Carola returned, quite truthfully.

'How rummy! Before I came here Mummy wrote to about ten different schools, and we had heaps of fun going through all the prospectuses and seeing which we liked best. We chose this because Mummy liked the sound of it and *I* liked being on an island.' Jean wound up with a laugh. 'We were *both* pleased that way, you see.'

Clem, whose school had been chosen much more dramatically, grinned. 'Dad chose for me—and nearly had to go on his knees to the Abbess to get her to take me,' she said.

'Why on earth?' Gillian demanded, instantly curious. 'Had you been so awful at your last school?'

'Not worse than usual,' Clem told her placidly. 'No; but the School happened to be full up that term before there was any idea of sending me. It must,' she added reflectively, 'have been quite an experience for Dad. He's accustomed to saying what he wants and getting it.'

The others left it at that. Everyone in the School knew that Clem was the daughter of the well-known artist Adrian Barrass, and as his undutiful child had once remarked, a genius thinks the only thing that matters is that he should go the way *he* wants, regardless of other folks and their rights.

Gillian began to explain how she had come to the School. 'Mummy knows a Mrs Carr, and her girl Elsie was here ages and ages ago. Mrs Carr said if they'd half a dozen girls they'd have sent the lot here, so Mummy said that was good enough for her and Daddy, and they sent for the prospectus and that was that. I came.'

'Our treasured little Jumbo!' Clem murmured. 'Tell me one thing, will you, Gill?'

'O.K. What is it?' Gillian demanded.

'Have you *always* been such a curiosity shop?'

'Clem Barrass, you pig!' poor Gillian cried with deep indignation. 'And if I *am* curious there are lots of worse faults! You're not an archangel yourself, so just shut up about me!'

Clem chuckled, but subsided. She was quite fond of Gillian, but could not forbear teasing her on occasions. Gillian, who was a sweet-tempered creature on the whole, contented herself with a muttering which died away as the new girl dropped another unexpected brick.

'Why do we have a Sale for that Sanatorium?' she asked.

Everyone within hearing turned and stared at her. The prospectus explained and they were always well aware that School and Sanatorium were very closely linked. The Chalet School undertook delicate girls because the San doctors overlooked the health of the girls, and Matron, who was, as Jo Maynard had once said, one of the foundation-stones of the School, had taken special training in such work. In Tirol, many of the pupils had been at the Chalet because they had relations up at the great sanatorium on the Sonnalpe, which was at the opposite side of the beautiful Tiernsee where the School had first made its home. Since they had been in England, this had not been quite so much the case, but the prospectus laid emphasis on the fact that health was particularly guarded here, together with a brief explanation, and most girls knew about it before they arrived.

'Look here!' Clem exclaimed, 'I really think—oh, bother! Grace!'

Peggy Bettany, the Head Girl, had risen at the prefects' table and her fellow-grandees were rising too. The talk had to cease for the moment, but Clem resolved to get hold of Carola as soon as she could and find out what she did and didn't know about the School.

'I'm right,' she thought as she helped to clear the table. 'There is some queer mystery about her coming here. Wonder what it is?'

Other girls were beginning to feel the same, though none of them had got as far as Clem. Luckily for Carola, it had not yet occurred to Gillian, who would never have rested until she got to the bottom of it unless someone had shut her up finally. Gillian was a slow-witted young person, however, and Clem made up her mind to see that no one should rouse her suspicions.

'Just the same,' the form prefect thought as she pulled her evening velveteen over her head, 'I don't mind admitting I'd like to know on my own account. There's something most frightfully odd about it all!'

Chapter X

A WINTER'S WALK

FEBRUARY was only a week old when winter suddenly came in earnest. They had great gales of wind which were so violent that no one could go out of doors and the ferries stopped running. Then the wind died down and the calm brought with it snow, and for two days and nights it snowed without ceasing. And, to quote Biddy O'Ryan, as if that were not enough, the snow turned to hail one night and the hail brought with it keen hard frost.

Even in the Big House, with its double windows and central-heating, the girls complained of the cold. Woolly cardigans were dragged over blazers and ankle socks appeared over stockings. Matron and Nurse had a busy time dealing with a large crop of chilblains and colds and quite a number of people appeared with bandaged fingers.

Poor Bride, always a martyr to chilblains, even developed them on her ears, but Nita Eltringham, one of the prefects, outdid this by producing one on the tip of her nose and went about with the end of that feature swollen and crimson.

However, the frost proved useful in one way, for on the Friday morning Miss Annersley stopped all lessons, bade the girls wrap up well, and sent them all out for walks which had been in abeyance for more than a week now.

'I've put on a jumper, my blazer, a cardigan, and my

big coat,' Gillian said with a shiver. 'I'm wearing two of everything underneath and I can't think of anything else except my scarf.'

'I *thought* you looked extra tubby,' Jean said amid the yells of laughter that greeted this announcement. 'I put it down to having no walks or games, though. Try two pairs of gloves to top off with—do!'

'Well, anyway, I stand some chance of being warm,' Gillian told her serenely. 'Which way are we going? Anyone know?'

'Ready, you Fifth Forms?' asked Miss O'Ryan's voice. 'All got your scarves on? Sure you'll all freeze if you don't wrap up. This is nearly as bad as Tirol.'

'Mummy said it was like Tirol in Canada,' Sybil remarked as they all trooped out after the young mistress. 'I can *just* remember it there, and how white the snow was when the sun shone.'

'And we all had to wear dark glasses in case of snow blindness,' Biddy supplemented as she led the way. 'There'll be no need for that today, anyhow.' She glanced up at the grey sky. 'There's a lot more to come down yet, or I miss my guess. Pair off, girls, and remember, you must keep moving. This way, all of you. We're going along to Kittiwake Cove first, then right along to the Merry Mermaidens. We'll come back by the high road, by which time I should think you'll all be ready for Mittagessen and a quiet afternoon. Go carefully; it's slippery with this frost.'

She was quite right. Slippery it was, and before long the girls were hot and breathless with trying to keep their feet on the frozen surface. Miss O'Ryan revised her first ideas about a walk, and presently announced that they would go to the Cove, but there would be no going along the cliffs. It was much too dangerous with the paths like this. The girls, floundering along, quite agreed with her. Walking properly was impossible. At any moment your partner might utter a wild squawk and grab you, and if you weren't prepared the pair of you might go headlong. Not that anyone wanted to turn back. It was far too good fun for that.

The way to Kittiwake Cove led down the side of a field, through a deep lane, usually full of ruts, and out to the cliff where there was a path cut deep into the rock, leading down to the Cove.

'Can we go down to the shore, Miss O'Ryan?' Bride Bettany coaxed.

'We'll see what the cliff path looks like first,' Biddy said cautiously. 'I'd like to be taking you all back with unbroken bones. I'll try it first myself, and if it's not too bad I'll let you come.'

With that they had to be content. In any case, at that moment Polly Winterton slipped, grabbed at her partner, Jean Ackroyd, and the pair of them staggered wildly about, trying to keep their balance, while the rest stood still to watch the fun. In the end they managed it, and then Biddy, with an eye to the keen air, moved them on.

'I feel like a hen on hot peas,' Sybil said presently to Carola whom she was partnering. 'We really ought to have nailed boots like we had in Tirol.'

'Well, something, anyhow,' Carola replied breathlessly. 'The backs of my legs are beginning to ache like fun—Ough!' as she just contrived to avoid sitting down violently.

'It may be easier in the lane,' Clem said hopefully. 'I

say! Listen to those kids yelling! I can hear Mary-Lou
above everyone else!'

On the sharp, clear air, they could hear faintly wild
shrieks coming from the direction of St Briavel's village
whither most of the Junior Middles had gone in charge of
Miss Bell, Miss Stephens, Miss Edwards, and Miss Burn.
The Juniors were kept to the grounds and the Seniors had
gone off in little groups, each with a mistress, so the School
was widely scattered over the island.

The girls gazed with interest over the well-known scenes,
now so different from what they had hitherto known. The
field was a wide white plain; the trees, bare and leafless,
creaking beneath the weight of frozen snow on their
branches; no birds or rabbits were to be seen and the
cows were all snug in their byres. Miss O'Ryan glanced
at it, and then turned anxious eyes at the sky. However,
she felt reassured when she saw it. Snow was certainly
there, but it seemed unlikely to come back for a while yet.
She led the way out of the field and into the lane where
the ruts had filled up, and walking was no more easy than
it had been.

'It's warmer here,' Gillian said suddenly. 'I suppose
the hedges act as a kind of protection.'

'Some protection!' Clem jeered. 'I shouldn't like to
be here in a wind. It 'ud be a bit draughty.'

'All right, girls? No one feeling cold?' Miss O'Ryan
called from the head of the file.

A chorus of protests arose. No one could feel anything
but warm, thanks to their wild struggles to keep their feet,
and most folk had crimson cheeks, even if they were rather
dishevelled by this time.

Miss O'Ryan surveyed them with a hidden smile. She

had expected this. 'Well, since you're all nice and warm, we'll go on,' she said. 'Be careful, though. We don't want any broken bones. Besides, I don't see how we could carry any one of you home if you did break a leg or so.'

With this most unschoolmarm-like warning, she turned once more, and finally they came out to the common-like space on the cliffs. Here, the ground sloped up to the edge of the cliffs, or the young mistress would certainly never have contemplated bringing her flock. Breathless as the early part of the outing had been, the girls found it even more so as they struggled up the slope, and finally found themselves opposite the opening to the cliff path leading to the Cove.

'I doubt very much if we'll be able to negotiate that at all,' Miss O'Ryan remarked, eyeing it thoughtfully. 'Sure, it's as slippery as can be.' She looked round. 'You can come to the head here between the rocks and wait a moment till I see for myself. No one is to come further than where I'm standing this minute. Bride, take charge, please.'

Bride went forward carefully, and the girls crowded into the space. They were not sorry for the shelter, for the wind came sweeping across the island from the north, chill and cutting, and making eyes and cheeks smart under its lash.

'I'm simply boiling!' Jean observed, 'all but the tip of my nose, that is. Gill, you're *scarlet*! You must be cooked alive with all the clothes you've put on!'

'I'm hottish,' Gillian agreed, 'but it's a nice change after being frozen to death for the last few days. D'you think Miss O'Ryan will let us go down, anyone?'

This question was answered by Miss O'Ryan herself.

She appeared, puffing and blowing, round the curve in the path, shaking her head. 'Sorry, but I'm afraid 'tis impossible it is. I've done quite a bit of alpine climbing in my time, and I wouldn't try to get down there without an alpenstock for anything you could mention. Besides, it's taken us quite a while to get this far, and we've all the way home to go. We'll have to turn and I'll bring you here another day when it's less of a break-neck business. Back you go, and no grumbling!'

The girls turned and began to go back. The mistress made no attempt to get them into line. She said afterwards that she thought it would be wiser to wait for that until they were safely back in the lane. At a word from her, Bride headed the crowd which crossed the cliff-top path, and began to struggle down the slope. She was a sure-footed creature, and old memories of Tirol were coming back to her legs. Moving carefully, she was soon half-way along to the lane. The rest followed, Biddy O'Ryan bringing up the rear to act as whipper-in.

'This is a lot easier than coming *up* was,' Clem said cheerfully.

The next moment her foot slipped, and with a wild yell she slid downwards, crashing into Bride and sending her flying as she grabbed at her, and the pair rolled down to the bottom of the slope, locked in each other's arms, and, as Biddy graphically told the rest of the Staff later on, yelling blue murder the whole way!

It was fatal for most concerned. One or two people began to laugh, and then discovered that they themselves had begun to slide, and once that happened they were fully occupied in trying to keep themselves on their feet. Polly Winterton, screaming the whole time, slid gracefully to the foot of the slope and ended up in a gorse bush. Gillian, with a truly thrilling squall, staggered wildly half-way down, sat down suddenly, and tobogganed on the tail of her coat the rest of the way. Loveday Perowne followed suit and arrived on top of her. It was left to Carola to put the finishing touches to what looked like becoming a regular football scrum. She skidded, swung completely round, and slid *backwards* to the bottom, clutching at all and sundry as she passed them, so that some folk went over at once, while others managed to keep their feet, but had, perforce, to slide the whole way, some ending up like Polly among the gorse bushes which dotted this part of the ground, and others arriving on their backs. All, it is hardly necessary to state, shrieked at the tops of their voices.

Miss O'Ryan, seeing what was happening to her walk, made the fatal mistake of trying to rush to the rescue. For half a dozen paces she kept her footing. Then she, too, slipped, and with arms outstretched like a tight-rope walker, joined the sliders, and brought up with a minor crash against a telegraph pole which she embraced affectionately.

She recovered herself almost at once, and turned round cautiously to see what was happening to her lambs. The next moment she was on the ground, rocking with laughter. Two girls, Annis Lovell and Tom Gay, who had been last, had gone down on all-fours, and were crawling down the slope with small regard for the knees of their stockings and their gloves, but considerably more safely than most of the rest had done it.

The girls at the bottom, seeing the mistress in convulsions of laughter, turned to look, too, and the sight of Annis and Tom set them off as well, so that by the time the pair joined up, the whole place rang with their mirth.

Tom, having reached the bottom, got cautiously to her feet and looked round with a disgusted air. 'What on earth is up with all you idiots?' she demanded.

'You!' Clem choked. 'Oh—*o-oh!* I shall be sick if I laugh any more!'

Miss O'Ryan, who was also on her feet by this time, assumed an air of dignity. 'Look at your stocking knees!' she said in shocked tones.

The pair hurriedly looked, and two more chapfallen persons it would have been hard to find at that moment.

'*Crumbs!*' Tom ejaculated when she could speak. '*Matey* will have something to say!' She glanced at her thick woollen gloves. 'Oh, lord! This means *hours* of darning! I never thought of that.'

'In the meantime,' Miss O'Ryan said with what severity she could muster, 'we had better try to get home before we meet anyone. You two are a pair of ragamuffins.' Then she added with some anxiety, 'Have you hurt your knees? Anyone hurt at all?'

Some of them were suffering from bruises and bumps, but no one had even thought of it since they had watched the exploit of the pair. No one was badly hurt, however, not even Bride who had gone with a real crash. Miss O'Ryan satisfied herself that any injuries were of a minor nature, and then set to work to get her flock home before anything worse could happen.

'Now then, pair off,' she commanded. 'Tom and Annis, you go to the middle of the croc. We may not meet anyone; on the other hand, we may, and it's no advertisement for the School the pair of ye are at present.'

In the general upheaval, she was forgetting all resolves, and becoming richly Irish. Bride Bettany, who had been a very junior Junior in the days when Biddy O'Ryan had been a stern but much loved prefect, nudged Primrose Day, another of the same vintage year, and the pair of them chuckled. They remembered what the young mistress had been like in those days, and it was a treat to hear her relapsing from her very beautiful English into the Biddy O'Ryan they had known.

'I always *knew* Biddy would never keep it up all the time,' Bride murmured to Primrose.

'Well, could you expect it?' Primrose asked reasonably. 'She's always had an Irish accent ever since *I* could remember.'

'And before that,' Bride informed her. 'Come on! She's yelling for us to join up—— *Auntie Jo!*'

She made a wild leap forward as a tall, well-known figure suddenly appeared at the end of the lane, and fell full length as a natural result.

Jo gave her a quick look as she struggled to her feet. What she saw was reassuring. 'I knew you liked me, Bride,' she said sweetly, 'but I didn't know your liking was mixed with sufficient awe to make you prostrate yourself at my feet.'

Bride greeted this pleasantry with a wild giggle. 'Oh, Auntie Jo,' she protested. 'Anyone would flop with the roads like this. You should just have seen us coming down that slope a few minutes ago!'

Jo looked round the laughing throng. 'I did notice you all looked as though you had been in a free-for-all of the most violent kind. Tom Gay! What *have* you done to your stockings? And Annis Lovell, too? Don't tell me you tried *crawling* down!'

'Sure, that's the very thing they did,' Biddy told her. 'The rest of us came down on our feet—more or less.'

'Carola came *backwards*,' bubbled Clem. 'I do wish you'd seen it, Mrs Maynard.'

'You can't talk!' cried the justly indignant Carola. 'You barged into Bride and the two of you rolled down fighting like a pair of wild cats!'

'Dear me!' Jo looked suitably impressed. '"A good time was had by all," in fact. We heard wild howls proceeding from this direction, so I volunteered to come and see what all the row was about. Tom and Annis, I'd advise you to enter School in the middle of a large crowd, otherwise Matron will tell you *all* about your stockings. Coming, everyone?' She swung round, and strode alongside them, chatting gaily as she went.

'Auntie Jo, how *do* you do it?' Bride demanded with point when they were nearly at the end of the lane.

'Do what?' Jo demanded.

'Walk so easily. The rest of us are sliding——' She did it at that moment and only Jo's hand gripping her arm kept her from going full length again.

'You're as bad as any baby learning to walk,' her aunt told her. 'As for me, I raked out my old nailed boots. Haven't used them since our last winter in Tirol—no; I was forgetting. I was in India that winter. The winter before, then—but I've kept them well-greased and they've come in very handy today, thank you. I had to come to bring some things to Matron, and the ferries were running at long last. If this frost goes on, however, it wouldn't surprise me if they didn't have to shut down again. Hi! mind your feet, Primrose!' as Primrose executed an involved slither.

'Shut down again, Jo?' Biddy opened her eyes widely. 'Why?'

'The strait looks like freezing over. It's skinned at the edges, anyhow. If that spreads and the ice thickens they wouldn't run the ferries. It wouldn't be safe.'

'But I thought the sea *didn't* freeze,' Bride protested as they turned into the field.

'Oh, it can. It doesn't often happen in this part of the world, but what about the Baltic? And the sound between Prince Edward Island and the mainland freezes over, too. It takes a pretty hard frost for it to happen, but it has been known, even here.'

'Goodness me! Then could we skate on it?'

'Well, hardly! It doesn't make smooth ice, you know.'

'Then if that happens, how are we to get to Carnbach— I say! Was that snow?' Bride broke off to look upward, an example followed by everyone else.

She was quite right. Floating down from the grey skies were one or two flakes, and it was quite clear that there was more to follow, and very quickly. Jo, with years of experience behind her, turned to the girls imperatively.

'It's going to come a young blizzard. We can't be caught in that on an open field. Scram, all of you! Keep to this edge, and stick together! Don't wander, whatever you do! Biddy,' in the emergency she forgot the formal title, 'you come behind with me and we'll guard the rear. Bride, you, and Primrose, and Tom, and—yes, Nancy Chester, act as whippers-in at the sides. Get cracking, all of you!'

So urgent were both voice and words that the girls took fright and stumbled along at top speed. Jo, however, knew what she was talking about. She and the rest of the

Seniors had once been caught in a snowstorm in Tirol. They had been quite near the School at the time, but so bewildering had been the dizzying dance of the fast-falling flakes that they had nearly gone past it. And then they had been on a fenced path with the Tiernsee at the other side. Here, if anyone strayed, it might be some time before she was found, and already the snow was coming faster.

Mercifully, they had not very far to go before they were pushing through the gate leading into the orchard, and before things became too nerve-racking they were streaming along the path two of the men, who saw to the gardens and furnaces, had dug out earlier on, and entering the side-door that led to the Splasheries, followed by a warning from Miss O'Ryan to change at once and go to their common-room.

Chapter XI

A SPOT OF GERMAN CONVERSATION

AS Jo had truly said, they were in for a blizzard. She herself insisted on setting off at once to reach home. Luckily, she had no fear of losing herself as the road down to the ferry-landing ran between fenced fields. She just managed to catch the last ferry that was to run for the next two or three days and landed safely at Cartref where, much to her joy, she found her husband awaiting her, he having run over from the Sanatorium for a few hours, which lengthened to a long week-end. There could be no question of his risking the road through the mountains in such a storm as this was.

Jo set to work on her new book, seeing there was little chance of going out, while he cleared up quite a good amount of clerical work which had had to wait for just such an occasion. In the mornings he escorted their eldest son Stephen, a sturdy youth of nearly seven, to the Kindergarten school farther along their road and Jo managed to run along at noon to fetch the boy home. That was all the 'out' any of them enjoyed during that time.

As for the School, the girls had to content themselves with extra gym and country dancing for exercise. No one was going to allow them to venture out in such a storm. They managed very well on the whole. The Heads promised that when it was fine weather again they should be allowed more time for walks and games practices. Joan

Sandys, the Games prefect, grumbled considerably about the time that was being lost, and one or two of the keener folk did their share of grousing, but on the whole the girls behaved very well—for the first few days, at any rate.

Trouble began on the Monday when Miss Annersley announced at Prayers that though French was improving throughout the School, with a few rare exceptions their German conversation was far from being what it ought to be. She therefore desired them to speak nothing but German throughout the day. This was a shock, as Monday was generally devoted to French, Tuesday being the day for German.

'How ghastly!' Clem growled once they were in the sanctuary of their form-room. 'I do think the Abbess is being mean. Who *wants* to talk that awful jaw-breaking stuff, I'd like to know?'

'Not me,' Polly said with more lack of grammar than was necessary. 'I loathe it, and I can't say more than a few words, anyhow. Strikes me I'll have to be silent for most of the day.'

'Not in lessons you can't,' Jean reminded her. 'We've got to talk it then, whether we like it or not.'

Carola, who had been looking as dismayed as the rest, now turned a horrified look on Clem. 'What on earth shall I do? We've had only four German days since I came——'

'We've had more, but you missed them,' Clem explained. 'Oh, well, we'll just have to manage as best we can. Try your hardest, Carola.'

She got no further, for Miss Slater entered at that moment to take them for arithmetic. Now, although they would not have believed it, Miss Slater was no more pleased than they with the Head's edict. She spoke fluent French, but her German was only shaky. However, unlike the girls, she could arrange her lessons to suit herself, and having heard before Frühstück what was to be the order for the day, she had occupied every moment of her spare time in preparing tests for her forms. She snapped out an order to sit to the girls and then proceeded to cover the board with questions nicely calculated to find out all their weakest spots. They groaned inwardly, but something in the mistress's eye, as she surveyed them, kept them from voicing their disgust aloud. Meekly they took the paper she had handed out and set to work to do what they could. On the whole, Carola decided, as she wrestled with an intricate decimals of money sum, it was better than having to do arithmetic in German. The room remained silent for the whole of the forty minutes devoted to the lesson. The bell rang and Miss Slater, after collecting her papers, departed for her next form. Miss O'Ryan passed her in the doorway and the girls prayed for another test.

It was not for nothing, however, that Biddy O'Ryan had spent her early years in Tirol. She spoke excellent German and had no idea of forgoing a lesson she considered important just because it had to be given in German. She set to work on the growth of the English colonies in North America and went ahead in great style.

The trouble started when she addressed a question to Polly Winterton, who stared blankly at her. Polly could work when she chose, but she had spent only one term at the School, and had come completely ignorant of any language but her own. One term, even with two days a week of speaking nothing but German, had not taught her nearly enough to follow Miss O'Ryan's fluent remarks, and she had no idea what she was being asked.

The mistress opened her eyes widely as Polly, having risen to her feet, stood silent and crimson and made no effort to answer the question.

'Ich warte,' Miss O'Ryan reminded her after a minute of this.

'Ich ver stehe nicht,' Polly stammered—it was one of the few German phrases she really knew.

Miss O'Ryan's blue eyes opened widely. 'Wie lang sind Sie hier gewesen?' she demanded.

Polly guessed the meaning of this. 'Only since last term,' she said, falling back on English in her dismay.

'Sprechen Sie deutsch!' Miss O'Ryan reminded her gently.

'Ich kann nicht. I don't know it,' Polly explained.

Still speaking in German, Biddy repeated what the girl had said. 'Nun sagen Sie,' she said firmly.

Polly knew this and did her best to repeat the German. It took seven repetitions before she said it sufficiently well to satisfy Miss O'Ryan. At last, however, that young lady announced herself satisfied, repeated her first question very slowly, and waited for some sort of answer. By this time, however, Polly was so gravelled that she was quite unable to guess at the drift of the German, and Miss O'Ryan had to give it up and pass the question on to Clem, who understood well enough and could even manage an answer, but whose German accent left everything to be desired.

Very patiently the mistress repeated her words and made the fuming Clem go over and over them until they sounded more like German. At last: 'Gut. Setzen Sie sich,' she said; and turned to Carola who came next.

Carola was all at sea in any case, and had already decided that her best move was to say so at once.

'Please, Miss O'Ryan, I don't know any German,' she informed the mistress. 'I've never done any till I came here and I haven't learnt much yet. I—I haven't understood a word of the lesson.'

A gasp ran round the room at this temerity. As for Biddy, 'Sure, I nearly flung my book at her,' she told the enthralled Staff later on when she was retailing the story for their delectation. 'And will you be telling me why a girl who has been here a whole term can't answer a single simple question in German? What's *happened* to the School?'

'The fact of the matter is,' Hilary Burn replied, 'that while a few of us do know German and can speak it pretty fluently, we have several folk who either didn't know it, or who had just enough to scrape through their exams. It was different in Tirol where everyone spoke it, and you sort of sucked in with your breath.'

'But the French isn't nearly so bad,' Biddy persisted. 'Why is the German, with extremely few exceptions, so utterly appalling?'

'You can keep the German for all of me,' Miss Slater said bluntly. 'I'm one of the people who only knew enough to pass exams. When school ended I tossed my German grammar aside with thankfulness. I've always hated it, and I wish to goodness it hadn't occurred to anyone to renew it here. I can tell you, the kids have all my sympathy. It takes me all my time to manage enough to teach anything on German days, and when I *can* manage it I set them tests and exercises to work out.'

Biddy, who had always had a gift for languages, stared.

'But it's an easy enough language to learn,' she argued. 'Look here, what you want is to spend a holiday in Germany or Austria with the natives. You would soon pick it up then. Why don't ye? I can give ye half a dozen addresses if that's all.'

Miss Slater looked coldly at her. Biddy O'Ryan might be a mistress at the School now, but the maths mistress still inclined to regard her as one of the girls who had been a regular nuisance in maths lessons. Hilary Burn, who had left the School before Miss Slater had joined it, saw what was in the latter's eye, and came to the rescue.

'Never mind all that now, Biddy,' she said. 'Tell us what you did about young Carola.'

'Well, I was so taken aback ye could have knocked me down with a feather,' Biddy explained. 'However, I said, "Hier dürfen Sie nicht englisch sprechen. Versuchen Sie, ich werde Ihnen helfen."'

'And did she understand you?' Mlle de Lachenais asked.

'Not a word, beyond the fact that she couldn't speak English just then. She stood gaping at me till, as I told you just now, I felt like throwing my book at her.'

The Staff laughed, and Miss Wilson coming in just then to make inquiries about Staff evening which was to take place after half-term, the subject dropped.

As for Carola and the rest of Lower Fifth B, apart from three of them, they were all in sympathy with anyone who couldn't speak German. As German had to be their language for the day, and few of them could express their feeling adequately that way, they had to wait until Wednesday, when English was the order of the day. All the same, with two days of German, one after the other, and a rather shocked Staff hounding them on, several people contrived to learn a little more than they had known before. Clem, who had taken the language very light-heartedly up till then, paid a little more attention to her accent, and Polly Winterton knew at least *one* sentence for the rest of her life.

Unfortunately for the School at large, the entire Staff, having had the School's shortcomings brought to their notice so thoroughly by Biddy O'Ryan, considered it their duty to make some improvement. In consequence, German days rapidly became a burden to everyone. By the time half-term arrived, the Middles were all in a state of revolt, especially the Junior Middles. Even the Seniors were heard to murmur.

The climax came when Vi Lucy, an ornament of Lower Fourth, had to repeat 'Ich weiss nicht wirklich was zu sagen' ('I really don't know what to say') seventeen times before Miss Edwards pronounced herself satisfied. Vi was raging by the time she was released. She left the Junior maths mistress with sparkling eyes and flushed cheeks and made a bee-line for her own particular gang, which included Mary-Lou Trelawney and Verity-Anne Carey.

Unfortunately for her, in her anger she let loose in English, and Miss Wilson, coming along, got the full beauty of her tirade. Vi had not spared any slang, and the Head dealt with her faithfully. By the time Miss Wilson had finished, the young lady was realising dazedly that she was docked of a week's pocket-money in the way of fines, never to mention having to learn the whole of 'Der Erl-König' by heart, with the prospect of repeating it to Mlle de Lachenais by the next evening without a mistake.

'And please see that your pronunciation improves, too,'

'Bill,' as she was generally known in the School, wound up. 'Now you may go and make the most of what is left of your games time. Explain to whoever takes you that you have been with me.'

Vi departed, seething, to explain as best she could to Dickie Christy, who was in charge of their netball that afternoon, and got a very cold reception. As she found it difficult to say all that had to be said in German, and at first gave Dickie the impression that she had gone to Bill of her own accord, this was hardly to be wondered at. When the prefect finally got to the bottom of the affair, she added insult to injury in Vi's estimation by saying, 'Well, perhaps that will remind you that slang of the kind you seem to have used is forbidden, anyhow, whatever may be the official language for the day. Now go over to the other court and ask Judy Rose to let you join her team.'

It was no use arguing with Dickie, even if Vi could have found the German for it. Dickie was Second Prefect, a very important person, and furthermore, a person who was jolly enough in general, but possessed a gift for sarcasm that made her juniors wary of rousing her anger. Vi, her form's captain, went across to join with the fourteen people who were poor at netball and were practising passing and shooting under the guidance of Judy Rose, another of the prefects.

If it had ended there, it might not have mattered so much, but the Staff convened a meeting at which it was decided that the prefects must have been very lax over slang. The two Heads called the grandees of the School to their study and spoke very seriously on the subject and then dismissed them, smarting and indignant.

'When you think,' wailed Daphne Russell, 'how strict

we all were about it last term and how some of those young demons played us up for it, it really is enough to—to dry up the milk of one's human kindness and finish for keeps one's belief in human nature!'

'They didn't keep it up for long,' Frances Carew reminded her with a chuckle. 'Peggy soon put a stop to their little games.'

'I know that. What I'm getting at now is the way the Heads have yattered about pulling them up for slang *again*! As if we could always be on their tracks! How does anyone think we can do it?'

'Ring off, Daph!' Peggy herself spoke. 'Of course, most of this comes from the business with Vi Lucy. I must say,' she added impartially, 'she seems to have excelled herself in the way of language. I had Mary-Lou on the carpet for telling Phil Craven to shut her head, and when I'd finished, she said, "That's nothing to what Vi Lucy knows. You ought to hear *her* when she gets going— or Clem, either."'

Dickie Christy laughed. '*Or* Mary-Lou herself. Funny kid! She can say things like that, and yet you know that most of the time it isn't sauce. I wouldn't have taken that sort of thing from most of those youngsters, but from Mary-Lou it's something different.'

Peggy nodded. 'I know. I think it's mainly because she lived entirely with grown-ups all her early years. And though she comes out with statements of that kind, it's neither cheek nor telling tales. As for young Vi, with brothers like John and Barney, what else can you expect? Really,' she went on, 'I suppose it begins with the German.'

'Oh that German!' Judy Rose groaned. 'I can manage with French, but German gets me down every time. Why on earth we've got to use it I can't think. Dad says that, so far as he can see, the School won't be going back to Tirol for years to come. How could it until Russia clears out of Austria and leaves the Austrians alone?'

Peggy eyed them all thoughtfully. Daphne, her great friend, saw it, and at once leaped to the conclusion that something was going on in the background and Peggy knew about it.

'*Is* anything likely to happen, Peg?' she asked.

'About Austria? Nothing at all, I should think. Judy's dad hit the nail on the head when he said we couldn't go back to Tirol yet.'

'Then is there an idea of somewhere else?' Daphne insisted.

Peggy shook her head. 'I really don't know anything. It was just something Auntie Jo said one day during the hols.'

'What was it?' A whole chorus demanded this.

Peggy considered. 'Well,' she said finally, 'it was words to the effect that if Tirol was out of the question for some time to come, there was still Switzerland. Mind, I don't suppose it was any more than her own ideas,' she went on, stemming the tide of exclamations that greeted this with waving hands. ' —Be *quiet* and let me finish!— Just the same, it's an idea that *might* come to something.'

There was a moment's silence while the prefects digested this.

Dickie was the first to speak. '*Switzerland!* I hadn't thought of that as a solution. Not that it's likely to affect me,' she added. 'I'm eighteen in June and leaving school at the end of the year. Cherry would come in for it, of course—and young Gaynor, too, I expect.'

'It wouldn't affect a good many of us,' Frances Coleman

agreed. 'You're leaving—I'm leaving—Nita's leaving—
so are Mollie and Barbara. Peggy will have another year,
I suppose: that's what comes of being an infant prodigy.
Daph, what about you?'

'Oh, I'm having another year,' Daphne replied. 'I
shan't be eighteen until next December and I'm to have
a year in Special Sixth and go in thoroughly for languages.
It would be super if we had a year in Switzerland. Where-
abouts would it be, do you think, Peg?'

'Bernese Oberland, I expect,' Peggy replied promptly.
'They're opening a branch of the San there, and the San
and the School have always been part of each other. Mind,
girls, I don't know any more about it than I've told you;
and please don't go round chattering about it, for it may
be only my imagination. Still, I do agree that they seem
to be making an extra fuss this year about our German.
If we went to the Oberland, German is the native tongue
there, I believe.'

'Well,' Dickie said, 'all this is interesting enough, but
it isn't deciding how we should deal with slang in the
School. That's our present job. Ideas, please, everyone.'

Needless to state, this bland request dried up everyone.
As pretty Mollie Avery complained, you just can't think
when you have a bomb flung at you like that. The girls
were fined as a rule for the worse forms of slang, and
hitherto it had been quite enough. No one liked to be
short of pocket-money each week. However, Miss Annersley had ordered them to do what they could to improve
the general usage of English among the younger girls, so
they must try. They sat in silence and racked their brains—
vainly, at first. Then Nita Eltringham suddenly said she
had a germ of an idea.

'What is it?' Peggy demanded. 'Trot it out at once.'

'Well, you know how they—or the kids, at any rate—hate messing about with dickers? If we catch them using slang let's make them hunt out the proper meaning of the words and write them out so many times. It'll help their spelling as well as their understanding of English, and if we insist it must be in their best handwriting it won't hurt *that*.'

'*And* it'll take up their free time, which they'll loathe, so they'll try to reform,' Dickie agreed. 'I think it's a wizard idea, Nita. What do the rest of you say?'

'Oh, I'm game to try it. I'll try *anything* that'll save us from a lecture like the one we've just had. What do you say, Peg?' Daphne turned to Peggy who nodded.

'We'll try it. It can't hurt them; it *may* do the trick. Anyhow, we've got to do something about it, and no one else seems to have anything to suggest.'

'When do we begin?' Frances asked. 'Tonight?'

'I think not. Half-term starts the day after tomorrow. We'll hint at awful things if they don't pull up, to give them something to think about over the week-end. When we come back I'll put up a notice about it and we'll start in then. Won't they hate us, though!' Peggy giggled. 'Where on earth did you get the idea, Nita?'

'Remember last week-end I had a cold and Matey made me stay in bed on Sunday? Well, when you crowd had gone to church she brought me some books from the library. I think she must have been in a frightful hurry when she got them, for they were all from the Junior library, and two of them were *aged* things—a school story and an adventure story. I read the school story because I'd never even heard of it before—*Barbara Bellamy, School-*

girl. Barbara Bellamy was a weird kid who had been brought up by a professor father and never talked slang at all. One of the girls said something about sapping, which seems to have been the slang they used for swotting in those days, and this *Barbara* went on with a lot of rot about sap being the juice of the tree and books being the juice of learning—or something like that,' Nita concluded hazily. 'She seemed to think it quite a sensible word used that way. When Dickie asked for ideas it came into my mind. That's all.'

'Well, I rather like it,' Daphne said definitely. 'O.K. That's settled then. Come on! There's the bell for tea. Remember to spread intriguing and ghastly hints about what's going to happen after half-term to anyone who uses outrageous slang, all of you. As Peggy says, we may as well give the little dears something to think about over the week-end.'

Laughing, the prefects trooped off downstairs for tea, and before the School broke up for half-term, all the Middles and a good many of the Seniors were being given to wonder what awfulness was in store for them if they didn't reform their mode of language in short order.

Chapter XII

HALF-TERM BEGINS

EASTER fell very early this year, so it had been decided to give the girls a long week-end at half-term and carry on with school until the middle of April. The Easter week-end would be a holiday, but they would have a bare three weeks before the summer term began, and as that was twelve weeks long, things would even themselves out.

'Suits me all right,' Jo Maynard had said airily when she heard from Miss Annersley what the arrangements were. 'Other things being equal, we sail for Quebec at the end of April, so the girls won't miss any of this term. Also, it will give me time to see about outfits. I must take them looking decent or Madge will say things!'

'It makes a filthy long term,' grumbled Bride Bettany in private to her sister Peggy.

'We'll be able to go home for half-term, anyway. And don't use such disgusting language,' Peggy retorted.

'We shan't be home for Easter, though, and I do love Easter at home,' Bride replied sadly, conveniently forgetting the last part of her sister's speech.

'It only happens once in a way. I've looked up Easter in young Len's Missal, and it isn't in March again for eight years, which won't affect you—or even Maeve. And honestly, Bride, you simply must stop using so much slang.

You're Upper Fifth and will be Lower Sixth next year, so you'd better be preparing for it.'

Bride made a face. No more than her Aunt Jo did she like the idea of having to grow up. 'I wish I could stay my present age for the next five years,' she said.

'Oh, talk sense!' the exasperated Peggy cried. 'You can't stay a kid for ever. Now you trot off and stop grousing.'

Bride departed, but she was no more reconciled to the future than before. As for the others, the Middles, at any rate, were content to take what came. They would think of grumbling over the belated spring holidays when Easter arrived.

Half-term began on the Thursday morning and would continue until Tuesday evening. With six days in hand, most of the girls were going home. Sybil Russell would spend the time with her aunt at Cartref. The Ozanne girls, whose home was in Guernsey, were to stay with their relations in Armiford, and so would the Lucy girls. Others were staying with friends, and when Matron had finished her inquiries she found that only ten girls would be left at the school.

'Who are they?' Miss Wilson demanded. 'Any prefects among them?'

'No; they are all off this time. Carola Johnstone from Lower Five B is the eldest to stay. Jean Ackroyd from the same form will be here, too. The rest are Doris Hill, whose people are in the south of France, Barbara and Kathleen Watson—they would have to spend a day and a half getting across to Orkney, and it isn't worth it—the O'Connor girls for the same reason, except that it's Ireland in their case, and Thyra and Signa Björnessen who always have to be arranged for. That's the worst of having foreign children,' concluded Matron.

The two Heads thought. Then Miss Wilson spoke. 'Well, you're going to Gloucester to stay with your cousins there, aren't you, Hilda? Which of the Staff are off?'

Miss Annersley fished a list out of her desk and looked over it. 'Miss Norman is staying and so is Hilary Burn. What are *your* plans, Nell? You haven't said anything yet.'

'Because they've been so nebulous. If I wasn't needed here, I thought I'd take advantage of Madge Russell's offer and go to stay at the Round House. Then I could keep an eye on what was going on at Plas Howell. However, it looks as if that must be off, now.'

'Rubbish!' Matron said trenchantly. '*I'm* staying. I had word this morning that my sister's two grandchildren have begun with whooping-cough, so I can't go there. I've made no other plans, so I shall stay here. If Ivy Norman and Hilary Burn and myself aren't enough to cope with ten girls we'd better give up our jobs at once.'

'Well, one of us certainly ought to go and see what's cooking,' Miss Wilson said. 'Whatever we do finally, there will always be part of the School in England now. Nothing's settled about the Oberland yet, though we can have Frau Hessell's house, Frieda says, and welcome. It's quite a big place and we could build on to it in time. A portion of the School will be here for years to come, though, and now that the Russells have bought Plas Howell from Ernest Howell, the School is definitely fixed there.'

'There you are then. You go and I'll stay.' Matron scanned her list again. 'Carola and Jean are Lower Five B. Doris Hill, Barbara Watson, and Judy O'Connor are Lower Fourth. Kathleen Watson, Norah O'Connor, and

Thyra are Lower Third A; the other two are First Form. Nothing to worry us there. We'll put them all into the big dormitory so that they can be together and no one need worry. Mercifully, the weather has decided to behave itself at last.' She glanced out of the window where the garden was glowing under a bright February sun and the borders already showed regiments of green spikes to hint at glories to come when the bulbs were up.

It was not settled quite so easily, but before the three who were, as saucy Jo was fond of reminding them, foundation-stones in the School, had parted, it was agreed that Matron should be in charge and the other two adhere to their original plans.

Thursday morning found the School up and hard at it by seven o'clock. More than half of the girls must be at either Swansea or Cardiff to make train connections. Those who were being fetched by parents expected to be off before eleven, and Frühstück had been ordered for half-past seven.

The ten left behind were inclined to be very doleful about it, with one exception—Carola. She had expected nothing else, so was not upset. Besides, Mrs Maynard had been over for the previous Saturday evening and had hinted at some plan for herself and Jean.

Dickie Christy, who lived in the island, appeared after breakfast when the two members of Lower Fifth B were lounging in the common-room.

'I say, you two,' she began, 'you're coming around to us this afternoon. Dad's pal, Kester Bellever, is coming for the night and I thought it 'ud be a good idea if you met him.'

'Will they let us come?' Jean asked, rousing up from

her earlier listlessness. She had hoped to spend the holiday with an aunt in London, but a letter on the Monday had told her that the said aunt had had to go north to Scotland unexpectedly and would not be home again until the Saturday night. Jean had been very depressed over this, but Dickie's words cheered her up again. 'I say, that'll be wizard, Dickie. I've been dying to know him ever since that talk he gave us last term.'

'Well, you will after this afternoon,' Dickie told her. 'Of course they'll let you come. Only too glad, I should think. If it's rotten luck for you to be left, it's just as bad, if not worse, for Matey and the mistresses. Matey simply *bounded* at the suggestion.'

'I hadn't thought of that,' Jean replied. 'Are we the only two, or are the kids coming as well?'

'The whole boiling of you,' Dickie replied. 'I'm coming for you at two, so mind you're ready. I must fly now. Cakes to make!' She laughed and left them feeling very much happier, and then Carola proposed that they should ask leave to go down to the ferry-landing and see the others off.

Matron was quite agreeable. 'You two ought to be old enough to be trusted,' she said. 'Miss Burn and Miss Norman are taking the others for a walk, but if you two like to go over to Carnbach for the morning, you may— so long as you catch the twelve-thirty ferry back in time for Mittagessen. Have you any money?'

'Yes, we went to Bank with the rest last night,' Carola said.

'Very well, then. Go to the Bunch of Violets for your elevenses and don't eat so many cakes that you can't eat your meal. Don't forget your scarves, either. I know the sun's shining, but the wind has a nip in it yet. Now be off, or you'll be too late.'

They needed no second telling. They raced along to the Splashery to get into coats, berets, scarves and gloves, and change their shoes in short order and were ready to join the long 'croc' which marched down to the ferry. It was rather pleasant to be thought old enough to be trusted like this. Doris Hill was the next eldest of the left-behinds, and she was only thirteen and, incidentally, a chum of Mary-Lou's. Carola and Jean, both fifteen, though Carola was a week older than Jean, felt themselves very grown-up beside Doris.

Once they had seen the happy, jolly crowd into the motor coaches they waved goodbye and then set off to the shops. It was too early for elevenses yet, so they amused themselves by looking at the windows. Then Carola suggested that they should see something more of the little town, so they turned down a broad, hilly road that ended in a pleasant little park through which they wandered.

'Well, we've seen that,' Jean said as they came to a gate at the farther end. 'Shall we go out this way and see where we get?'

Carola glanced at her watch. 'Only ten yet. We don't want elevenses for another hour at least. O.K., Jean. Let's do that.'

They left the park and found themselves in a long, tree-lined road with biggish houses standing in their own gardens on either side.

'This looks rather a nice place,' Carola said as she led the way.

Jean looked down it wistfully. 'It reminds me of home. Our road is just like this.'

Carola gave her a quick glance. She was sorry for Jean, so she set to work to distract her mind. 'Let's imagine the kind of folk who live in each house,' she suggested. 'Now this one belongs to two old maids, I think. Did you ever see a primmer place? Even the curtains seem to have been hung with measurements for their apart part all over.'

'I think this one belongs to a naval family.' Jean indicated the two models of ships standing in either window of the ground-floor.

'They might be Merchant Navy,' Carola pointed out. 'Who on earth do you suppose lives in that one over there? They've different coloured curtains at every window. It looks like an advertisement for someone's dyes!'

'P'raps it is.' Jean began to giggle. 'Doesn't it look *awful*?'

They went on to the next house which was larger than the first three in the road. It looked strikingly clean and fresh with its brown and cream paintwork. The curtains at the windows were of beflowered silk, and no one could have said it looked prim, for the spacing at every window varied.

'They've a big family of kids here,' Carola said decidedly.

'How do you know that?' Jean demanded.

Her friend pointed to the window over the door where a row of toy animals and dolls were gazing forth. 'Look at that! Oh, and there's a big, old-fashioned wooden engine at the far end. They've boys as well as girls.'

'You can't be sure. Girls play with engines as well as boys; I did myself when I was a kid. Daddy had his old puffer, and I always played with it. Besides, anyhow, there might be just one of each.'

'With all those toys? Talk sense!' Carola said derisively.

In their interest, all thought of manners had been banished and they were leaning against the wall, staring at the house. Suddenly the front door opened and a tall, fair girl in the early twenties came out, accompanied by a huge St Bernard dog. She raised her eyebrows at the sight of the two schoolgirls. Then she suddenly smiled.

'Hello!' she said amiably while the pair started and went red. 'Were you wanting Jo—I mean Mrs Maynard?'

'Is—is this her house?' Carola cried. 'And how did you know——'

'By the uniform, of course.' The young lady gave them another smile. 'I wore it myself for nine years, so I'd be fairly safe to know it, wouldn't I?'

'You were a Chalet School girl?' This was Jean.

'In Tirol as well as here,' the girl replied. 'Now tell me your names. Are you coming in?' She opened the gate invitingly.

'Oh, I don't think we'd better. I—we——' Carola ran down.

'Don't be silly!' was the bracing retort. 'Come on in and see Jo. I'm Daisy Venables, by the way.'

'The *doctor*?' gasped Jean. 'The one who's won all the medals and things?' She eyed Miss Venables with awe.

'Primula Venables' sister,' Carola supplemented this.

'Yes; that's me,' Daisy agreed. 'Now tell me who you are.'

'I'm Jean Ackroyd and this is Carola Johnstone,' Jean explained.

'The girl who ran away to school?' Daisy gave another of those friendly grins. 'I've heard all about that, Carola. It was a new one on me. I've heard of girls running away *from* school, but you're the first who ever went the other way round. Well, are you coming in? If not——'

'Daisy Venables, do you mean to say—Carola and—let's see—Jean, isn't it? What on earth are you doing in Carnbach? Have you come to visit me?' Jo herself had appeared in the doorway. Now she came swiftly down the path. 'Come along in; and Daisy, if you really want to meet Biddy at eleven for coffee, you'd better scram. It's ten-to now.'

'Oh lord! And it takes at least a quarter of an hour to reach St David's Road! O.K., Jo; I'm off! Come on, Rufus!' Daisy gave the lead a gentle tug and set off, accompanied by the big dog, at a great pace.

Jo, left behind, cast a grin after her, and then turned to the abashed pair standing by the gate. 'Well, are you coming in?'

'I—I think we'd better not,' Carola stammered. 'We were just spending the time till eleven and then Matey said we were to go to the Bunch of Violets for elevenses and catch the twelve-thirty ferry back. If it's as late as that, we'd better go.'

'Just as you like. Anyhow, you two are coming over on Sunday for the day. I was going to write to you this afternoon. That's tuppence saved, anyhow. Come straight over after church. Do you know how to get to the shops from here? No? Well, it's easy enough. Go right down the road, turn right, and carry on, and you'll find yourself in the High Street. You can carry on from there, can't you?'

They thanked her and she waved goodbye to them and returned to the house, while the pair, gradually cooling down from their embarrassment, hurried along the road.

Daisy Venables had vanished, and they saw nothing more of her, for the Bunch of Violets, the café favoured by the School, had not been the one she and Miss O'Ryan had chosen.

Carola and Jean enjoyed coffee and cream cakes—synthetic cream, alas!—and sat talking over their unexpected meeting with Mrs Maynard. So long did they gossip that when Carola finally looked at her watch it was to find that they had only ten minutes left in which to catch the ferry. They paid their score and set off at top-speed to the landing. They caught the boat by the skin of their teeth, and spent the whole of the crossing in recovering their breath and tidying themselves after their mad race. Still, they were in time, and despite their cream cakes orgy, brought healthy appetites to Mittagessen.

Dickie arrived at two o'clock, and they enjoyed a delightful time at the Christy home, finding Kester Bellever a most interesting person, full of stories about birds both here and abroad. After tea, at which Dickie's cakes figured largely, they all joined in a thrilling game of Murder, and their screeches could have been heard up at the school if anyone had been listening.

Commander Christy and his friend joined in, and Kester Bellever as detective proved himself a most efficient person. By the time he had detected three murderers they had lost any shyness of him they might have felt, and when they had to say goodbye, little Signa Björnessen threw her arms round his neck and kissed him affectionately.

'I think you are so nice,' she told him. 'I wish you were *my* uncle!'

He laughed. 'I think I'd better adopt the entire School

as nieces,' he said. 'Wait till next term, Signa, and you shall come with the others and see my island and my funny little house.'

Signa trotted off with the rest, quite satisfied with this. Dickie, who had undertaken to escort them home, chuckled over the little episode.

'Uncle Kester used to be a lonely sort of person,' she told the two fifth-formers.' He hasn't any relatives but some distant cousins, and he adopted Gaynor and Cherry and me as nieces. It looks like becoming a habit with him now. Well, here you are! Glad you've all enjoyed it. Carola and Jean, I'm coming over with you on Sunday. Wait for me after church, will you? Bye-bye, everyone.'

She turned and ran home while the others went sedately up the holly-hedged path and in at the front door—a half-term privilege.

'Had a good time?' Matron asked as she served their Abendessen.

With one voice the ten replied, 'Super!'

'Good! Well, all but Jean and Carola must go to bed after this. Jean and Carola, you can have another hour in the common-room, but mind you're in bed by half-past nine. I'll be up about then to put the lights out.'

Chapter XIII

UNEXPECTED BATH

WHEN the ten arrived in the dining-room next morning they found only Miss Burn and Miss Norman waiting for them. Matron was nowhere in sight. They sat down after Miss Norman had said Grace to a delicious meal of poached eggs, toast and marmalade, and the milky coffee that was their usual beverage.

'Is Matron not well?' Carola asked Miss Norman as that lady handed her her coffee.

'Quite well; but we need a rest from work as well as you folk,' was the brisk reply, 'so each of us takes one day off. This is hers. She's celebrating by having her breakfast in bed, and then she's going off somewhere by herself.'

'What are we going to do, Miss Norman?' Doris Hill asked eagerly.

'When you've made your beds and tidied up, we're going to Pembroke to see the castle,' Miss Norman told her. 'We didn't tell you before for it's definitely a fine-day expedition. However, we could hardly ask for a better day at this time of year, so we'll go. Mind you put on woollies under your coats. The castle stands high and the wind is still chilly. Jean and Carola, when you've finished your Frühstück, run along to the kitchen and ask Cook for the picnic baskets.'

'Are we picnicking somewhere, then?' Carola asked joyfully.

'We are—at Bosherston lily pools.' Miss Norman settled down to her own breakfast and added, 'It's Miss Burn's idea. Ask her about it.'

Ten pairs of eyes promptly turned on Hilary Burn, who laughed. 'I spent part of my summer holidays at Tenby,' she explained. 'The lily pools are simply lovely, though you really ought to see them in June or July when the lilies are out. It's quite a thrill to see a bud rising out of the water and going "pop!" as the calyx bursts open. I stood for ages on the causeway which cuts across the pools at one point just to watch them coming up. If there's time and the weather holds, we'll have a look at St Govan's Chapel. That's built in a fissure of the cliff, miles from any house—at least it was when St Govan lived there— and in storms the spray is flung clean over it.'

'Who was St Govan?' Jean demanded.

'A Welsh hermit. Near by is his well, which is a holy well, of course——'

'Can you wish in it?' Barbara Watson interrupted eagerly.

Miss Burn laughed. 'I haven't the remotest idea. I suppose you could if you liked, but I don't know that it's a wishing-well. You have a shot, Barbara, and tell us if you get your wish.'

'Is there anything else to see there?' Carola asked. She knew the Gower coast, but that is farther west, and Cousin Maud had never gone to Tenby, so it was as new to her as the others.

'The Stack Rocks where thousands of seabirds nest in the season—though I don't think that's now,' Miss Burn told her. 'We shan't have time to see much more, I'm afraid. Remember, this is only February, and it grows dark early. However, if only the weather holds, I think you people will have a really interesting time of it.'

'And no essay to write about it all after, thank goodness!' Doris spoke fervently. She did not like writing essays, and all too often for her liking, trips were followed by essays on what they had seen.

'Oh, I shouldn't count on that,' Miss Norman said demurely. 'Miss Bell may ask for an essay on "What I did at half-term." You never know. Neither Miss Burn nor I will ask for one, though, so you *may* escape. Any more coffee, anyone?'

Doris made a face, and Barbara chuckled. 'I *like* writing essays,' she said. 'That's an awfully easy one to write, too, 'cos you only have to remember what you did and describe it.'

'Oh, well, you must just wait and see,' Miss Norman returned, inwardly deciding to ask Miss Bell to leave half-term alone for an essay subject. 'You finished, Carola and Jean? Then we'll excuse you. Pop along to the kitchen for the baskets and set them outside the door. Then you can go upstairs and see to your cubicles. Say your Grace first, Carola!' For that young lady was out of her chair and making for the door.

She came back to stand behind her chair and repeat the School Grace to herself. 'I forgot,' she explained.

'And take your crocks to the hatch,' Miss Burn added. 'Be quick!'

Carola did as she was told, and then went racing off after Jean who had remembered everything. She was at the kitchen door when Carola reached her, and Cook was handing over the big baskets she had packed overnight, except for the sandwiches.

'Going to Bosherston, are you?' she asked as she gave
Carola hers. 'My, I wish I was coming with you! My
home's not so far from there. There you are, Miss. I
hope you have a good time.'

'Thank you, Cook. I'm sure we shall,' Carola said. 'And
I hope you can get off some time soon to go home. Is this all?'

'Why, how much more do you want?' Cook demanded
with her jolly laugh. 'There's sandwiches, and pies, both
meat and fruit, and cakes and biscuits, look you.' Then
she relented. 'There's a bag still with the flasks of coffee
and milk, but that's enough for you to carry at once.
Gladys will bring the bag to the door. Got your beds to
make, haven't you? Best hurry up, then.'

Carola thanked her, hurried after Jean to put her
baskets on the wide step at the front door, and then raced
off upstairs to make her bed and tidy her cubicle before
she went down to get into coat and beret and change
into stout walking-shoes. They were all quickly ready,
and when the two mistresses appeared were already in
double file.

'All well wrapped up?' Miss Norman asked. 'Yes, I
know it's not chilly at the moment, but remember what I
told you about Pembroke. In addition, I expect it'll be
dark before we get back to Carnbach and it's never warm
on the water at this time of year. Lead on, Carola and
Jean. We don't want to miss the ferry.'

They set off, the girls carrying the big baskets between
them and the mistresses following. The crossing was made
as peacefully as usual, and when they marched off the
ferry-landing they found a funny little bus awaiting them.

'Oh, I wondered how we were going,' observed Judy
O'Connor.

'No use having an ordinary coach,' Miss Burn explained, 'so Miss Annersley ordered this for us. All in? No baskets or anything left behind? Very well, then.' She shut the door and the driver, who had kept his motor ticking over, set off.

It was, as Miss Burn had said, a lovely morning. The snow had gone, though traces of it still lingered on the summits of the hills. The February sun shone down on a world that was showing the first faint greening on bushes and trees and the grass was beginning to lose its dead, wintry look. The road ran along valleys where streams chuckled merrily round their stones and small villages were busy and full of life. It was too early for the spring ploughing, but there were signs of new life everywhere. Later, they drove round Milford Haven, making for New Milford, where they crossed in the ferry to Pembroke Docks.

One or two of the younger ones wanted to get out and look at the shops, but the mistresses were adamant. Time was passing, and the castle could not be properly seen in half an hour or so, and they wanted to go to Bosherston for lunch. The small folk had to content themselves with eyeing the bustling streets wistfully. Then they had passed through the busy area and were running along a broad highway till Judy O'Connor suddenly set up a shout.

'I see the castle! Look! Oh, what a *lovely* castle!'

They all looked eagerly in the direction in which she was pointing, and saw the towers and battlements, with the great keep rising above all, perched on the top of the cliff which had made a natural protection for the place in the Middle Ages. Trees and bushes clung to the cliff, and, as they came nearer, they could see that the castle had been built on a promontory washed on two sides by the river, thus adding to its natural defences.

'It's like a castle in a fairy-tale,' Doris said. She turned to Miss Burn who was sharing a seat with her. 'Does anyone live there?'

Miss Burn shook her head. 'Not now. It looks very complete from here, but when we are inside you will see that it is ruined.'

'Oh, what a pity!' Doris cried. 'It looks so lovely!'

'Why is it a ruin, Miss Burn?' Carola asked. 'Who did it—Cromwell?'

'He had a hand in it,' Hilary said with a grin. 'The weather did a lot more, though. The last owner began to restore it and did a good deal, but it would need a fortune to rebuild it properly. Anyway, who wants that? I'm afraid castles as homes are a thing of the past. You be glad that it's properly looked after nowadays. It's Crown property, by the way, though it was leased to Sir Ivor Phillips. Here we are. Tumble out! No; you can leave the baskets. We aren't going to feed here. Your camera, Carola? Oh, that's another matter.'

Miss Norman had been the first to leave the bus and the girls were soon after her, Miss Burn bringing up the rear. They paid their entrance money and were soon through the great arched gateway and standing on the grassy platform which was once the busy courtyard of the castle.

'One moment before you begin to explore,' Miss Norman said. 'You are to keep together and no one is to try any silly tricks of climbing. A good deal of the castle is unsafe and we don't want any accidents. That's all. If you want to take any snaps, Carola and Jean, wait until we've seen all there is to see. Now come along.'

It was a wonderful castle. The girls walked along the ramparts as far as they could. They peered through the grilles of the water-gate and went up the keep. When they had seen everything and climbed everywhere they were allowed, Carola and Jean took a series of snaps and promised copies to everyone who wanted them if they turned out well.

'Only if they like to buy them,' Miss Norman protested. 'Copies of snaps come expensive if there are several of them, and you want ten copies of each. If you don't want to keep the money yourselves, girls, you can put it into the fines box for the San. But no one is going to expect you to *give* them away like that.'

Then they entered the bus again and were whisked off to the Bosherston lily pools where they sat on the causeway and ate their lunch, gazing at the great pads of lily leaves that covered the water.

'I'd like to come here in the summer when the lilies are out,' Carola said. 'It must be marvellous then. It's wonderful now.'

'So it is,' Hilary Burn agreed. 'Mind, Signa! Be careful or you'll tip into the water, and we don't want to have to find somewhere to dry you off! Hold her, Judy.'

Little Signa, who had been kicking her heels rapturously against the stonework, desisted, and lunch finished without incident.

'How far do the pools go?' Jean asked.

'Oh, a long way down. You can walk through the woods to either end in summer, but I think we won't just now. It's too muddy, and the paths will be slippery, not to speak of hanging right over the pools in places and the water is deepish. Besides, lilies mean weeds as well. Finish your lunch, and then we must go on to St Govan's if you want to see it. Come along, girls. Come on to the dry land and help repack the baskets and we'll be off. Careful now, Signa.'

One by one they sidled off the causeway to the grassy patch by the side, and Miss Norman heaved a sigh of relief when she saw excitable Signa safe ashore again. The girls set to work to fold paper bags and sheets and tuck them back into the baskets. Hilary Burn carefully settled the emptied flasks into their bag and Jean and Carola counted the mugs before packing them. The two elder O'Connor girls were standing looking at the pools and the two little ones were at the end of the causeway arguing between themselves whether if you stepped on to one of the lily-pad islands, you would go through or not. Signa thought you wouldn't; Bridgie O'Connor thought you would. Suddenly Judy uttered a cry which was echoed by her sister Norah.

'Oh, Miss Burn—Miss Norman! Look! A water-rat —a big one!'

Before anyone could say or do anything, Signa cried, 'Oh, where? Oh, let me see him!' and dashed back along the causeway with little heed for its narrowness or where she was going.

Carola had just finished the mugs and stood up. She was nearest, and even as Miss Norman called, 'Signa! Come back at *once*!' the elder girl was crossing after naughty Signa with swift, sure steps.

'I *must* see the water-rat!' Signa called back.

Carola had almost reached her. Already her arm was outstretched to catch the little sinner, when Signa made a false step. Her foot slipped and she overbalanced. With a wild cry she splashed into the water, and the next moment Carola was after her.

Mercifully for everyone, the water here is not deep nor are there many weeds, though quite enough to cause alarm. Miss Burn was along the causeway in a flash, while Miss Norman very sensibly kept the other girls from following.

'*No*, girls! Stay where you are! Jean, run quickly to the bus and see if the man is there. He went to have his dinner, but he ought to be back. Bring him and also the rugs from the back of the bus. Thank God we thought of bringing them. Thyra, stand *still*!'

Thyra, frustrated in her effort to dash after Miss Burn, burst into tears and Doris Hill had to go to the rescue. Thyra was only nine, and Doris, four years older, was quite a big girl in her eyes. She clung to Doris, sobbing pitifully, an example suddenly followed by Bridgie, who howled at the top of her voice and occupied her two sisters very completely.

Meanwhile, Signa, in falling, had been caught by the weeds, and Carola and Miss Burn were working frantically to pull her up. Miss Burn wrenched and tore at the things holding the little girl in a vice-like grip, while Carola, who had managed to get her arms round the child, hauled valiantly to bring her head above the water.

Help was close at hand, mercifully. A man and a big retriever dog, attracted by the noise Thyra and Bridgie were making, suddenly appeared at the other end of the causeway. He took in the situation in one glance, snatched a big knife from his pocket, and was by the side of the two rescuers, slashing at the weeds almost before anyone had seen him. The weeds gave under the sharp edge of the knife.

Carola contrived to pull Signa's head above the water, and a minute or so later saw Signa's limp little body come up, when the dog who, at a word from his master, had remained on the causeway, stretched forward and gripped her coat with his teeth, taking part of the weight off Carola who was shivering with cold by this time, though she clung to Signa like grim death. A moment or two later, and the man had taken the child and was carrying her to where the white-faced Miss Norman was waiting, while Miss Burn helped Carola to scramble up to the causeway, and then followed herself. By the time they reached the little group, Signa had been laid down on Miss Norman's coat, and the man, kneeling across her, was turning her head to one side and clearing her mouth of mud and weed. Then he set to work with artificial respiration while the terrified girls watched him, too frightened even to cry now. Signa looked as if she were dead.

Miss Norman turned to her colleague. 'Take those other children to the bus, please, and dose them with hot coffee. There are two flasks left. I sent Jean for the rugs. Take one, and get Carola out of her wet clothes and roll her in it. Take some coffee yourself.'

'No,' Hilary said sturdily. 'I know about this and it may take us both. You take the girls, and I'll stay here and help.'

There was sense in what she said. Miss Norman knew it and made no attempt to argue. She marched the girls off, including the icy Carola who could scarcely walk, even with the help of the mistress's arm. Her teeth were chattering, for lake water in February is a chilling thing, and she was looking very blue and pinched. Half-way up the steep pitch that leads to the main road they met Jean and the bus driver, both laden with the rugs Miss Norman had insisted on bringing in case the evening turned out chilly. She stopped Jean and took one from her. The man went plunging down the slope at top-speed.

'Hurry with those rugs, Jean,' was all the mistress said as she turned to Carola once more. 'Come along, Carola. We're nearly there, and when you're out of your clothes and have a hot drink you won't feel so bad. Come, dear: you mustn't stand still.'

'I—I'm so *tired*,' half-sobbed Carola who, between cold and shock and the weight of her streaming clothes, found it very difficult to move at all.

'I know, but you'll feel better once you're in the bus.' Miss Norman was inexorable. Signa she had had to leave to Miss Burn and the stranger. She could only hope that they would succeed in reviving the little girl. Her most present duty was to make as sure as she could that Carola felt no real ill-effects from the adventure. So she coaxed and bullied alternately until at long last she got the girl to the bus, where she made the others stand round while she stripped her of her clothes and rolled her in the rug, scrubbing her over it until the blue look began to leave Carola's face and she was able to drink a mugful of the hot coffee without her teeth chattering too much on the rim of the mug.

By the time this happened, a little procession was coming up the slope, the stranger leading with Signa in his arms, rolled in a rug, and the driver helping Miss Burn who looked almost as blue as Carola had done. Signa's head lay against the man's shoulder and she was very limp, but the grey look had left her face, and Miss Norman needed no one to tell her that the child was alive.

'She's come round,' said the man as the mistress came to them, 'but she must be put to bed at once. My house is a little way up this road and I'm taking her there. Your man will bring the bus along and then Miss Burn and that elder girl can come in and have hot baths and fresh clothes, and with luck I think you'll escape even colds. Rough!'

The big dog came up beside them and stood wagging his tail and looking up with intelligent eyes. His owner nodded to the driver, turned off, and marched along the road with long strides, while Miss Norman got the rest of the coffee into the shaking Miss Burn, and then they all piled into the bus and the driver drove them to the house where Rough was waiting at the gate.

A lady was at the door looking for them, and she took Miss Burn and Carola off upstairs at once, only pausing to push open the door of a pleasant sitting-room with a hospitable, 'In there and sit down. I'll be with you as soon as I've settled these two.'

'Go in and sit down and keep quiet!' Miss Norman told the girls fiercely before she ran upstairs after the others, intent on finding out how Signa was.

The lady saw her, and when they reached the bedroom landing she nodded to a door and said, 'In there. My brother is seeing to her. She'll be all right soon, though.'

'Thank you!' gasped Miss Norman before she turned into a pretty bedroom where Signa, rolled in a blanket, was already in bed, while a jolly-looking girl in the twenties was rubbing her hair dry. A fire was burning in the fire-place, and already Signa was looking more like herself. As the mistress came in, she opened her eyes, and gave her a little smile. The man was ready with a cup which he held to her lips.

'Drink this—all of it,' he commanded; and Signa obeyed.

When she had finished, she gave a little sigh. Her long lashes fell, and she turned on her side. The girl with the towel took the cup, while the man bent over the child. Presently he stood up.

'Fast asleep, thank God! I don't think she'll take any harm now. Where's Miss Burn and the other child?'

'I don't know. Your—the lady took them away,' Miss Norman said. She was stooping over the sleeping Signa, watching her with anxious eyes. The little girl's lips were pink again, but she still looked pale, and her damp hair lay limp about her face.

The stranger smiled a little. 'Don't be alarmed. I'm a doctor—Dr Graves at your service—and my sister here is a nurse. She will stay with the kiddy for the moment. Meantime, I want to see those two. They had both cut their hands on the weed and I want to see to them. You come downstairs and my other sister will give you all some tea. I'm sure you need it after a fright like this.'

He took Miss Norman away, despite her murmured protests. He was anxious to dress the cuts of the other two, but to his practised eye the mistress was suffering badly from shock, and he wanted to get her downstairs to his other sister.

In the end, Carola, after a boiling hot bath, fresh clothes, and a good tea, declared that she felt quite fit to go back to school. Signa, of course, must stay where she was, and Miss Graves suggested that her sister should stay with her, and they would keep the pair for the week-end. Miss Burn, too, would remain until the doctor was sure that she had taken no real harm. She had been much longer in her wet clothes than anyone else, and her hands were very badly cut with the weeds. Dr Graves had insisted on her going to bed as soon as she had had a bath, and he had given her a sedative to allay the shock. She still looked very wan when Miss Norman visited her, and she agreed that she dreaded the drive home. If she were all right by Monday, however, the doctor said he would drive her to Carnbach.

So the party which had set out so gaily in the morning returned minus three of its members and with the rest in very subdued mood.

'I might have known!' Matron said when she had heard the whole story. 'I don't believe we've once had a term since this school began without some sort of sensation. Well, you can all go to bed and to sleep, and tomorrow the girls may satisfy themselves with quiet walks and a party at night. Oh yes, my dear! You'll sleep all right. *I'm* going to make sure of that. You're having a dose, and so is Carola. I don't suppose the rest will need it. Come along and take Prayers, and then bed is the order of the day.'

And it was so.

Chapter XIV

MISS WILSON PRONOUNCES

'NEVER again!' Miss Wilson declared. 'Never, once again, do both Miss Annersley and I go off and leave the School to its own devices during half-term! There are limits!'

It was Tuesday evening, and the Staff, having seen all but the prefects safely to bed, were relaxing in the Staff-room, drinking coffee, eating chocolate biscuits, smoking, and otherwise refreshing themselves. Most of them had turned up during the afternoon, but Miss Wilson had missed the bus and been obliged to come on by the coastal train which had landed her at Carnbach with barely time to make the last ferry. In winter, this was at six-thirty, so it was not until after Abendessen that she had been informed of Friday's disaster. Miss Annersley was not returning until next day, so her co-Head was left to comment on the affair, which she had done with the full force of her vocabulary.

Matron, who had just joined them, gave her a quick look. 'That is an absurd thing to say,' she said firmly. 'If the entire Staff had been there I doubt if they could have prevented Signa from dashing across that causeway unless someone had been holding her very firmly at the time. That child ought never to be let out without a collar and lead!'

'What's the latest news of Hilary?' the Head asked her anxiously.

'Temp. down, thank goodness, and the chest trouble clearing up. Miss Graves was on the 'phone to me at seven and she said that her brother thinks all danger of pneumonia is ended. She's very weak, of course, but that's only the high temperature. She ought to be back at school by next Monday unless anything else turns up. He doesn't expect it. Hilary is very strong and sturdy. If she had been able to get out of her wet clothes when Carola did, the worst would have been just a bad cold. It was staying there until they brought Signa round that did the damage.'

'Carola behaved jolly well,' Miss Norman remarked. 'She kept her head amazingly. Dr Graves said that trying to pull Signa's head above water as she did was the wisest thing she could have done. She may have come here in a very irregular way, but I, for one, am very thankful that she did. The rest of the girls were no good—ran round in circles and howled to high heaven! That wasn't much use to Signa.'

Miss Wilson, who had found time to go to her study and glance over the mail which had been awaiting her, suddenly grinned.

'What's the joke?' Miss Slater demanded.

'I have some news for Carola, and I'm wondering just what she will think about it.'

'Oh? What's that?' Miss Denny looked inquisitive.

'Well, I see no reason why you shouldn't know. It doesn't affect us, but—well—listen to this.' Miss Wilson took a letter from the pocket of her cardigan, opened it, and then read aloud: '"I am writing to ask you to tell Carola that I am engaged to be married to a Mr Lucas I met on the boat. He has a sugar plantation out here, and some day, when Carola is a year or two older and, I hope, a very different girl from what she is at present, we intend to invite her to spend her summer holidays with us. Of course, this means that even if she had still been with me I must have asked my cousins to make other arrangements for her, as we are to be married here and my house in Boscombe sold with all its contents.'''

At this point, Miss Wilson stopped and cocked an observant eye at the others. They rose just as she had hoped.

'Well, of all the selfish creatures she beats the band!' Biddy O'Ryan exclaimed. 'Sure, the way she talks you'd be thinking Carola was no more than a pet dog or a Persian cat!'

'But why, my dear Nell, does she write in this way about Carola?' Mlle Lachenais asked placidly. 'I like la petite. I find her intelligent, well-mannered, all one could ask in a schoolgirl.'

Miss Wilson flushed with annoyance at herself, for she had let slip enough to rouse the suspicions of the entire Staff unless she were very wary. Orders were that no one was to speak of the way Carola had come to school. Then she suddenly remembered Miss Norman's remark about Carola having come irregularly, so it was clear that some of them, at any rate, either knew or suspected. Quickly she made up her mind that the best thing was to make a clean breast of the situation.

'I'll explain,' she said, 'but first I want to say that what I'm about to tell you must go no further than this room. Agreed, everyone?'

'Naturally,' Miss Denny answered for the others. 'What's the mystery about this new child? Don't tell me she's another princess on our hands! Elisaveta was enough for any one school.'

'Oh, it's nothing like that,' Miss Wilson assured her. 'I'll just tell you the whole story and then I hope we can bury it decently for the future. But, whatever you do, try to keep it from the girls. Some of the little idiots would think she'd done a marvellous thing in gate-crashing on us the way she did; and the more sensible might be inclined to look down on her for making such a fool of herself.'

'Gate-crashing?' Miss Denny pricked up her ears, and Grizel Cochrane, who was sitting near her, dropped the intricate piece of knitting on which she was busy, and turned wide grey eyes on the Head.

Miss Wilson nodded. 'Just exactly that. Carola quite literally gate-crashed us. I'll explain and then you'll understand.'

In as few words as possible, she told the story. Some of the Staff were inclined to be amused at Carola's calm assurance. Others were rather shocked. Those already in the know helped out now and then, and Biddy O'Ryan, when the Head had finished, added a pithy if uncomplimentary few sentences about Miss Curry.

'So *that* explains why she turned up practically minus proper uniform,' Miss Cochrane said. 'I *thought* it was queer that any girl's people should be so absorbed in departing on a cruise of the Caribbean that they couldn't even spare the time to have her properly outfitted for school. It also helps to explain how she has heard so many of the really big musical folk. I've wondered about that more than once.'

Miss Wilson glanced at her. 'You never said anything to us about it.'

'Well, to tell you the truth, I rather thought she was drawing the long-bow, and if it had gone on I meant to come to one of you and suggest you talked to her about the beauties of truth,' Grizel drawled.

'I wish you'd try to give people credit for decency, Grizel,' the Head said impatiently. 'Is it necessary for you to look on the worst side? Surely, at your age, you must know that there are thousands of folk in the world who are as nice in these matters as you are!'

Miss Cochrane's pretty face was flooded with crimson. However, she could hardly resent this plain speaking openly, though she felt very indignant about it, and mentally scored a bad mark against Carola for being the cause of her receiving it. Grizel Cochrane had a very hard streak in her character which all the care and training of the Chalet School during her schoolgirl years and, later, when she had returned to teach, had not succeeded in eradicating. Motherless at an early age, she had first been left to the care of her grandmother who had spoilt her outrageously; and later, when her father married again, had been called to order by her stepmother with a sharpness and even unkindness which had strengthened her faults. Finally, she had been disappointed in the choice of a career, her father insisting that she should devote herself to music for which she had a superficial gift, while she herself had longed with her whole soul to be a physical training mistress. As he held the purse-strings, Grizel had been forced to give in, but though she was a brilliant teacher and her girls did well, it was largely through fear of her bitter tongue that they worked so hard for her.

Miss Wilson knew this, and could have bitten her tongue

out as she finished her little speech. However, it was too late now. She felt thankful that Mlle Berné took up the tale.

'Well, ma chère, I agree that it is best to keep cette petite histoire from the girls. La pauvre Carola! I am glad indeed that she is here. But were not her parents very angry about this?'

Miss Wilson nodded. 'More angry with Miss Curry than with Carola, however. Jack Maynard knows Dr Johnstone and when he flew here to——'

'*What?*' It was a chorus, and she flushed and looked sheepish.

'Oh, bother! That's another thing we've kept dark. He's stationed in Calabar at the moment, making a study of native diseases. He flew here to settle about that wicked child and we all thought it wiser that no one should know just what she had done, so he stayed with the Maynards, and Hilda went over with Carola and saw him at Cartref. He let fly to her about his cousin and Jo tells me he had quite a lot more to say to her and Jack. Carola never heard of it, of course.'

What more might have been said on the subject no one will ever know, for just then there came a hurried bang on the door and Carola herself appeared, with tousled hair and eyes looking as if they would drop out of her head.

Miss Wilson jumped to her feet. 'Carola!' she exclaimed.

Matron was there too. 'What's wrong? Are you ill?' she demanded.

'It's not me but Con Maynard,' Carola replied, looking scared. 'I—I think she's been walking in her sleep. I've got her back to bed but I thought someone ought to know and go to her.'

Matron was off without more ado. The Head asked quietly, 'How do you know Con was sleep-walking? Why weren't you in your own room?'

Carola turned red. 'I woke up and felt thirsty, so I was going to the bathroom to get a drink of water,' she explained. 'Then I saw Con walking along the corridor with her eyes wide open.' She gave an irrepressible shudder. 'She did look uncanny! They were all staring and I guessed she was walking in her sleep. I've read somewhere that you shouldn't startle sleep-walkers awake, so I just said, "Why, Con, you come back to bed this minute! You oughtn't to be here now." Then I took her hand and went with her to her dormy. She didn't wake up, and I got her back into bed all right. Then I thought you ought to know, and Matey—I—I mean Matron— wasn't in her room, so I came here.'

'I'm glad you were so sensible about it,' Miss Wilson said quietly. 'It's all right. Con does walk in her sleep sometimes, but she hasn't done it for more than a year and we all thought she had outgrown it.' She darted a warning glance at Biddy O'Ryan, who seemed to be on the point of choking. Then she added, 'Well, now you had better go back to bed. Miss Edwards, will you take her up, please? You might give her some warm milk once she's in. That will put you to sleep again, Carola, as well as relieving your thirst. Good-night!'

Miss Edwards rose and escorted Carola back to her cubicle, where she gave her a glass of hot milk, and waited until she had finished it.

'Feel you can sleep now?' she asked casually as she took her glass.

'Yes, thank you.' Carola's blue eyes were already

growing opaque. Miss Edwards tucked her in, picked up the glass, and departed.

Arrived in the Staff-room, she found Biddy O'Ryan and Miss Wilson deep in reminiscence of a certain night years ago in Tirol when Biddy, then a sinful Junior Middle, had thrilled her dormitory to the limit by telling them the woeful tale of the Banshee of Castle Rathdearg. Unfortunately, Alixe von Elsen, one of Biddy's partners in sin, was a highly imaginative young lady and, as Biddy had told Jo Bettany next day when that lady made inquiries as to why Alixe should have walked in her sleep, uttering the most awful howls imaginable, 'I told them the story and Alixe tried to *be* it!' Hence Biddy's chokes when Carola arrived with her dramatic announcement about Con!

Matron followed Miss Edwards into the room in time to catch the tail-end and chuckled. 'Well, apart from Con herself, there's no one in that dormy likely to indulge in telling tales after lights-out. Tomorrow I'm making inquiries to find out what those monkeys have been eating. Con's all right now. Carola had tucked her in so tightly she'd have had some difficulty in getting out again, and she was sleeping quite quietly. I'll ring Jo tomorrow, though, and let her know. Con may be the quiet one of those three externally, but her brain is easily excited. Hot milk every night for her for the next few weeks. We can't have that sort of thing going on.'

'Con won't love you,' Miss Stephens, who was Con's form mistress, observed. 'She'll drink any amount of cold milk; but she told me once that she loathed it hot.'

'Oh, well, it won't hurt her, and it's soothing,' Matron retorted. 'Carola all right, Dollie?'

Miss Edwards nodded. 'I doubt if she was awake when

I closed the dormy door behind me. Oh, well! we don't get much money, but we *do* see life!'

'I believe you,' Miss Wilson said drily. 'Well, it's growing late and we can't do anything more about anything at the moment. I vote we end this session and seek our beds. I'm tired.' She yawned as she spoke. 'Thank goodness, Hilda will be back tomorrow, and I can turn the lily-pool business over to her.'

'There's one thing,' Matron said as she watched the younger mistresses begin to put the room to rights. 'Signa's mother is an Old Girl, and she does know what things can be like here. Thora always was a sensible girl and she's not likely to make a great fuss.'

'I should imagine,' Miss Norman said with some bitterness, 'that she knows all too well what her younger daughter is like. Thyra is her mother over again, but that monkey Signa must be a hop-out-o'-kin.'

'Oh, I don't think so.' Miss Wilson gave a sudden gurgle. 'Have you forgotten that awful sister of hers—Astrid? I've always wondered that my hair didn't turn white ages before our wild adventure at the end of the time in Tirol, considering how that little demon played us up. If you ask me, Signa is merely a second Astrid.'

'I'd forgotten Astrid.' Miss Norman began to laugh. 'What a life she led us all! But it was nice naughtiness, Nell. She was bad, but not horribly bad. I suppose you're right, and it's coming out in her young niece. Well, I'm off to bed. Good-night, everyone! Dollie— you coming?'

Miss Edwards nodded. 'Just let me gather up my work. You off, Grizel? Good-night, then.'

Grizel Cochrane nodded good-night and departed. Ten

minutes later the room was empty, Mlle Berné, the last to leave, switching off the lights after a final look round to be sure that everything was as it ought to be. Satisfied, she shut the door and hurried upstairs, meeting Matron in the corridor.

'Con is fast asleep,' that lady said. 'So is Carola. I shall let Jo know about her daughter, all the same. I would very much like to know what has started the trouble again.'

Mademoiselle laughed. 'Perhaps she has been eating too many sweets or apples,' she suggested. 'I know that the dear Jo saves her own sweet ration for her children. So does Daisy Venables, who is at home for the present. And then there is Robin's ration, too. Jo told me that when Robin went to Switzerland she left her sweet coupons behind for the children. It would be possible. After all,' Mademoiselle's black eyes twinkled wickedly, 'this is just the last day of half-term. If I were you, Matron, I'd ask Jo what she has been giving her children.'

Matron chuckled. 'How indignant she'll be! Upon my word, I think I'll do it just for the fun of hearing what she has to say.'

'Oh, do—and pray let me be present when you do it,' Mademoiselle cooed sweetly as she turned to go. 'Bonne nuit, chérie.'

'Good-night,' Matron replied as she turned in at her own door, still chuckling at the thought of Jo's fury when she was called to account for her daughters' diet during half-term.

Chapter XV

ADVENTURE FOR CON

NEXT day Matron duly rang up Jo, who protested wildly against the idea that she had allowed her family anything indigestible, half-term or no half-term. Before Matron had finished with her, she was literally squeaking, so indignant was she, and when she finally hung up, the School's domestic tyrant was one broad grin.

'That shook Jo,' she remarked to Mademoiselle, who had been present and shamelessly listened in. 'Well, unless they've had any contraband, which I greatly doubt, it's clear enough that food has nothing to do with Con's attack. I must see Bill about this. I'm having no somnambulism in the School if I know it.'

Mademoiselle was unable to solve the problem and was, in any case, due for a lesson with Special Sixth, so she laughed and went off and Matron turned to the next job in hand.

Jo arrived during the afternoon, still indignant that anyone could think that she would allow her children to gormandise, and, secretly, a little anxious. It was Matron's 'free' day and she had gone off to Swansea as soon as Mittagessen had ended. Miss Annersley had returned with the noon ferry and she had to listen to Jo's diatribes as Miss Wilson was teaching.

'You must feel a good deal better for having got all that off your mind,' the Head observed when Jo ran down at last. 'You'd better come across later on and let Matron have the benefit of it. I don't know why *I* should be the only one to be scolded—especially as I had nothing at all to do with it.'

Jo laughed shamefacedly. 'Sorry, Hilda, but I really can't understand why Matron of all people should accuse me of such doings. She ought to know me better than that,' she added in injured tones.

Miss Annersley eyed her thoughtfully. 'I should imagine she couldn't resist the temptation,' she said. 'You nearly always do rise, Jo.'

Jo glared at her. Then she giggled like a schoolgirl. 'Oh, well, I suppose I'll have to forgive her. All the same,' she went on, 'I don't like this sleep-walking business coming back. Nor will Jack when he hears of it. But what can possibly have started it is more than I can say. I *know* they had only their usual simple meals, and they didn't have many more sweets than usual. Daisy's gone, or I'd have asked her what they had when she took them out yesterday morning. But even if she treated them to cream cakes with their coffee, *once* of that shouldn't have set Con off again.'

'Suppose you stay for tea and see them and find out?' her friend suggested. 'She patted the parcel of bedroom slippers the pair had left at home and which Jo had made an excuse for coming. 'They need know nothing but that you came to bring these. We'll invite them, shall we, and see what we can find out. All the same, if Daisy really did treat them liberally to cream cakes, I'm surprised at her.'

Jo nodded. 'It isn't like her, is it? Thanks, Hilda; I think that's a good idea. Are you busy?'

Miss Annersley nodded. 'I go to the Sixth for poetry when the bell rings. And there it is. You must look after yourself until tea-time. Why don't you invade the Staff-room and see who's there?'

'Excellent idea! So I will! By the way, what's the news about Hilary?'

'Recovering steadily now the temp. has gone down. Matron was on to Dr Graves this morning and he said there was no reason why she shouldn't return next Monday, though she must be careful for the next few weeks of course. Thank heaven neither Signa nor Carola seems to have been affected by it. We were a little anxious about Signa, but she's eating well and sleeping well. By the way, Thora may be coming across next week if she can get away. She can't come before as she isn't out of quarantine till then.'

'Out of quarantine? What on earth do you mean?'

'Oh, I forgot, you wouldn't know. She's had all three of the boys down with chickenpox. Axel was the last and his quarantine ends next Monday. Nothing bad, she says, merely tiresome. Now I *must* go.'

Miss Annersley had been collecting her books while she talked, and now she left the room. Jo ranged round it for a minute or two. Then she, too, departed for the Staff-room, where she found Biddy O'Ryan correcting books, and settled down for a good chat.

Len and Con duly came to tea with their Heads and mother and were cautiously sounded. It turned out that Daisy had treated them to nothing more deadly than sugar-topped buns, so Con's somnambulism was not to be explained that way. She looked well enough, and she and her sister brought their usual healthy appetites to the meal, so Jo went home thinking that it must be a final hang-over from the former trouble.

Three nights later, such part of the School as was still up were startled by wild yells proceeding from one of the Junior dormitories. Matron got there first, of course, but Miss Wilson and Biddy O'Ryan were not far behind her, Peggy Bettany, the Head Girl, also appeared, Miss Annersley sending the rest back to their rooms with a dignified. 'There is no need for all this excitement, girls. One of the Juniors must have been having a nightmare. Go back, please.'

They went—all but Mary-Lou Trelawney and her faithful chum, Verity-Anne Carey. They hung on a little, and were rewarded with a reminder that their bedtime came in half an hour's time, but if they really wanted to go earlier, they could. The pair departed at top-speed, leaving their Head smiling grimly.

Meanwhile, Matron had found the cause of the trouble. Con had been having nightmare, and had wakened screaming, thereby rousing her whole dormitory. When Matron erupted into the room she found the other little girls all clustered round the now-weeping Con, who wept loudly and noisily for her mother.

They were shooed back to bed, and Miss Wilson took the sobbing Con off to her own room where she was speedily soothed back into calmness. Matron administered a cup of hot milk when the storm was over, and a pacified and sleepy small girl was finally tucked back into bed and thereafter slept peacefully till next morning.

'I think I'll have her in San if this sort of thing occurs again,' Matron said next day when severe questioning of the entire dormitory had elicited the facts that no one had smuggled food in, nor had they been telling stories after lights-out. In fact, all they had done was to go blamelessly to sleep until Con's yells woke them. 'What about letting Jo know?'

Miss Annersley shook her head. Before she had left, Jo had confided a secret to her friend, and that lady was determined not to worry Mrs Maynard if it could be avoided. 'I'll write to Jack at San,' she said. 'By all means take Con if you think it wiser, Matey. In that case, though, Len must be warned to hold her tongue. Jo was really anxious about the little monkey when she was here on Wednesday.'

Matron raised her brows. 'Oh, like that, is it? Well, it's only what we could expect, Jo being Jo. Will she go to Toronto at Easter, then?'

'Oh, yes. Plenty of time before October. They're returning at the end of June. It will probably do Madam all the good in the world. She's missed her Margot very badly, and as she's taking her entire family with her, she'll be happy again.'

Matron nodded. Jo was her darling, though wild horses wouldn't have dragged it from her. She quite agreed that if the Maynard family was to have an addition in the autumn it would be just as well for their mother not to have anything to worry her. Her hands would be full enough without that.

'We'll tell Len that Con's tummy seems to be upset as she's having bad dreams and we don't want to bother her mother about it,' the Head decided. 'That will keep her quiet. In the meantime, I'll write to Jack as I said and I expect he'll come over to see his daughter for himself at the first opportunity.'

So it was left. Con was sent to the School San for the week-end, and Miss Annersley wrote to Dr Maynard giving him a full account of what had happened. As she had expected, this brought him over on the Tuesday after a week-end in which Con had behaved as any normal little girl ought. Con was thrilled to see her father, and he begged leave for her and Len, took them off home for the afternoon and returned them about six. Then he demanded an interview with Matron and the Heads.

'Well?' Miss Annersley demanded when they were comfortably settled in the sitting-room the two Heads shared.

'Nothing to account for it. They stick to it that they haven't been eating anything but what the rest have and they don't lie awake telling hair-raising tales to each other. She's growing very quickly just now, and I'm inclined to set it down to that. I've had a tonic made up for her—here it is, Matey. See she takes it and keep her quiet. She ought to be all right soon. Don't say anything to Joey. She's been very good about it, but I know that she has fretted over Margot, and just at present I'd rather she was spared anything more. You know what an excitable creature she is and there's nothing really wrong with Con that I can see.'

'All very well, so long as Jo doesn't come haring over to see the girls,' Miss Wilson told him.

However, a week later Jo rang up agitatedly to say that Stephen, who had been poorly and fretful lately, had come out with a rash and she feared measles.

'Heavens!' Miss Wilson, who had taken the call, was thoroughly upset. 'And Jack had the girls over to see you last week!'

'It *may* be just German measles,' Jo said. 'Stephen isn't really ill—just poorly, and as cross as a bear with a sore paw. The girls didn't see him, either, as he and Charles were at a birthday party that day. I should stick 'em into quarantine and hope for the best.'

This optimistic point of view robbed Miss Wilson of her breath for the moment, and Jo had rung off before she recovered sufficiently to tell that lady her views. 'Bill' left the telephone and went off to Matron, who declared that as the children had not met she didn't think it likely the little girls would take it. She agreed, however, that it would be best to quarantine them, and not only them, but the entire form.

And then Mary-Lou complained a week later of feeling headachy. Matron whisked her off to San, but by the next morning she was a lovely shade of rose-pink, and the School had to face the fact that they had German measles in their midst.

Next day Verity-Anne joined Mary-Lou before breakfast, and by midday seventeen Middles and five Juniors were keeping them company. Len Maynard was among them, but not Con, who remained splendidly well the whole time. Jo, on being told, laughed and said that, after all, it was a mild affair. Stephen was up and about again, and Charles, who had begun two days after his brother, was demanding lots to eat. In the end, out of the whole School, thirty-seven went down. The rest escaped. Three dormitories were turned into sick-wards and the people turned out had to go where they could. Matron had her hands full, and so had Nurse. The prefects were turned on to more dormitory duty and some of the Senior Middles were also pressed into service, among them Carola. Clem had been one of the first to succumb, along with three more from the same dormitory.

Carola was sent to sleep in the end cubicle of the Junior dormitory of which Con Maynard was an ornament. She took a special interest in that young person, having been attracted to her from the first. Consequently, when one night she was roused by a cry from Con's cubicle, she slipped in and found the child trying to get out of bed, still fast asleep.

Carola was in a quandary. She knew that someone in authority ought to be fetched, but she did not like to leave Con alone in case of what she might do. Neither did she want the other small girls to know of it. She got the sleeping Con back into bed and tucked her in firmly. Then she sat down beside her for a little. Con seemed to have settled down again, so after ten minutes of this, Carola made sure that the bed-clothes were securely tucked round her and slipped out to go in quest of someone.

Matron was sleeping in the wing where the patients were, so she could be of no help. Carola went down to the next corridor and tapped on Miss Wilson's door. There was no answer, so, greatly daring, she opened the door. The light was on and the bed was empty. No help to be found here. Carola withdrew, and tried the next room. Here, too, she drew a blank.

By this time she was growing cross. Where on earth were the Staff and why couldn't they be in bed when they were wanted? Carola tried the next room, got no answer, and opened the door to find herself looking into Matron's spare linen-room. Well, really! Crosser than ever, she shut the door with more than the suspicion of a bang and tried the next. Here she struck oil, for it was Biddy

O'Ryan's room and that young lady was in bed and asleep. In fact, she was so soundly asleep that Carola had to shake her before she could rouse her.

Biddy sat up, her masses of long black hair showering round her, and turned sleepy eyes on the intruder.

'Well, and what are *you* wanting, may I ask?' she demanded.

'Oh, Miss O'Ryan, would you come to Con Maynard?' Carola begged.

'Con?' Biddy was still rather foggy.

'Yes; she woke me up with crying out and I found her trying to get out of bed——'

'Walking in her sleep again?' Biddy was out of bed in a moment and pulling on her dressing-gown. 'Fish my slippers out from under the bed, Carola. Why on earth did you leave her, anyhow?'

'I got her back into bed and sat with her a while—*ages*, in fact,' Carola explained. She did not mean to exaggerate, but those ten minutes of sitting in the dark beside Con had seemed hours. 'She was sleeping all right, so I tucked her in tightly and then came to find someone, only no one seems to be in their rooms. You're the first I've found.'

Biddy nodded and picked up her torch from the bedside table. 'I see. Well, come along, though if you sat with her so long and she stayed put, I expect she's all right.'

The two ran softly upstairs to the dormitory, and Biddy made straight for the cubicle where Carola had left Con, Carola following. Switching on her torch, but careful to keep the light lowered, Biddy drew aside the curtain and the pair peered in. The bed-clothes were lying in a heap on the floor, and Con had vanished!

Carola's face was horrified. She was about to exclaim, but Biddy kept her head and set a firm hand across her mouth.

'Hush, will ye?' she said in an undertone. 'No need to wake the rest. She can't have gone far, anyway. We'd best search here first.'

Tiptoeing from cubicle to cubicle, they made the rounds. All the beds except Carola's own were occupied and no Con was to be found. She had evidently roused up after Carola left the room and gone out. Biddy dropped the last curtain and led Carola out into the corridor.

'Now,' she said, 'let's think. She hasn't gone to another dormy or someone would have waked up and we'd have known about it by this. We'd best try the bathrooms. I don't want to bother the Heads yet, as it may not be necessary if we can find the imp and put her to bed again. I'll go this way and you go that. Try every bathroom.'

But though they conscientiously tried every bathroom and then every dormitory on the corridor just in case, as Biddy said, they drew blank everywhere.

Thoroughly roused by this time, Biddy led the way to the other corridors, but they had no better luck. However, they did wake up Peggy Bettany who, as Head Girl, had the privilege of sleeping by herself in a tiny room, and when she heard that her small cousin was missing, she came out to help with the search.

High and low they sought, but no Con was to be found anywhere. By the time they had been over the whole house, not omitting the kitchen regions, and only leaving the infected part alone, Biddy was seriously alarmed.

'We'll have to get Miss Annersley,' she said when they came out of the Junior common-room, which was the last.

'This is beyond me. Carola, you ought to be in bed, you know.'

'Oh, Miss O'Ryan, please don't send me!' Carola implored. 'I simply must help to find Con. I—I sort of feel responsible. If only I hadn't left her so soon!'

'Well, don't howl about it,' Biddy replied bracingly. 'That's no help to anyone. You stay here with her, Peggy—or no; it's on the draughty side. You two go into Senior common-room. It's still pretty warm there. I'll go and get Miss Annersley.'

She went off and Peggy took Carola's arm and pulled her towards the Senior common-room where the ashes in the big fireplace were still warm. The Head Girl looked very grave and Carola took fright.

'Peggy, you—you don't think she—well—could she get out of a window?' she asked timidly. They knew Con could not have escaped by a door, for the outer doors were all locked and bolted.

'It looks like the only solution,' Peggy said, 'but I don't see how she could possibly. The windows down here are all latched and those in the dormies can only be opened so far—and that's not far enough for even a kid like Con to squeeze through. I just don't understand *where* she can have got to!'

Nor could Miss Annersley when she arrived with Biddy. She questioned Carola closely, and then told her not to be so upset. She had done the best thing she could. All the same, she could not disguise the fact that she was very anxious. She refrained from sending Carola to bed, for she saw that the girl was working herself up to such a pitch that she would never sleep.

'You and Peggy had better dress,' she said. 'Miss

O'Ryan, too. In the meantime, I'll call Mademoiselle and we two will go over the house again. If we can't find Con, then I'm afraid it means that she has got out some-how. Carola, was she dressed or in her pyjamas?'

'I don't know,' Carola said. She shivered. 'If—if she's outside in her pyjamas——'

Biddy O'Ryan dashed from the room to return in a few minutes. 'She must have dressed in her sleep,' she said breathlessly, waving a small pyjama jacket in one hand and a pair of trousers in the other.

'But—but how could she?' Carola gasped. 'I wasn't away long enough—at least, I don't *think* so. I don't know. I had to knock at two or three doors before I found any-one. But I didn't *think* it was as long as that.'

'Sure, they *have* only about four things to put on,' Biddy said. 'That wouldn't take long.'

'Go and dress, you three,' Miss Annersley said sharply. 'Then come——'

Her words were cut short by a sudden fearful bellow from just under their feet. They all jumped, and Peggy cried, 'That's Con! Where on earth can she be? Not outside, surely!'

She dashed at the door and began tugging at the heavy bolts, but Miss Annersley stopped her. 'No; she must have got into the cellars somehow. I don't know how. I always understood that Karen kept that door locked. It's all right, Peggy. Come quickly, girls! Biddy, give me that torch, please.'

Biddy handed it over, and the four made for the kitchens. Miss Annersley led the way to a small entry behind the kitchen door, and pulled open the door within. She flashed the torch down the stairs whence was coming a series of howls that the most tragic banshee Ireland ever produced could not have bettered.

'Con!' she called. 'It's Auntie Hilda. Don't yell like that or you'll wake the entire School. I'm coming!'

The howls softened though they did not cease. The Head ran lightly down the stairs, and presently reappeared with the queerest little object in her arms.

'Shut the door,' she said as she came into the blessed glow of the kitchen light. 'Biddy, go and hunt in the pantry for milk, will you? Con, stop that howling at once. It's all right. Auntie Hilda has you and you're quite safe.'

Carola came and knelt by her side as she sat in the big chair that belonged to Karen the cook, who was an old friend and had come from Tirol. She kissed what she could see of a black-smeared pink cheek. Con was a most appalling-looking little object. She had dressed as far as knickers and blouse and had one stocking on. The other foot was bare. She must have been in the coal cellar, for she was black from head to foot. A spider's web, thick with coal dust, adorned her black curls, and she must have stumbled over something, for one sleeve was torn, and a long graze was reddening on her arm.

'Don't cry, Con,' Carola said. 'It's quite all right.' She looked shyly at the Head. 'I know she can't go into San, Miss Annersley, but could she share my bed?'

'Or let me have her,' her cousin said, coming with a duster from Karen's drawer and removing the cobweb. 'It's all right, precious.'

'I was alone—and in the dark—and it was full of lumps! And so something went tick-tick, and it wasn't a clock!' Con wailed.

'The electric light meter,' Miss Annersley said at once.

'I'll take you and Len down in the morning and show you the little wheel that keeps turning all the time. Biddy, is that milk ready yet?'

'Just!' Miss O'Ryan poured it into a cup and brought it, and the Head held the cup to Con's lips.

'Drink it up, Con, and stop crying,' she said briskly. 'You're quite safe now, and you'll wake up everyone else if you howl like that. Nine is much too big to be a baby. What would Mamma say?'

If the Head had petted her there is no doubt that Con would have kept up her wails. This matter-of-fact way of dealing with things reassured Con as nothing else could have done. She stopped howling, though her chest still heaved with sobs and she choked over her milk. She was calmer when it was finished, however, and Miss Annersley gave the cup to Carola who was nearest, and then stood up, Con still in her arms.

'I'm taking Con to have a bath,' she said quietly. 'Carola, go and seek some clean pyjamas for her and bring them to my room. Miss O'Ryan, you might just go the rounds with Peggy and see if Con's yells have roused anyone. If they have, just say that one of the Juniors has been upset and I'm dealing with it. Thanks for your offer, Carola, but I think Con had better spend what's left of the night with me.'

Con put up a filthy arm and embraced her Head with it. 'I was *so* frightened, Auntie Hilda,' she said with a hiccup.

'Never mind. It's over now and you're going to sleep with me for a treat,' Miss Annersley said cheerfully. 'Switch the light off, Peggy, and shut the door after us, please.'

She bore Con off to be undressed, sponged down, and her grazed arm and knee bathed and bound up. By the time this was done, Con was asleep again and never knew when she was snugly in bed, Miss Annersley's arms round her so that she could not walk off again in her sleep. By this time, Peggy and Carola were also asleep. Only Biddy O'Ryan was left to finish her round and then climb wearily into bed with a deep sigh and a hope, voiced aloud, that no one would disturb the School for what remained of the night.

'And that's only four hours,' she said as she switched off her light and lay down. 'What a life!'

Chapter XVI

CAROLA DOES A LITTLE COOKING

JACK MAYNARD arrived that evening in answer to a somewhat agitated telephone call from Miss Annersley. He still insisted that Jo must know nothing of Con's exploits. All three of the little boys had had German measles, and though none of them had been more than poorly and peevish for a day or two, he felt she had had enough. In the meantime, he proposed to find out what was at the bottom of Con's nightmares and sleep-walking.

They were into March by now and the weather had turned fine and sunny with fresh breezes. Dr Maynard accepted the invitation of his friend Commander Christy, father of Prefect Dickie, to spend the night with them and see his daughter on the morrow. He had rung up Cartref before setting off, to inform Jo that he was going to see a patient at a little distance so that she would not ring up the Sanatorium, and had carefully avoided Carnbach as far as he could. She was not to know of his visit to St Briavel's.

As he had crossed by the last ferry and came to the School after dinner at the Christys, the pair were in bed and asleep when he arrived. Miss Annersley still had Con in her own room and was sitting there doing her work in the evenings.

'I thought it wiser for the next week or two,' she explained as she took the doctor up. 'I hope to heaven,

Jack, you can find out what has upset Con like this. They stick to it that they aren't eating anything but what the rest have, nor is anyone telling stories at unlawful hours, which was the other thing I thought of.'

Jack Maynard grinned. 'Still brooding on Biddy's doings?' he asked teasingly.

'Well, it's the only other cause I can think of,' she replied defensively. 'It may be some quite little thing. Children won't tell, quite often. I hope you can get something out of her.'

'Well, I'm here till the day after tomorrow, so I'll do my best.' They were in the room by this time and he bent over the camp-bed where Con lay sleeping profoundly, her long black lashes making little fans on her pink cheeks. 'Looks fit enough.' He straightened up and they went to the desk at the far side of the room. 'I'm inclined to think you may be right and someone has told them stories. Con's an imaginative little person—much more so than the other two. What wouldn't affect them might upset her. O.K., Hilda; I'll have a proper go at it tomorrow.'

A murmuring from the camp-bed reached them and both turned in time to see Con throw back the clothes though still fast asleep. Her father went quickly across, laid her back and tucked her in.

'No, Con,' he said firmly. 'Lie still, my pet.'

A minute or two later he gently roused her. 'What were you dreaming, Con? Tell Papa.'

Con opened her brown eyes and stared at him sleepily. Then she sat up with a little scream of rapture. 'Papa! Oh, how lovely? When did you come? Is Mamma here, too?'

'Not this time. What were you dreaming about, Con?'

Still drowsy and therefore not on her guard, Con replied at once. 'It—it was the big horse.' She gave a shudder.

'What horse, pet?'

'The one that lives at the bottom of waterfalls and comes up and takes little girls away to live with it until it eats them. Oh, Papa, it isn't *really* true, is it?' She clung to him, her eyes dilated with fear, and he held her in a safe, warm clasp.

'True? Of course it isn't! How on earth could the poor thing breathe at the bottom of a waterfall?' he demanded, with such an air of plain common sense that she relaxed with a long breath.

'O-oh! I hadn't thought of that. Of course it couldn't. Then it is only a kind of fairy-tale? Oh, I'm so *glad*! That's super!'

'And anyway,' he went on, 'where's your waterfall in this part of the world? Honestly, Con, what *has* become of your wits? But you needn't worry, even if you live with fifty waterfalls round you! No horse of any kind whatsoever could be stabled under a waterfall, so you can be very sure there isn't any such beasty. Now lie down again and go to sleep. Your guardian angel is always beside you, and you needn't be afraid of anything. Got that?'

She nodded as he put her back into bed and tucked her up. 'It's all right. I'm not afraid—no-ow.' She ended on a little yawn, and fell asleep again.

'Who's been telling the poor bairn about kelpies?' Jack demanded when at length they left the room. 'That bad Clem?'

Miss Annersley shook her head. 'That's no kelpie!

It's a Norse superstition and I can guess who was at the bottom of it.'

'So can I—young Signa or that sister of hers. Well, I'm glad to know what's caused all the fuss. I don't suppose you'll have any more trouble with her now. Keep her quiet for a day or two with plenty of milk and eggs and early bed. Lay an interdict on weird tales. Keep her in the fresh air as much as you can. That's all. Is she having her tonic?'

The Head nodded. 'Trust Matey to see to that!' She drew a long breath. 'Thank goodness we've got to the bottom of it! Well, tomorrow I shall interview Miss Signa and put a stop to all such stories. The bad little things! And they assured us they—oh, I see!'

'See what?'

'Signa obviously told those stories when they were playing. We only asked if they'd been doing it after lights-out. It wasn't Thyra. You forget, my dear Jack, that she's Upper Third and—well—it's rather a case of the Jews having no dealing with the Samaritans.'

He laughed and said good-night. Next day he bore his girls off for a long walk in the afternoon, and they returned rosy and fresh and with enormous appetites. What was more, greatly to the relief of everyone, Con stopped sleep-walking and had no more nightmares, so that episode ended after Signa had been interviewed and told she was to tell no more frightening tales to the others.

'But they're so lovely,' she had argued. 'It's such a *gorgeous* feeling when your spine all *cruddles* up!'

Miss Annersley was hard put to it not to laugh. She controlled herself, however, and merely repeated her ukase.

In any case, the weather was fine enough for the Juniors to be out most afternoons, playing rounders, which gave them little time for stories, frightening or otherwise.

And then Carola, just to keep things from becoming monotonous—or so Jo said when she heard the tale—produced a new legend to add to the many the School cherished.

Long before this, when the School was in Tirol in fact, a domestic science class had been introduced as part of the curriculum. Every girl as soon as she reached Lower Fourth attended for the whole of one day in the week and was instructed in all kinds of housework, including mending of linen and, best of all, cooking.

This class had, in its time, made School history. No one was ever likely to forget what happened when Cornelia Flower had given out garlic cloves instead of the more usual variety to flavour the apple pies her form was making. Another time, Joyce Linton, sister of Miss Linton who had taught in the School until the previous summer when she had married, had set out to make saffron cakes and used flowers of sulphur instead of saffron. There were other episodes quite as startling, and now Carola added one that took the fancy of everyone who heard of it—including Lady Russell in Canada.

On a certain day towards the middle of March it seemed good to Frau Mieders, who had been domestic science mistress from the beginning of the class, to teach the two Lower Fifths the art of deep-frying. They began with fish coated with thick batter before it was fried, and potato chips, all of which were devoured with much enjoyment at Mittagessen. The Lower Fifths smirked complacently at the compliments they received on all sides on the de-

licious first course they had provided, and certainly their
heads were all a little swollen by their success.

'Please may we make doughnuts for tea?' suggested
Clem Barrass, who had recovered from her German
measles and was back in school again.

Frau Mieders, who had planned a programme of
various scones, looked doubtful. 'Doughnuts?' she queried.
'But why doughnuts, Clemency?'

'Well, they're done in deep fat—I remember that from
the time we were in the Rockies,' Clem, who had travelled
widely with her parents at one time and another, explained.
'We *have* the deep fat——'

She got no further just then. Frau Mieders threw up
her hands in horror, and exclaimed loudly and fluently at
the idea that they could use deep fat in which fish had
been fried for any form of bun. Clem, who was a canny
young person and had learnt to hold her horses when
necessary, waited until the mistress had recovered, and then
tried again.

'I'd forgotten that,' she admitted, 'but *do* let us try them.
Everyone would be fearfully bucked to have doughnuts
for tea. Can't we?'

Frau Mieders went to the shelf where she kept her
treasured array of cookery books, and took down the new
Canadian one that Lady Russell had sent her from Canada.
She found the recipe—two or three of them in fact—and
read through, the class watching her eagerly.

'I have no sour milk,' she said at last. 'Still, I could
turn some with a little vinegar, no doubt.'

This was new to the Fifths, who exclaimed at it, and she
had to explain before going any further. When they knew
it, however, she continued: 'Also, I see it says they must

be fried in lard. Now, of this I have but little—certainly none for frying.'

'But couldn't we use vegetable oil same as we did for the fish?' Gillian asked. 'That's a Canadian book, isn't it? The Canadians must have heaps of lard. Just think of all the pigs they kill in Chicago.'

Peals of laughter greeted this, and two or three people asked if Gillian knew no more about North America than that? She laughed, too, being a thoroughly good-natured girl, and Frau Mieders, with a smile, hushed them, reminding them that art was going on further along.

'*Couldn't* we use vegetable oil?' Clem asked. 'It didn't make any difference to the fish, did it? I should think it would be O.K.—I—I mean quite all right—for doughnuts.'

Frau Mieders promptly turned to the fish section and read the fried fish recipes. Then she nodded slowly. 'I think it might do. At any rate we will try it. *One* doughnut to be made for each girl and one over for a friend. We cannot waste materials,' she added firmly.

The fact of the matter was that since the proprietor of the School had sent her the book the opportunities for using it had been all too few, and she was not sorry for the excuse to experiment.

'What do we need?' Vanna Ozanne asked briskly.

Frau Mieders read out the recipe for them to write into their recipe books and then sent Rosalie Browne to the store cupboard to find the big flagon of vegetable oil kept there. Alas! When Rosalie produced it, it was only about a third full. The faces of the girls fell considerably at this. They were all agog to try their hands at doughnuts, but now it looked as if that were out of the question. It was left to the ever-fertile Clem to solve the difficulty.

'Couldn't we use *olive* oil?' she queried. 'That's vege-table oil, all right, and Matron has a *huge* jar of it. I'm sure she'd lend us some if we asked her.'

'Shall I go and see?' asked Carola, who was nearest the door. She loved her cookery lessons, never before having had the chance to compound much beyond toffee and fudge, and very rarely even that. Doughnuts promised to be really interesting, and she was quite as keen as anyone to try her hand at them.

Frau Mieders was a kindly soul who rarely said 'No' if she could manage 'Yes.' She nodded, and Carola shot off at once. The rest were told to read over their recipes, see what they needed, and begin to collect the ingredients.

Carola was away a little while, but explained it by saying that she had not found Matron in her room and had had to look for her. What she did *not* say was that Matron proved quite unfindable, so she had simply looked round the tiny room where all medicants were kept, found the big jar of yellowish oil, and calmly helped herself—Frau Mieders had given her a large container as she went out of the kitchen.

She set the thing down in a corner after emptying the contents into the big fish-kettle the mistress pointed out to her. Frau Mieders herself set it on top of the Aga cooker they always used as being safest for the girls, Carola went to collect her materials, and silence fell on the kitchen while the girls set to work to mix their dough.

'What about jam?' someone asked when most of the dough was out of the mixing-bowls and on the floured boards. 'Do we put it in to cook or after they come out?'

None of the recipes in Frau Mieders' book told this—never mentioned jam, so far as that went; but when the girls assured her that doughnuts must *always* have jam in them, she decided that it should be put into a pocket in each little ball before the said balls were dropped into the fat which was beginning to boil. She produced a great jar of rhubarb jam and the girls delightedly inserted spoonfuls into their balls.

At length they were ready, and while four of the cooks collected the dough balls, some of the others were set to cut out large squares of brown paper to hold the sugar in which the doughnuts must be rolled when they came out of the oil.

'Funny how the smell of fish and chips always hangs about,' said Jean Ackroyd as she rolled a ball between her hands to get it round. 'I can smell ours yet!'

'Yes, it's what you might call a penetrating smell, isn't it?' Clem agreed. 'When I was at school in York I sat next a girl whose people kept a fish-and-chip shop and she always reeked of it, poor kid.'

Frau Mieders laughed. 'I do not notice it—but then I have a catarrh of the nasal passages and can smell nothing these five days.'

The girls murmured sympathy and she turned to the business in hand, the wire frying basket was half-filled with doughnuts and carefully lowered into the boiling oil, and the girls came in turn to stand and exclaim as the small balls they had produced swelled to proper doughnut size, which was almost twice as large as they had been.

'If they liked our fish and chips, I'll bet they *love* our doughnuts,' Rosalie Browne remarked with conviction as Frau Mieders pronounced the first boiling 'done,' and lifted the basket to let it drip before turning the doughnuts out on to the sugar-covered papers.

By four o'clock there were four large heaps of nicely-browned and sugared doughnuts, and the kitchen had been restored to the perfect neatness about which the mistress was always most particular. The hot oil had been set aside in the scullery to cool sufficiently to allow it to be poured off into the flagon, and all the windows opened to get rid of the fish-and-chips smell which still hung round.

When the last utensil had been washed and wiped and put away in its proper place and every vestige of mess dealt with, they were dismissed just as the bell rang, to get ready for tea. They bestirred themselves, and were down first, eagerly watching the faces of the rest as they saw the treat in store for them.

The Sixth came in shortly after the cooks and the rest were not far behind. The exclamations at sight of the platefuls of swollen brown and white beauties on the tables made the Lower Fifths preen themselves more than ever.

'I hope you had the decency to send samples to the Staff,' Peggy Bettany remarked to Clem Barrass as she sat down.

'Frau Mieders took a plateful for them,' Clem replied. 'Bread-and-butter, please.'

The School had an unwritten rule that no girl was to eat cake or buns until she had eaten at least two pieces of bread-and-butter. Mary-Lou who, like *Amy* of 'Little Women' fame, was fond of delicacies, hurriedly choked down her two pieces and then, with a smug smile at the rest who were still busy with bread-and-butter, took a doughnut and bit a huge chunk out of it. The Lower Fifths watched her eagerly, prepared for an exclamation of delight. They, by the way, had been eating in a much more ladylike manner.

Mary-Lou's reaction was anything but what they had expected. She solemnly chewed her mouthful, gave a gasp, jumped to her feet, upsetting her chair in her hurry, and vanished incontinently from the room, regardless of Peggy's stern command: 'Mary-Lou! Where are you going? Come back at once and ask for leave!'

'Choked,' Dickie Christy said. 'That's what comes of trying to hog your food instead of eating it decently.'

She might have had more to say, but Vanna Ozanne and Tom Gay had both helped themselves and bit into their doughnuts with every anticipation of a treat. Vanna followed Mary-Lou from the room at even greater speed. Tom hurriedly removed *her* mouthful with more haste than elegance, and exclaimed, 'Cripes! What *have* you kids put into the things? They're ghastly—frightful!'

'They're *not*!' exclaimed half a dozen indignant voices.

'But they *are*!' Tom maintained, hurriedly picking up her cup. She gulped down her tea and then went to the urn for more. '*Urrh!* Of all the beastly tastes!'

Peggy rapped on the table with the handle of her knife. 'Less noise, please,' she ordered. 'Tom, stop making those awful faces. You aren't poisoned, anyhow.'

'I'm not so sure of that,' Tom retorted, swallowing down her tea and pouring out a third libation. This she carried back to the table. 'What on *earth* have you kids been doing? The thing just reeks of bad fish!'

'*Bad fish!*' The Lower Fifths were nearly speechless at this. Clem managed to collect herself, however.

'That, I'm certain, they don't! We had a clean fish-kettle that Frau Mieders took off the shelf and the frying fat had never been *near* fish of any kind. It came straight from the bottle!'

By this time, various of the cooks had helped themselves and were tasting gingerly. It was plain, even to them, that Mary-Lou, Vanna, and Tom had real reason for their behaviour. Peggy Bettany took one, and lifted it to her mouth. Before she could bite into it, however, the door opened, and Matron appeared on the scene.

'Who got the oil for frying from my room?' she demanded.

Carola stood up. 'I did, Matron. I couldn't find you, and Frau Mieders was waiting, so I—I just took some.'

'Indeed?' Matron glared at her and Carola wilted visibly. Then the School tyrant looked round the room. 'Where are Mary-Lou and Vanna?' she demanded.

'They—er—*left* the room,' Peggy replied, suppressing their manner of leaving since Matron seemed to be angry about something.

'Had they had any of this latest concoction of yours?' Matron queried.

'Well—yes,' Peggy admitted, looking at the doughnut she still held.

'I see.' Matron turned again to Carola. 'Can't you read, eh, child?'

By this time, Carola was convinced she had come near poisoning everyone, and her voice was shaky as she replied, 'Yes—oh, yes!'

'Didn't you read the label on the bottle?'

'I—I couldn't. It—it was so oily,' Carola stammered, nearly in tears now.

There was an electric pause while the girls wondered

wildly what was coming next. *Had* Carola got hold of something that would make them sick?

Suddenly Matron's stern face creased. Her eyes twinkled, and she had to bite her lips to steady them. 'I see. Well, girls, I'm afraid you won't enjoy your doughnuts this time. I advise you to let them severely alone.'

'But—*why*?' Clem demanded, wide-eyed.

'Because Carola took the wrong bottle.' Matron paused again. Then she flung her final bombshell among them. 'Those doughnuts of yours were fried in *cod-liver oil*!'

Then she departed, leaving the entire School staring at each other and the unhappy Lower Fifths with startled eyes and dropping jaws.

Chapter XVII

CAROLA SOLVES A PROBLEM

NEEDLESS to state, once the School had got over its first shock it revelled in the latest 'yarn.' Carola was assured that no one would ever forget it. She was asked with mock sympathy if her sense of smell had returned yet; requested for other new recipes; told that she really ought to write a cookery book as it was bound to be original if nothing else!

She bore the teasing very well at first. Then she lost her temper one day when Mary-Lou, all innocence, pressed a note into her hand—a note that purported to come from Karen the cook, begging her to say if she would advise using Epsom salts or salts of lemon in place of the proper article for flavouring the soup?

Carola read this effusion and then went in search of Mary-Lou, who had meant to join her own gang for safety but had delayed as she had just thought of a delightful joke she wanted to play on Polly Winterton. She was leaving the bathroom when Carola ran her to earth and there was no one near. Mary-Lou, looking up, felt rather apprehensive as she saw the angry blue eyes looking down at her and the flushed face. She gave a little giggle from sheer nervousness and that was oil on the fire. Carola said nothing. She simply took the younger girl by the shoulders and gave her a good shaking, finally shoving her away with the remark: 'Perhaps that will teach you

to keep your silly tricks for your own crew!' before she
flung off, leaving the Junior Middle feeling that it might
be as well to leave Carola alone, as well as very indignant
at the shaking which had been thorough.

Luckily for all concerned, Mary-Lou was an honest
young thing and she owned to herself that *perhaps* she had
deserved Carola's fury. Anyhow, she wasn't going to tell
any tales and no one but their two selves ever knew anything about it. Even more luckily, the very next morning
Miss Annersley reminded them after Prayers that there
was only a fortnight left before their Sale, and thereafter
Carola's exploit sank into the background. Lessons had
to go on as usual, but apart from them and their games
periods, the girls talked, thought, and *dreamed* Sale.

It was always an important event in the Easter term.
Nor was the School ever satisfied with just a 'plain' Sale.
One year they had used fairy-tales, and Snow-White and
the Seven Dwarfs, the Sleeping Beauty, Rapunzel of the
Golden Locks, and several other fairy-tale characters had
had a good airing. Another time it had been a Willow
Pattern Sale, when the girls all turned Chinese overnight
and the stall-frames were transformed into quite good like-
nesses of pagodas and Chinese houses. This year, they
were to represent many nations. Special Sixth, who had
charge of the tea-room, would be Indian ladies and had
already been practising the art of wearing a saree. The
two Fourths were to be Red Indians and had charge of the
needlework stall which was to be turned into a tepee—or
as nearly one as possible. The Thirds had pleaded to be
allowed to be Maories and were to make of their sweets
and cakes a Maori 'Pah.' The Sixth, who were to have
fruit and vegetables and flowers, had insisted on being

Persians, and devoted a good part of their spare time to manufacturing for themselves slippers with turned-up toes and the round, fez-like caps Persians are supposed to wear. The bric-à-brac stall with fretwork, pottery, shell-covered boxes and photograph-frames and other oddments had been given to the Second Forms who were to be Chinese, and the Kindergarten had charge of the lucky dip as usual and were to be Eskimos. The two Fifths had undertaken the toy stall and, at Clem Barrass's suggestion, were to be Scots in kilts, bonnets, and plaids.

'We ought to have *one* of our own lands,' Clem said wisely, 'and Welsh hats would be the limit to make!'

'And what's the matter with an Irish stall?' Miss O'Ryan had demanded when they told her.

'You haven't *got* a national costume,' Clem told her, grinning.

'We'd best see just what we've got,' Bride Bettany said to the others. 'I vote we have a show tonight and see what's finished and what's still left to be done. Then we'll know where we are.'

They agreed to this with acclamations. It was decided to ask leave to use Upper Fifth, which was a large room, for the show and certain of the mistresses were to be invited to come and pronounce on it.

'We've needlework this afternoon,' Jean said. 'Let's ask Mademoiselle to let us get on with our work for the Sale.'

'So've we,' Tom Gay retorted. 'We come after you. O.K. It's quite a scheme, Jean. We'll do it, too—if Mademoiselle'll let us, that is. Here, Nella Ozanne, you're her blue-eyed boy at the moment. You can ask her.'

Nella, twin sister of Vanna, assented placidly. Mademoiselle was a good-natured little person and willingly agreed. So the two Fifths—or rather three, since there were two Lower Fifths—spent part of the afternoon in working for their stall.

After tea and prep, the girls sped off to bring their collection from its cupboards and drawers and then set it out. Abendessen came all too soon for them, but when it ended, they had twenty minutes or so before Prayers in which to finish and select the Staff who were to be privileged to see their show. Finally, it was ready, and Clem and Bride went off to invite the mistresses.

The two Heads, Mademoiselle, Miss Burn (now quite recovered from her accident), Biddy O'Ryan, Miss Norman, and Miss Dene (the school secretary) were all summoned and came agog to see what the girls had been doing.

They exclaimed with surprise as they saw the quantity and variety laid out. There were cuddly toys made of material or knitted rag dolls, beautifully dressed; piles of dolls' clothes of all sorts and sizes; a heap of little carpets made by Audrey Simpson, a very quiet member of Lower Fifth A, with canvas and wool; boxes of bedding and bed-linen; sets of toy furniture and separate items as well; in short, everything they could think of and make. But the gem of the whole collection was undoubtedly the dolls' house.

Tom Gay had been responsible for the house itself. She had made it out of tea-chests which she had taken to pieces, cut to the sizes she wanted, and put together to form a veritable mansion. There were four rooms on the ground floor as well as the hall, from which rose a staircase with a

landing half-way up and a turn in the stairs: and only
Tom knew how much labour and temper had been spent
on this last item! Over the door was a bathroom, fitted
up with a tin bath and all the other etceteras, which were
the only articles of furnishing the girls had bought. Four
bedrooms were over the sitting-rooms and kitchen and in
the roof were two more rooms. All the sides were on hinges
and opened. The roof was a thatched one, the thatch
being of yellow raffia. The house had been painted outside to imitate the old black-and-white houses of Armi-
shire, and inside, every room was properly papered with
the exception of the kitchen and bathroom. They had
been painted.

Tom had given her house lattice windows which swung
open delightfully, and the front and back doors also opened
and shut.

Carola examined it carefully, for about the tenth time.

'I still don't see how it sticks together,' she complained.
'There isn't a nail in sight! Go on, Tom! *Tell* me!'

Tom grinned. 'I'd be ashamed of myself if I had to use
nails for putting a thing like this together,' she said. 'It's
all dovetailed, and I've used wooden pegs where I simply
had to do any reinforcing, though it's mainly dovetailing.'

Carola gasped. 'Well, I think it's super,' she said simply.

Tom went richly purple. 'Oh, rot!' she said brusquely.

The furnishings were as delightful as the house. Nella
Ozanne, who was amazingly clever at both fretwork and
wood-carving, had produced a stately set of dining-room
furniture in simple Chippendale style with padded chair-
seats and a little sideboard whose one drawer really pulled
in and out. She had also made chairs and tables for the
drawing-room and a delightful little china cabinet into

which the girls had put tiny papier-mâché vases, painted and decorated by the artistic members of the form. Jean Acheson, another fretwork enthusiast, had contributed the morning-room furniture and someone else had attended to the kitchen, which had an imitation range made of wood and painted black. The fireplaces were of copper wire, also painted, with little wooden mantelshelves over them. Polly Winterton had drawn and painted the pictures that were glued to the walls, Tom refusing flatly to have her work marred by tacks.

The best needlewomen in the forms had made the curtains, table-covers, and wee cushions that gave the place such a well-finished appearance. They had also made the bed-linen for the little four-posters Nella had managed for two of the bedrooms. The other two bedrooms had beds made of matchboxes, and matchboxes glued together, framed in stout pasteboard and painted, provided tallboys and low chests of drawers. Audrey's carpets were laid on the floors except in the kitchen, bathroom, and nursery, and for these they had used American cloth which they had painted in tiny squares, or, in the case of the nursery, with sprays of flowers. The dressing-tables and wardrobes had slips of looking-glass framed so that the dolls' family might look at themselves. As for the dolls, they had been provided by an artistic member of Special Sixth who had been interested in puppetry and had contrived a very pleasant-looking family which the Fifths had supplied with extensive wardrobes.

The Staff simply gasped when they had taken it all in. They knew the girls had set out to outdo anything they had done before, but this excelled their imaginings.

'Well,' Miss Wilson said when at last she stood back,

'I haven't the least idea what you propose to do in the way of a competition, girls, but I honestly think you must charge far more for an entrance fee. What do you say, Miss Annersley?'

'I agree,' Miss Annersley said promptly. 'You can't make it less than five shillings, and anyone who wins it at that has simply *found* it! What ideas have you about the competition, by the way.'

There was an awful pause. The girls had all racked their brains to solve this problem, but so far no one had done it. Nancy Chester of Upper Fifth had suggested that intending competitors should guess the complete cubic content of each room and then of the house itself, and had been howled down for such an appalling suggestion.

'You couldn't do it yourself,' Bride Bettany had pointed out severely, 'so why should you try to let anyone else in for anything so utterly ghastly? You think again, my good girl!'

'Well, it's the only thing I can think of,' Nancy had retorted defensively. 'We generally get a good number of fathers along, and men always seem able to do things like that.'

'Well, we're not having it,' Tom squashed her promptly. 'Think again!'

Rosalie Browne had proposed that the competitors should be asked to choose a name, and then the School could vote on the list and the winner would get the house, but that, too, had been vetoed. There was good reason, therefore, for their stricken silence at Miss Annersley's bland question.

She surveyed their crestfallen faces with laughing eyes. 'Not found anything *yet*? Oh, you'll have to do better

than this. There's only a fortnight left, you know. Put
your brains in steep and see if you can evolve something
worth while. The house deserves it, you know.'

The Staff left shortly after that, having seen everything
and complimented the Fifth Forms on their industry and
ingenuity, and those young ladies instantly went into a
huddle, to quote Bride, on the subject of the competition.

'The name business is definitely *out*,' Primrose Day said.
'Bill said that last term, you may remember. What we
can do instead is beyond me. I never *was* a brainy
creature.'

Bride, sitting on the corner of a table, swinging long,
brown-stockinged legs, mused a moment. Then she looked
up. 'We mayn't have guessing the name of the house,
but do you think they'd let us name the family and make
them guess *that*?' she asked hopefully.

'We can *try* it, I suppose,' Tom said gloomily. 'What
d'you think of calling 'em?'

'Something appropriate, anyhow,' Gillian said. 'We
can't pitch on anything like Smith, or Jones, or Brown.
They're too ordinary.'

Sybil Russell grinned. 'Before we start working our
poor brains too hard, what about going and seeing if the
Heads will pass that?' she suggested.

'Good idea!' Tom looked round. 'Here, Bride, you
beetle off to the study and put it up to them and see what
they say.'

'O.K.; but I'm not going alone, so don't you think it,'
Bride responded, sliding down from her table. 'There's
got to be one from each form. Here, Prim, you can represent Lower Five A, and—and—you can take Lower
Five B, young Clem. Come on!'

'We'll go on with our work while you're gone,' Elfie Woodward, an ornament of the Upper Fifth, said. 'We're out to make the biggest sum, aren't we? Then let's stop huddling up like this and get cracking.'

There was common sense in what she said. The Fifths had plenty of work to finish, so they went to the cupboards, fished it out, and when the three delegates returned a quarter of an hour later, they came in to a busy room. Everyone dropped what she was doing, however, and a chorus of eager voices demanded, 'Well? What do they say?'

'Well, it's not washed out altogether,' Bride told them. 'They say we can keep it in mind, and if we really *can't* do any better, we can use it—*may*, I mean—but they don't think much of it. It was Bill who said that, by the way,' she added with a grin.

'As if we needed anyone to tell us that!' Tom said with scorn. 'Well, if we can't do any better, I suppose we must make it do; but I'm none too satisfied with it, I can tell you.'

'I don't think any too much of it myself,' Bride agreed, 'but I simply can't think of anything else. Have a shot yourself!'

Tom grinned. 'Not much! I've no brains for that sort of thing. I made the house. It's up to the rest of you to find a comp. for it.'

'We don't seem to have much success, do we?' Primrose said.

'Well, there's one thing,' Nancy Chester remarked decidedly. 'We fix it for ourselves. No going outside the Fifths for an idea! Don't you go and ask Auntie Jo, Bride, d'ye hear?'

'As if I should!' Bride cried indignantly.

Carola, who had been wondering if it would be any use
to suggest doing that very thing, went scarlet, but no one
was noticing her at the moment, so she was not called on
to explain her sudden blush. She finished off her thread,
broke it, and held up the little knitted frock on which she
had been busy to shake it out.

'Finished?' Clem asked. 'It's sma—er—wizard. You
really are a decent knitter, Carola. Look, you folk!'

They eyed the gay little frock in primrose yellow with a
tiny Fair Isle border in reds and blues round the hem, and
agreed with Clem's dictum. Then they turned back to the
question of the competition. Carola folded up her frock
and laid it in her workbox until she could press the seams.
She had nothing else on hand at the moment, so she
strolled over to the house, opened the sides, and stood
gazing in admiration at the contents. Tom looked up and
saw her.

'Hey!' she called across the room. 'The house isn't
likely to give you any ideas, no matter how much you
stand there trying to mesmerise it! If you've finished
your own job, come here and hold these bits while I glue
them together, will you?'

Carola slowly closed the sides of the house. Then she
went over to where Tom was waiting. She held the pieces
of wood which Tom put into her fingers without saying a
word. Tom paused to look at her.

'I say, you're not stuffy about what I said, are you?'
she asked doubtfully. 'I didn't mean anything.'

Carola started awake and shook her head. 'Of course
I'm not stuffy, I was just thinking. Tom! You've used
lots of different kinds of stuff in it, haven't you?'

Tom stared at her. 'I should just think we had! What do you call the furnishings? Are you crackers?'

Carola looked at her and then gave a chuckle. 'It sounds rather like it, I suppose. No, I'm not. It's only— I've got the ghost of a germ of an idea for the comp. Don't talk to me, Tom. I want to work it out.'

Tom grunted, but said no more, concentrating on fitting the dovetailing of a workbox she had been making. Carola held the pieces she had been given until the glue began to set. Then Tom took them from her, giving her a curious look. Carola went back to her seat, set her elbows on the table, buried her chin in her hands, and stared thoughtfully at nothing. The others were too busy to notice her, so everyone jumped violently when she suddenly bounced up, exclaiming, 'Eureka! I've got it, I do believe!'

'Got what?' Bride demanded crossly as she sucked the finger Carola's outburst had caused her to prick with her needle. 'What's biting you?'

'The comp.! I believe I've got a real idea at last!'

With one accord they dropped their work. 'You've got an idea? What is it?' Tom wanted to know.

'Let's have it,' Clem ordered. 'Is it any good?'

'It had better be!' Polly Winterton spoke darkly. 'You made me jump so, I've smudged green right across my sky.'

Carola paid no heed to them. She turned to Tom eagerly. 'Tell me, Tom, what did you use to make the house— materials, I mean?'

Tom reached out and felt her head. Carola shied away.

'I'm *not* crackers! Don't be such an ass, Tom! Answer my question and tell me what materials you used.'

Tom gave it up and condescended to reply. 'Wood—

and glue—and raffia—and glass for the window-panes. What are you getting at?'

'And there's the canvas and wool for the mats—and the muslin for the curtains—and the silk for the inner ones in the drawing-room—and—oh, heaps of things!' The words came tumbling out. Carola was almost incoherent with excitement. 'Oh, don't you *see*, all of you? There must be dozens of different kinds of material in it. Let's count them up and make a list. Then we can tell people there are so many and ask them to name them, and the one that gets the fullest list gets the house! *Now* do you see?'

There was silence for a moment as they took it in. Then they saw and the noise they made was enough to have brought someone in authority down on them if everyone had not been so busily occupied that they had no time to bother about the Fifth Forms.

'It's a smashing idea!' bubbled Primrose, using forbidden slang in the excitement of the moment. 'We ought to be able to get quite a long list. There's the cotton for the bedding——'

'*And* linen,' Sybil supplemented this. 'I bagged three of Uncle Jack's best linen hankies for the best sheets and pillow-cases.'

'Whatman paper for the pictures and water-colour paint!' This was Polly. 'And then there's the cellophane over them and passe-partout for the frames!'

'There's the paint for the outside, if you come to that,' Bride put in. 'It's oil-paint, so it's another material. Carola, it's a super idea! Come on, all of you! Get a pencil and paper, Carola—you're doing nothing—and we'll remember while you write the things down.'

They calmed down a little after this. Carola was supplied with someone's pad and someone else's ink-pencil, and while the rest resumed their work, she sat writing.

At first it was easy enough. They could think of all the obvious things. When she had scribbled them down, she shook her head, however. It was not nearly enough—only twenty-two articles.

'We've got to have at least double this,' she said definitely. 'It won't be any real competition if this is all. I'm sure there's crowds more if we can only think of them. What did you stuff the mattresses with, for instance?'

'Cotton-wool,' Sybil replied at once. 'And I took some kapok from one of Auntie Jo's cushions that was leaking a bit for the little pillows and cushions.'

'You seem to have got going fairly well on Auntie Jo's things,' Bride grinned at her cousin.

'Oh, well, I knew she wouldn't mind when it's for the Sale,' Sybil replied insouciantly. 'I didn't take *much*; and I *did* sew up the seams for her when I'd got what I wanted. I thought that was only fair.'

Carola looked up. 'How d'you spell "kapok"?' she asked.

'"K-a-p-o-c-k",' Clem obligingly spelt. 'At least, I think so.'

Carola wrote it down and then asked, 'What about those nifty little dinner mats in the sideboard drawer? Who made those?'

'Me.' Primrose took a hand. 'They're cork. I cut them out of medicine-bottle corks. That's why they're all round. I just *couldn't* get the oval shape, though I blunted my penknife badly over them.'

'And what about the chandeliers in the sitting-rooms?

Tom, you made those, didn't you? What are they made of?'

'Copper wire and gilding. The candles are wax tapers I found in a box at home. I really wanted to light it by electricity, but I wasn't sure how to manage the wiring safely,' Tom confessed. 'I had to fall back on wax candles instead.'

'Oh, well, they look wizard,' Polly replied. 'And those wee shades Primrose made for them are smashing! What are they made of, Prim?'

'Cellophane in the dining-room, so you can't use *that* again,' Primrose said. 'The drawing-room ones are parchment I pinched from home.'

'This form seems to have gone in for a lot of pinching altogether,' Bride said austerely. Then she chuckled. 'I did a bit myself. Those inner curtains in the drawing-room are a bit of silk brocade Mummy had in an old bag of Grannie's. I saw it one day and I thought it was just exactly what we wanted, so I—er—*lifted* it.'

They giggled appreciatively at this. Carola wrote down 'brocade' and then looked round for the next thing.

Jean supplied it. 'What about the paste we used for the papering? That's made of flour, isn't it? Put it down, Carola.'

So it went on, one after another remembering something, until Carola's list reached the bottom of the page twice over and she had to turn over and write on the back. At last no one could think of another thing, so they told her to count up what they had remembered and waited breathlessly while she did so.

'Thirty-nine!' she said when she had gone over the columns three times. 'Oh, can't we possibly get it to fifty? Oh, wait! The sponge in the bathroom! That's forty, anyhow.'

'The sawdust in the seats of the chairs! I got it from the sawmill near us at home!' Vanna Ozanne cried excitedly. 'Then that makes forty-one. Can't we *possibly* get nine more?'

'The leatherette on top of the writing-desk in the morning-room,' Nancy Chester said instantly. 'Oh, and brass! The door-knocker! It's a tiny brass ring, isn't it, Tom?'

Tom nodded. 'It is. And I've got an idea. I'll cut a tiny bit off my loofah and put *that* in the bathroom, and that'll make one more.'

'Then you'll have to gum it round the edges or something, or it'll fray out,' Clem told her. 'I've got a sliver of soap left. I'll wet it and try to shape it into a little tablet. We could dye it pink with red ink. I don't suppose the *dolls* 'ud mind if it came off on them!'

In the end, however, they had to give up with just forty-eight materials. However, they felt they had done really well, and when the Heads finally passed the scheme, Bride awarded the accolade to the genius who had thought up the scheme before the assembled members of all three forms.

'It really is a wizard idea. I was beginning to think we'd never solve that problem, but Carola's done it for us. I vote we cheer her!'

This was not allowed for a moment. They had no wish to be called to order for making a noise. But the happy Carola was delighted to take the will for the deed when Tom said, 'Cheer be sugared! D'you *want* to lose us all order marks, Bride? What an ass you are sometimes!

All the same, Carola's done us proud, and I move a hearty vote of thanks to her for a really super idea!' This last with a sudden memory of the many church bazaars and meetings she had had to attend. 'All in favour hands up —and *don't make more row than you can help*!' A forest of waving hands assured everyone how the girls felt, and Carola went to bed that night as happy a girl as you could have found anywhere.

Chapter XVIII

'A-SELLING WE WILL GO!'

'HERE you are, Natalie. Cook says that's the very last cup she can spare. How many does that make?' Jean Mackay set down a laden tray on the table in the Seniors' common-room as she spoke and looked anxiously at tall, stately Anthea Barnett—yes; she was the 'young monkey' Mrs Barnett had spoken of when she met Cousin Maud at Southampton!—who was head of Special Sixth this year, those very superior damsels who were having an extra year's school and specialising.

Anthea counted the cups and saucers. 'Well, that gives us sixty, so surely we'll have enough. I say, Natalie, you might fix that bead and bamboo curtain thing. It looks like collapsing any moment!'

Natalie rushed off to secure the Indian curtain which hung over a doorway and Anthea began placing the cups down the long trestle-table commandeered from the dining-room.

It was the morning of the Sale, and everyone was scampering everywhere, the whole place filled with noise and chatter, since rules were in abeyance for the time being. In Hall, the forms in charge of stalls were very busy setting out their wares. A concert was to take place in the Kindergarten, which was an army hut set to one side of the Big House, and a country-dancing display was billed for half-past three in the gym. In the prefects' room the Mr Young who had married Miss Linton in the summer, thereby leaving the School lamenting a very favourite mistress, had undertaken to do lightning portraits at half a crown a time. Altogether, the girls had decided that this ought to be the best effort they had ever managed.

The two Heads, who had been hard at it all the morning, strolled into Hall after elevenses to admire the general effect, and really, it was worth admiring. At the top of the room was the daïs on which the opening ceremony would take place. It was banked up with pots of ferns and flowering bulbs, and great jars of pussy willows had been disposed across the back on stands. To one side stood the 'igloo' of the Eskimos, constructed of bamboos with sheets spread over, and the outlines of the snow 'bricks' marked with black tacking. The 'dip' consisted of snow-balls made of cotton-wool, each containing some prize. Miss Norman had wisely insisted that those for boys must stand at one side of the igloo, and those for girls at the other. The small folk were very busy making neat piles and as excited as was good for them.

'I shan't be surprised if we have tears before the day is over,' Miss Wilson observed as she surveyed them. Then she made a dive forward. 'Signa! You bad child! What do you think you're doing?'

Signa went red and she dropped the red blackboard chalk with which she had been chalking at one side, 'Eskermo igloo for dips.'

Miss Norman looked at it with resigned horror. 'I might have known! Get a cloth, one of you others, and let me wipe it off. *No*—not you! It's only a frail affair and I don't want it pushed over. I'll do it myself. As for you, Signa, let me catch you doing one wicked thing again today, and you'll go to bed at once and stay there till tomorrow.'

That settled Signa, who had no wish to miss all the fun. She retired behind the others and made up her mind to be good until the Sale was over, at any rate.

The Staff moved on to admire the Persian effort where the girls had hung up draperies, and disposed fruit and vegetables in as artistic heaps as they could manage on their stall, while great jamjars begged from Karen had been roughly enamelled in what purported to be Persian designs, and were crammed with daffodils, tulips, early wallflowers, and narcissi. The big tin bowl from the School's 'Dommy Sci.' kitchen was a mass of violets, and they had filled one Dickie Christy had brought from home with primroses.

'A very artistic stall,' Miss Annersley commented to Peggy Bettany. 'Who gave all the jam? Matron again? How *does* she do it? She always gives us dozens of jars for the Sale, but I can't say that I've ever noticed the School going short at any time.'

Peggy grinned ruefully. 'We've been allowed one dessertspoonful each for the last fortnight,' she said. 'We knew Matey was giving jam when *that* happened.'

The Heads laughed, and went on to admire the Red Indian tepee which was draped with travelling-rugs of every lurid colour they could contrive and was decorated with 'Indian' drawings pinned up everywhere. Mary-Lou and Verity-Anne had written excitedly home for sundry curios, and these had been sent, and adorned the inside where the objects for sale were hanging from strings, or piled into big reed-woven baskets.

The Maories showed piles of sweets made by the Dommy

Sci. classes as well as cakes from the same source. Jo Maynard had sent a large contribution which her Anna had made, and various other nearby friends had also rallied round.

'Have a jam tart or a piece of fudge, do,' Mary-Lou pressed them.

'No, thank you, Mary-Lou. A jam tart would be two-pence lost, and even a piece of fudge can count,' her Head Mistress told her. 'I'll buy some fudge this afternoon, though, if there's any left by the time I manage to come round.'

'I s'pose you have to spend ages being polite to every-one,' Mary-Lou said sympathetically. 'I'll tell you what, though: I'll save you each a quarter, shall I, before it all goes? O.K. Vi—Doris! You are to keep two quarters of fudge for Miss Annersley and Miss Wilson. That'll be all right!' She beamed at the two Heads, who retired feeling mentally breathless, a state of mind to which she often reduced her elders.

'It isn't that she's cheeky—though I admit she can be when she chooses,' Miss Wilson said to her friend as they made for the toy stall. 'It's simply the calm way she has of treating the most grown-up of grown-ups as dear friends.'

Meanwhile, the Fourths were all engaged in giving Mary-Lou their opinion of her behaviour.

'Though, goodness knows, we ought to be used to you now,' Cherry Christy added.

'Really, Mary-Lou, you are the limit,' one of her chosen friends, Viola Lucy, chimed in.

Verity-Anne Carey smiled at them all. 'Don't worry. The Heads will only say, "It's just Mary-Lou!" and that will be that,' she said.

This was so true that the Fourths left it at that. In any case, they had plenty to do, and they knew well enough by this time that they could, as Viola said graphically, talk themselves black in the face and Mary-Lou would never turn a hair.

Having seen the Fifth Forms' show a fortnight before, the mistresses imagined that a mere cursory glance and a few words of praise would be all that was needed from them. When they reached the stall, however, they felt impelled to do more than that, for the girls had exerted themselves to the utmost, and the piles of toys laid out among thistles and gorse were really remarkable. Moreover, as Polly Winterton pointed out with some pride, they had gone one better than everyone else in the matter of wrapping paper. The School always bought two or three reams of white kitchen paper for these occasions and practically every girl in the three forms had spent her spare time for the past three days in painting their share of the paper with tartan patterns. Carola had a book of all the tartans, and they had passed it round and copied them, each girl taking one tartan and concentrating on that. They had neither shortbread nor Edinburgh rock nor tablet, such things having been handed over to the cakes and sweets stall by unwritten law. You chose your stall and stuck to it, only such things as properly belonged to it being placed thereon.

'That's a good idea,' Miss Wilson said, gazing at the wrapping paper admiringly. 'Whose idea was it?'

'Carola's,' Clem said. She giggled as she added, 'We had a go at painting the string, but it just didn't work. However, the paper won't look so dusty and *our* parcels will have quite a cachet!'

Miss Annersley burst into laughter. 'They certainly will! I only hope you have packers who know how to make up parcels securely. If not, I'm afraid all your pretty paper will be wasted.' She turned to her colleague. 'Do you remember our Fairy-tale Sale in Tirol? The Bishop wandered round with all sorts of oddments drooping sadly out of the very inadequate parcelling that was all some people had thought necessary to provide. Joey had to take pity on him and *she* provided him with an old fish-basket into which she packed everything. He told me later that his parcels were all quite safe when he got them home, but some of them had a distinctly fishy odour at first!'

The pair broke into peals of laughter at this reminiscence. Gillian Moggeridge, standing near, opened her eyes widely.

'Do they have *bishops* in Tirol?' she exclaimed.

'My good child, what else did you suppose?' Miss Wilson demanded. 'Really, Gillian!'

'Well, I didn't know. Somehow I thought it was only *us* had them—and the R.C.s too, of course,' Gillian explained.

'All Tiroleans are Catholics—or most of them, anyhow,' Miss Wilson told her. 'He was a Catholic bishop, naturally. Frieda Mensch's great-uncle, as a matter of fact—Oh, don't be silly! Frieda von Ahlen, Mrs Maynard's great friend.'

'Oh, I see,' Gillian murmured as the mistresses went on to admire the bric-à-brac stall of the little girls and congratulate their form mistress on the truly Chinese effect she had contrived with paper lanterns, imitation peach-blossom, and cardboard gables of enormous curves fastened to the top of the stall.

'Really, the girls have done better than ever,' Miss Wilson said when, their inspection over, they retired to their study.

'Yes; I think they have.' But Miss Annersley seemed dissatisfied about something.

'What's wrong?' her friend demanded.

'It's only that I wish we could have used something else for the Dip. I'm always afraid of cotton-wool; it *is* so inflammable!'

'Oh, nonsense, Hilda! In any case, none of the children are in it. Besides, there isn't an open fire anywhere about. But if you feel nervous, I'll tell Rosalie to print some big notices, "No Smoking," and have them put up round Hall. Then you needn't fear even matches or lighters. And talking of no smoking, I haven't had a cigarette today. Join me in one now.' Miss Wilson held out her case.

'That's an excellent idea.' Miss Annersley helped herself and lit up. 'People are so careless about matches.' She turned to the house telephone and called up her secretary, Miss Dene, and gave her the instructions. 'There!' she said, coming back to sit by the open window through which the March sun was pouring a glorious blaze of light. 'I think it'll be quite safe now.'

'Then sit down and get your breath. It's nearly time for Mittagessen, and after that we shan't be able to call our souls our own much before seven o'clock.'

Mittagessen was ended by half-past twelve, the School cleared the tables at top-speed and then streamed off upstairs to deck themselves for the afternoon. This took a little time, for the Maories had to be painted with tattoo marks and so had the Red Indians. The Indian ladies contented themselves with washing their faces in strong coffee and the Persians reddened their lips and left it at that.

'Thank goodness *we* don't have to bother with make-up muck,' Clem remarked as she struggled with her plaid which would *not* fold neatly across her. 'Now, all of you, you know exactly what you have to do, don't you? Carola, you and Jean go with Rosalie and Vanna to the little room by the door to give out paper and pencils. Rosalie will be at the door, but if she's called off, you'd better do that, Carola. Don't let anyone in who hasn't a ticket to show. Be sure you see that they put their names on the papers. When you've got two dozen, hand them over to Nancy Chester or Primrose Day to correct.'

'Let's hope they all write so that we can make it out!' Jean said darkly. 'You know how some grown-ups scrawl. We'd get our work returned if we dared show up such scribbles as *I've* seen—our doctor's prescriptions, for instance.'

'Oh, that's part of a doctor's job,' Clem told her airily. 'If they wrote too clearly, people would know what they were having and it might put them off! There! I've got this thing fixed at last! Ready, you folk? Then come on!'

'Just a tick!' Jean said. 'I want to buy some things from the Sale. How do I manage if I'm stuck in the little room all the time?'

'You won't be needed for the first twenty minutes or so,' Clem said. 'You'll have to rush round and get what you can then.'

However, when they reached the Hall, they discovered that this point had already struck their elders and betters, and Tom Gay, who was responsible for all arrangements connected with the house, called them together and informed them that it had been decided that there should be relays of them. The four already chosen would be 'on' for the first half-hour and then four others would relieve them, and they could do their buying before coming to help at the stall.

There was half an hour left now before any visitors would come, so they strolled round Hall, admiring the efforts of the rest of the School and marking various things they hoped to be able to buy.

'Those kids are nearly crackers with excitement,' Clem remarked, nodding towards the igloo where the Eskimos, clad in woolly garments of the appropriate fashion, were buzzing about like a swarm of hysterical bees. 'I wouldn't be their mistresses for something!'

Mary-Lou, looking most unlike a Red Indian with her yellow plaits and wide blue eyes, was near enough to hear this and giggled. 'I heard Miss Phipps telling them if they couldn't be quieter she'd pack half of them off to bed. I say, Clem, can I have a go for your dolls' house? I've never bothered with one before, but I do think it's a simply wizard effort.'

'Why not?' Clem demanded. 'You haven't the foggiest notion what the comp. is—no one has but ourselves and the Heads. You have a go if you want one. It'll give you something to think about.'

'That means it's something beastly,' her small friend said shrewdly. 'Oh, well, it'll be fun, anyhow.'

'You'll be fined if you use language like that,' Peggy Bettany, who had overheard her, observed. 'I suppose you'll think that fun, too?'

Mary-Lou's eyes widened with horror. 'This is the *Sale* day, Peggy,' she reminded the Head Girl severely. 'You couldn't do that today!'

'Just you go on using forbidden slang like that and you'll see,' Peggy retorted. 'You hop back to your tepee, and watch your language or fined you'll be! Trot!'

Peggy was Peggy, so Mary-Lou departed, not noticeably crushed, and the Head Girl went on her lawful occasions while the others moved on to admire the Second Form's Chinese stall which was in charge of Miss Edwards, their form mistress. 'Teddy,' as she was known to the School, was a good sort, but she possessed a tongue which kept them in awe, so this part of the room was fairly peaceful.

'You'll come and buy from us, won't you?' Len Maynard implored.

'I will,' Carola said. 'I want that little ware stand with the tapers in it. I say, I do like your kit, you two!'

'Mamma made it,' Con explained, standing beside her sister. 'It was an old frock she had in a play when *she* was at school. It's awfully gay, isn't it?' She held out the skirt of her coat, and extended one leg to show off the beflowered and betinselled cotton of which their Chinese coats and trousers were made.

'Jolly!' Clem said appreciatively. 'It's a lovely yellow.'

Betsy Lucy of the Fourth had been keeping an eye on the window. Now she suddenly squeaked, 'They're coming! I can see them!'

'Cripes! We'd best get back!' And Clem headed the rush back to their stall.

Miss Burn, coming from gym where she had been making certain that everything was in readiness for the country dancing, heard her unlawful remark and grinned to herself.

'I *ought* to haul young Clem over the coals for that,' she thought as she made her way to the top of the room, 'but I think I'll forget about being a good mistress for once. It was really very mild for Clem.'

Then the doors opened and the visitors poured in. No selling was allowed until the Sale had been declared open, but they thronged round the stalls, admiring and exclaiming at the work the girls had produced. The dolls' house, needless to state, came in for any number of congratulatory remarks, and the Fifths were smirking with complacency by the time Jo Maynard, who had made a bee-line for the Chinese stall first, had reached them. She surveyed them with a frown.

'Take those self-satisfied grins off your faces!' she ordered. 'If you're going to be as swelled-headed as that over the thing, I shall strongly advise the Heads to give you the plain needlework stall next time, and see how you like *that*!'

The smirks hastily vanished. Then Bride said anxiously: 'You're having a shot at the competition, aren't you, Auntie Jo?'

Her aunt nodded. 'Have I ever once failed to do it? I know it isn't choosing the name this time. What have you got in store for us?'

Tom grinned. 'Wouldn't you like to know?'

'Yes, I should,' Jo said frankly. 'What ghastly effort have you provided for us?'

'You'll find out presently,' Bride said soothingly. 'I say, Auntie Jo, if by chance you should win it you'll keep it, won't you? I mean, I know the Trips have La Maison des Poupées, but they've been completely goggle-eyed over this. They're even having a shot at it for themselves. They haven't a chance, of course. I don't know that *you* have, for that matter. But *if* you should get it, do stick to it for them.'

'O.K.,' Jo agreed. 'As you seem so certain I haven't really a look in, *if* I manage to win it, they shall have it. But don't you say anything to *them* about it,' she added hastily. 'No sense in *giving* them a disappointment!'

She was hailed at that moment by Biddy O'Ryan who wanted the latest news of Daisy Venables. Jo, cocking an eye at the Fifths, decided to remove Biddy to a less public spot before she gave it, and escorted Biddy to a far corner where she broke to her the news of Daisy's engagement to a young doctor at her hospital. She was puzzled, however, by Biddy's method of taking it.

'That's *one*!' Biddy said mysteriously. 'When are the rest to know?'

'One what?' Jo demanded; but Biddy refused to answer this.

'Sure, you needn't be minding me. Oh, look! Here comes the Opener!' Biddy hurriedly disappeared, and Jo, replying to the beckoning she was receiving from Miss Annersley, joined the opening party to be introduced, much to her wrath, as 'Mrs Maynard, Lady Russell's younger sister. We can't have Lady Russell with us today —I expect you know that she and Sir James are in Canada at the moment. Mrs Maynard is representing her, however.'

The Viscountess who was the Opener replied charmingly and Jo had to swallow her wrath and answer in kind. Then they mounted the daïs, and a tiny Eskimo, the School 'baby,' presented her with a bouquet.

Jack Maynard had been unable to represent the Sanatorium, so his place was taken by Dr Peters, another of the doctors there and an old friend of the School. He spoke briefly, explaining the object of the Sale; introduced the Viscountess, and then sat down. The Viscountess, with a smiling look round at the eager young faces of the stallholders, was very merciful. She congratulated them on such a picturesque affair, whereat Bride pretended to swoon with horror, but was jerked to her feet by Tom, who had no patience with such antics; said a few earnest words about the crying need for the Sanatorium and the great work it was doing; then she declared the Sale open and set an example to everyone by hurrying off the platform, without even waiting for the vote of thanks due to her, and demanding three separate dips for her three little girls at home.

After that, it was a case of business first, and everyone was kept hard at it. Matron's jam vanished 'like snow on a dyke,' to quote Jean Ackroyd's aunt who had turned up. The toys sold well, too, and before the afternoon was half over practically all the sets of bedding and every carpet, too. The people in charge of the competition for the house had scarcely time to breathe, as Nancy Chester said when she handed over to Audrey Simpson. So far, no one had come anywhere near the number of materials used, either.

'So there's a chance for you, Auntie Jo,' Bride said when her aunt appeared shortly after the country-dancing display and demanded to be told what she had to do.

She groaned loudly when she heard, but sat down and began to write with grim determination. As no one was allowed more than ten minutes for a list, some of them were scribbled in a manner that made the inspectors groan loudly.

'Anyway,' Bride said during a short pause, 'we've made twelve pounds ten with it already, so it's jolly well worth it. No, Mary; I simply can't make head or tail of that word. You'll just have to let it go.'

At long last, when most of the stalls had been pretty well cleared and people were packing up to go home, intending competitors ceased to come and the girls settled down to go through all lists which had reached thirty or over. Biddy O'Ryan and Hilary Burn joined them to help and they scanned those lists carefully. Then Hilary looked up at Biddy, who nodded.

'Yes; she's got it after all! So sucks to you, Bride Bettany,' she added, completely forgetting in her excitement that this was *not* the way for a mistress to speak to a pupil.

Bride grinned. 'I'm jolly glad. Good for her! But however she got so many is beyond me. Come on and let's tell the world.'

They poured out of the little room into Hall where Dr Peters was busy announcing the results of the various raffles. The Heads were standing beside him and the girls hurried up to the group.

'Dolls' house result,' Tom said, handing the slip of paper with the name of the successful winner on it to the doctor.

'Who is it?' he demanded as he took it. 'Anyone I know?'

'Look and see,' Tom grinned. 'You'll get a shock!'

He opened it and read. His eyebrows nearly disappeared into his hair and he whistled softly. 'Not really? I say!

What an excitement! Phoebe will be thrilled to hear this.' He spoke of his crippled wife whom all the girls knew well.

'Announce it—announce it!' Carola was nearly dancing with excitement.

He turned to show the Heads the name before he did so, however. Then he rang his bell for attention, and when there was silence, he said: 'I have just been given the result of the dolls' house competition. I congratulate the winner most heartily on her success.' He paused. Then he went on: 'The house has been won by—Con Maynard, with thirty-seven materials!'

Con, standing with her sister by the stall, stared at him. The rest of the gang shoved her forward.

'Go on—go on!' they urged. 'You've got to go and take it.'

Still in a maze, Con went forward, looking very small and childish in her Chinese dress. Someone helped her up to the daïs and Miss Burn took her hand and led her forward.

Everyone began to clap and then someone started to cheer. Con stood clinging tightly to Hilary Burn, half-scared at her triumph.

Dr Peters smiled down at her. 'Congratulations, Con,' he said, 'and now I must give you your prize.'

The cheering and clapping died down, to be succeeded by an outburst of laughter as Con said seriously, 'Thank you very much, Uncle Frank, but please can't someone else take it for me. I couldn't possibly hold it, you know,' she wound up.

There was more clapping and cheering, under cover of which Hilary Burn released her hand and sent Con back to join the others. The doctor held up his hand for silence again.

'I think you will all like to know that the dolls' house has netted twenty-five pounds five shillings,' he said. 'And now we have four more raffles for which to draw, so, if you please, we will continue.'

Chapter XIX

CAROLA TO THE RESCUE!

IT was seven o'clock. The last of the visitors had gone and the girls were busy dismantling the stalls. Miss Cochrane came into Hall to collect her purchases which she had left at the tepee until now. She looked at the small pile of articles she had bought and laughed.

'I certainly can't carry all that myself,' she said. She looked round. 'Here, Len! Pile those small things into one of those reed baskets; and you bring the larger ones, will you, Carola? Bring them to my music room. I'll have them there. I'll go ahead and clear a shelf for them. Mind you don't break anything.'

She departed on this and Carola and Len set to work to gather her possessions together. The small things were put into one of the reed baskets and Carola loaded herself with the three scrapbooks, teapot, small stool with its seat of woven sea-grass, and hand-painted tea-tray. Then they set off, to find Grizel Cochrane in her music room standing by the table reading a letter which had come for her during the afternoon. Her pleasant smile had vanished and she was frowning blackly.

As the pair entered, she crumpled up the sheet and thrust it into the pocket of her cardigan. 'Put the things on the table,' she said shortly as she went over to the mantelpiece and took a cigarette from her case lying there. She struck a match and lit up as she went to a cupboard.

'Can we help you to put them away, Miss Cochrane?' Carola asked.

'No, thanks.' Grizel still spoke shortly. 'Put them down and then run off.'

As she spoke, she tossed the match in the direction of the fireplace. She threw short, and it fell, still burning, into the reed basket Len was holding. The tinder stuff caught fire at once and flared up. The flame caught the flimsy material of Len's Chinese dress and in an instant the sleeve was a mass of flames.

Len screamed and so did Carola, who tossed down the things she was holding and was on to the terrified child, beating out the flames with her bare hands while Grizel, with an exclamation of horror, snatched up a rug and flung it on the blazing basket before going to Carola's help. The Big House was an old one with any amount of wood about it and there was a fresh breeze blowing.

The fire, smothered beneath the heavy rug, went out almost at once, but a good part of Len's coat was burnt before the flames there were subdued. Mercifully, she had stout underclothes and, as they discovered later, beyond a long scorch on one arm, she had come to little harm. It was a different matter with Carola. When the mistresses within hearing came tearing to the spot they were just in time to see her swaying and falling if Grizel had not caught her.

Miss Annersley took the unconscious girl from the arms of the music mistress, who stooped over her with a face as white as chalk.

'Go and fetch Matron, Grizel,' the Head said; and Grizel, shaking and terrified, went.

Miss Burn, who had been telling Miss Annersley some

news and come racing with her to the music room, picked up Len and carried her away to be soothed and have her burn dressed at once. Oddly enough, no one else had heard the cries, but Biddy O'Ryan met Grizel and, struck by her face, ran after her to Matron's room to find out what was wrong.

Matron, taking a much-needed rest in a chair by the fire, looked up in amazement when the pair entered. What she saw in Grizel Cochrane's face made her leap to her feet at once.

'Where is it?' she demanded, going straight to the point.

'My music room,' Grizel gasped.

Matron made for the door. 'Sit down at once,' she said curtly. 'Biddy, you look after Grizel.' Then she was off.

Biddy obeyed her. Taking Grizel by the shoulders, she made her sit down in Matron's chair, brought her a glass of water and then stood waiting till the elder chose to speak. At length Grizel looked up, and Biddy's heart stood still at what she saw in the dark grey eyes.

'Oh, Grizel, whatever *is* it?' she faltered.

'I set Len Maynard on fire,' Grizel replied dully. 'Carola tried to save her and—and I'm afraid she's very badly injured.'

'Len?' Biddy could scarcely whisper it.

'I don't know. She screamed dreadfully, so she's alive. Carola——' Her voice died away. She was unable to say any more.

Biddy was silent, too. She longed to go and help to see to Carola, for the girl had won herself a warm place in the Irish heart; but Matron had told her to stay with Grizel and Biddy knew that the music mistress should not be left alone yet.

Suddenly Grizel looked up again. 'It was an accident, Biddy.'

'I know that,' Biddy said brusquely. 'Don't be silly, Grizel. No one's going to think you deliberately set Jo's girl on fire.'

Grizel shuddered. 'That—that's almost the worst of it—Jo's girl. And Jo and Madame were both so good to me years ago!'

Biddy was not sure what to say or do, but she must try to get that look out of Grizel's eyes. Grizel was years older than herself. She had been teaching up at the Sonnalpe when Biddy first came to the School. The Irish girl had never liked Grizel Cochrane very much, but it was not in her to ignore the anguish she saw before her.

'Tell me, Grizel,' she said. 'Maybe 'twill make it a little better. We can't do anything for Len or Carola just now. You tell me.'

Grizel turned her eyes on the flickering of the cheery little fire and she shuddered again. 'It was my stepmother,' she said. 'You know I never wanted to go in for music, but my father insisted. I wanted to take up P.T., but he wouldn't hear of it, and I hadn't enough of my own to do it off my own bat. When he died he left me some money outright. More he put into a fund in charge of two trustees—his lawyer and my stepmother. I'm not supposed to have it till I'm thirty-five. All the same, if the trustees would agree, I could draw part of it. You never knew Deira O'Hagen, did you? She left before you came to School.'

'I've heard of her, though,' Biddy said.

'Yes; well, Deira and I became good friends after we'd both left. She married a New Zealander and went out

there to live with him. Last year he died and she found
that he'd muddled away a good deal of his money and
Deira was none too well off. She has one little girl who
was born a cripple, so she has to do something about it.
There was a business going—books and music—quite a
good thing. She hadn't enough capital to buy it herself
and she thought of me. She always knew I hated teaching.
She wrote and asked if I'd come in with her and I leapt
at the idea. I saw Mr Sothern, the lawyer, and he quite
agreed it would be a good thing. Deira had sent over
books and papers for him to vet it. He would agree to my
having the money. It all depended on my stepmother.
He wrote to her and so did I. I had a letter this afternoon
saying that she wouldn't agree to letting me have a penny
until I was thirty-five. I was to go on as my father had
wished. She never liked me, you know.'

Biddy said nothing for the very good reason that she
could think of nothing to say; but her heart ached for
Grizel.

'Well,' went on Grizel dreamily, 'I read that letter after
I'd told Len and Carola to bring my buys to the music
room. I'd just finished it when they arrived. I was
raging. I got up and went to the cupboard. I was lighting
a cigarette and I threw the match away. It landed on
the reed basket Len was carrying. Those things are like
tinder. It flared up at once and caught her sleeve. I
only waited to throw a rug on the basket—no use letting
the whole house go up. That's the story.'

There was a silence, broken by Matron who came to
fetch some things she wanted. She only shook her head
when Biddy eagerly demanded to know how the patients
were.

Len is only slightly scorched, but she's suffering from shock,' she said. 'Carola's hands are in a bad state. Dr Peters was still here, luckily. He's spending the night at the Christys'. He's in San with Carola now. Poor, plucky child! I'm afraid she'll pay heavily for her courage. By the way, Grizel, were you hurt at all?'

'No, Matron. Carola had most of the flames out before I reached them. I stopped to throw a mat on the basket. It was flaring badly.'

'The most sensible thing you could have done,' Matron said. 'Now, my dear, I see you've had a very bad shock, but you mustn't give way. We have our hands full as it is. Biddy, go and ask Karen for some strong coffee for her and see that she takes it. Then, if you feel that you can't help with the rest, go to bed. I'll come along some time and let you know the latest news. Cheer up! "All is not lost that is in danger," you know.'

She gave them a nod and went out again. Biddy stood up.

'I'm going to get that coffee. You stay quiet till I come back. Try not to worry, Grizel. It won't help anyone and will only make you unfit to help out.' She slipped away to return presently with coffee and the news that Miss Wilson had told the girls what had happened and they were having supper now and then the prefects would see the little ones to bed.

'So there's nothing we can do at present,' she concluded. 'You drink this and then go to bed and try to sleep.'

Once more Grizel shuddered. '*Sleep!* I don't feel as if I could ever sleep again!'

'Oh yes, you will. Sure, it's nonsense to talk like that.' Biddy held the cup to Grizel's lips. 'Drink this and you'll feel better. Drink it, Grizel.'

Grizel drank, and when the cup was empty, Biddy sat back watching her colleague with wary eyes. What she did not tell Grizel was the fact that she had gone to San and told Matron the outline of the story. Matron had given her a sedative to put in the coffee, and before long Biddy saw that it was taking effect. Grizel's eyes were growing drowsy, and she nodded.

'Come along, now,' Biddy coaxed. 'It's worn out ye are, ye poor creature. I'll help you to bed.'

She succeeded in getting Grizel to bed and before long was able to leave the room, sure that the other mistress was sleeping quietly. She went along to San again, but saw no one and dared not go in. However, before they finally went to bed after one of the most eventful days in the Chalet School's history, Miss Annersley sent for her and told her that the doctor said that Len would probably sleep herself all right, though she would have a very sore arm for the next few days. As for Carola, one hand was so badly burned they had had to put her to sleep before they dressed it and she was still sleeping.

'Mercifully, she is a sturdy, healthy girl,' the Head said, 'so I hope her nerves won't suffer too badly. But I'm afraid this will put an end to her music. The doctor is afraid that there is damage done to one finger which will weaken it seriously.'

'Oh, well, 'tisn't as if she meant to go in for it for a career,' Biddy said consolingly. 'And isn't it the good news about Len! Does Jo know, Miss Annersley?'

'Not yet. Dr Peters will go over first boat tomorrow and tell her himself when he has seen Len. She couldn't come here even if she knew, and there was no sense in giving her a bad night on Len's account. Thank God it *was* Len and not Con! Len is a matter-of-fact little person and Dr Peters thinks she will be over the shock very quickly. We're keeping her in San for a day or two to keep her quiet; but he expects she will be fit enough by Tuesday and then we break up. They have the trip to Canada in a couple of weeks' time, and that will be enough to take her mind off the whole thing.'

Biddy nodded. Then she knelt down beside the Head and looked up at her. 'I want to tell ye how it happened,' she said, becoming richly Irish in her earnestness.

'Do you know? We have all been so anxious about Carola I'm afraid I never thought of it till you spoke.'

'I do so,' Biddy nodded. Then, still kneeling, she told the story she had heard from Grizel.

Miss Annersley heard her in silence—a silence which lasted for some minutes after Biddy had stopped speaking. That young lady took alarm.

'Ah, now, ye won't be angry with Grizel,' she coaxed. 'Sure, the poor creature is ready to beat herself for her carelessness.'

'No,' Miss Annersley said. 'I am not angry. I am too sorry for her to be angry. Say nothing to her, Biddy, tomorrow. I must see her myself. I'm glad you told me, child.'

'And you'll speak to Jo, the way she won't be flaring out at Grizel over it?' Biddy wheedled.

Anxious as she was, Miss Annersley began to laugh. 'Oh, Biddy, Biddy! What a born wheedler you are! You must leave it to me to say what I think to Jo,' she went on seriously. 'And now, I have a piece of news for you that I *think* will be no real surprise to you after all.'

'If it's that Hilary Burn is going to marry that nice Dr

Graves, 'tis no news at all, at all,' Biddy told her calmly. 'We've all been expecting it this last fortnight. And did ye hear about Daisy?'

'Daisy? No! What about Daisy?' the Head asked quickly.

'Didn't Jo tell you?'

'My dear girl, I never saw Jo to speak to after the opening.'

'Oh, I see. As Mary-Lou said, you had to spend time being polite to people. Well, Daisy's engaged, too—to a doctor at her hospital. Jo's very bucked about it, because, as she says, it'll mean that Daisy has a home of her own now. I know she's had one with Madame and then with Jo, but it's not quite the same thing.'

Miss Annersley nodded. 'I'm very glad for Daisy. And now, Biddy, it's after eleven and time that both of us were in bed. Good-night, and sleep well. Carola's life is in no danger, though she will have a good deal of pain to endure for the next few days, poor child. We have a great deal to be thankful for.'

'We have that!' Biddy stood up. 'Good-night, Miss Annersley, and thank you very much.'

Grizel had her interview with Miss Annersley next day after Dr Peters had been to see the patients and been able to assure the anxious Heads that Len would soon be well again and Carola was going on as well as possible. What was said, neither ever told, except that Grizel hunted Biddy out and told her briefly that Miss Annersley had offered to back her in the new business until she could use her own money. She was leaving at the end of the summer term and would sail for New Zealand almost at once.

'Well, I wish you all the luck in the world,' Biddy said.

'Thanks, Biddy. You've been a real stand-by. Thank you for telling the Head—everything. I knew I had to, but I didn't see how I was ever going to do it.'

'Oh, well, maybe I'm inheriting Jo's mantle. You know Dr Jem always did say she was a champion butter-in. I thought, maybe, I was taking too much on myself, but I knew 'twould be a hard thing for you to do. And isn't it grand about Hilary?'

'*Hilary?*' Grizel eyed Biddy as if she thought she were mildly insane.

'Haven't you heard? Hilary's engaged—and so is Daisy Venables!'

Biddy ran off after that, for she was due to take duty with the Juniors, so she was unable to watch Grizel's reactions to the news.

As for Jo, Miss Annersley had gone down to the ferry to meet her, and after reporting on Len who was very sorry for herself and inclined to be very cross, she told Grizel's story as eloquently as she could. Jo was inclined to 'flare up' as Biddy had said; but by the time the Head had walked the pair of them right past the Big House and nearly to the other end of the islet, not to speak of talking herself nearly hoarse, that lady had calmed down.

'It's Grizel,' she said finally, 'just Grizel! All right, Hilda; I'll say nothing—or very little, anyhow. And now, what about Carola? Jack and I are *in loco parentis* at present. Is she really ill?'

'Her one hand is in a bad state, but it *will* heal in time. She is inclined to be feverish, too, but that will pass off. Don't worry, Joey. By the time you sail for Canada, I expect she'll be on the high road to recovery. As for your *in loco parentis*, Nell and I are taking that on while you're away, so suppose you leave her to us and concentrate on your own affairs.'

Jo had three interviews before she went home again. The first was with her daughters. Len had been moved into a little spare room so that Carola might be kept quite quiet. The two small girls were together and Miss Wilson had had the wonderful house moved up so that they could play with it. Therefore, Len's first greeting to her mother referred to that.

'Look, Mamma! Isn't it lovely? And Con says we three are to share it. Isn't it super of her?'

Jo grinned. 'Only what I should have expected. I never knew you three when you *didn't* insist on sharing. Well, Con, my lamb, you're a clever child and you beat your mother hollow. *I* only thought of thirty-one materials.'

Con surveyed her mother with solemn brown eyes. 'I just thought and thought about all the things in La Maison des Poupées and what they were made of, and I seemed to remember dozens. *Only*, Miss Alton saw my list after and she said I must have extra spelling next term if I couldn't spell better than that.'

Jo chuckled heartlessly. 'I suppose you were in such a hurry you just went by the sound. That sort of thing won't pan out where the English language is concerned, my lamb. Well, and what have you been doing to yourself, young Len?'

'It wasn't me—'twas the basket,' Len cried. 'It blazed up like billy-oh and then my coat caught and I thought I was going to be burnt to death, only Carola knocked me down and sat on me and hit me and the fire went out.'

'A good time was had by all, in fact,' her mother chuckled again.

'Mamma.'

'Yes? What is it, sugarpie?'

'I shall never be a martyr.'

Jo sat down limply on the bed and regarded her eldest girl with startled eyes. 'Who wants it? And what on earth makes you think that? What *is* all this in aid of?'

'Well, I couldn't,' Len said defensively. 'Not if I had to be burnt to death, anyhow. It hurts too jolly much.'

'Well, there's no need for you to think of it at present, anyhow. And if God meant you to be a martyr, He would give you the courage, so you needn't worry about that any more. I've something to tell you about Auntie Daisy. What do you think? When we come home from Canada in the summer she is going to be married, and you three and Primula are to be her bridesmaids! How's that for news?'

Just as Jo had meant, the pair forgot about being martyrs and beset her with questions about 'Auntie Daisy' and her wedding. When she finally left them, they were considering with great solemnity just what would be the best thing to give her for a wedding-present.

'Well, that's so much done!' she thought as she closed the door behind her after assuring them that she would be on time to take them home for the holidays next Tuesday. 'The next thing is Carola, poor kiddy! Oh, no; the next thing is obviously Grizel!'

The little room was at the farther end of the corridor where Grizel's music room was, and just as Jo turned to head for the San the music room door opened and Grizel emerged. She went white when she saw Jo and her eyes fell. Not quickly enough, though, for Jo to have missed the look of apprehension in them. She swept forward, crying, 'Oh, Grizel! My poor lamb! *Don't* look like that at me! It was an accident, and anyway, I shan't eat you!'

'An accident that should never have happened!' Grizel spoke almost harshly. 'Whatever I might have been feeling, I'd no right to go chucking matches around like that. If—if anything had happened, Jo, I should have been to blame.'

Jo pulled her into the room and shut the door. 'I can't say that's untrue, Grizel. I'm not going to lie about it. But you get it into that thick head of yours that it's over—finished! After today, I shall never speak of it to you again. Understand?'

'If—oh, I'd never have forgiven myself if—if——'

'Ah,' said Jo with unusual gentleness of tone, 'we can all say that about lots of things. I'll only say this and then you and I are going to forget. When things go wrong, it's just as well to learn to hold your horses a little. Count a hundred, Grizel—count a hundred before you fly off the handle. That's all. Now, my dear, I want to wish you every happiness and every success in your new life when it begins. You've got to write frequently and let us know all about it, mind. Oh, and, by the way, Mollie's out there. Oh, don't be an ass! Jack's sister—our Miss Maynard. She lives outside of Auckland. I'll write and tell her to look out for you as soon as you sail. You'll go by boat, I suppose?'

'Of course I shall! Where's the money coming from to fly?'

'Anyway, you'll love the voyage. I know how I loved the voyages to and from India. Now I'm off to San. Goodbye; be good!'

She was off, but what she had said sank deep into Grizel Cochrane's mind. The whole affair was to make a very big difference in her character, and the Grizel who returned to England on a visit five years later was a very different woman from the one who had so nearly caused a tragedy in the Chalet School.

Jo ran lightly down the corridors, and presently was tapping at the door of San. Nurse came to answer it, and agreed to let Mrs Maynard visit her patient for ten minutes. Jo had to rub it in very hard that she was, as she had said, *in loco parentis* before Nurse would grant even this grace. However, she got her way and Carola, opening languid eyes, saw the clever, sensitive face with its beautiful eyes bent over her.

'Mrs Maynard!' she whispered. 'How is Len?'

'Sitting up and taking notice,' Jo told her, sitting down beside her. She stooped and kissed the girl. 'Thank you, Carola, from the bottom of my heart, for what you've done. We owe Len's life to your quickness. I'm certain of that.'

The languid eyes brightened and Carola smiled a little. 'I'm glad she's not much the worse.'

'Very little indeed. So now, you've got to forget about the whole thing and set your energies to getting better. You break up on Tuesday and we set off to Canada in just over a fortnight's time. I want you with us *part* of the time, anyhow.'

'Has anyone told Dad and Mother?' Carola asked.

'Not yet; that's *my* job and I wanted to see you first. Any message for them?'

'My love. And please tell them I simply love the Chalet School and I'm awfully glad I'm here, if—if I did——'

'Storm it in the most outrageous manner,' Jo finished for her. 'By the way, if ever you are moved to put out a fire again, you might look round for something of a thick cloth nature and not use your poor hands. Not much sense in that!' quoth Jo. 'There's quite a good cloth on the table. Why didn't you use that?'

Nurse, coming to send Jo away, reflected the grin that overspread that lady's face as Carola made her usual excuse.

'I—I didn't think!'